MASTER OF THE GAME

"You said you preferred a sport you can master," Vanessa laughed. "Is this your favorite?"

Lord Brickendon caught her hand between his and brought her a half-step closer. No frivolity filled his eyes, for they were dark with stronger emotions. "Ducks and Drakes," he said so softly she had to lean even nearer, "is easier to master than a woman's capricious heart, but sometimes the enjoyment gained from a sport comes from the attempt to conquer it."

"Is that what you wish? To conquer a woman's heart?"

"No, for something so precious must be freely given, or it is never truly won." He drew her hand to the ruffles on his shirt and pressed her fingers over the steady thump of his heart.

*   *   *

Jo Ann Ferguson

The Wolfe Wager

ZEBRA BOOKS
KENSINGTON PUBLISHING CORP.

For Nancy Bulk and Sharon Winn,
whose phone numbers will always
be on my automatic dial—
Thanks for being my friends!

Chapter One

The elegant room resounded with prattle and laughter, as the scent of French perfume and smuggled wine drifted from each person the tall man passed. He did not tarry to take part in any conversation, but offered a smile to a bald-ribbed dowager who appraised him candidly before turning to the young woman beside her to whisper. The young woman's eyes widened as she glanced in his direction, her face flushing to an appealing shade.

His grin broadened, for none of the marriage-minded misses and their sponsors would be able to find anything to fault with the appearance of Ross Hogarth, Lord Brickendon this evening. His cream-white shirt was closed with a cravat of the same color, and the sedate shade of his dark coat and deep blue waistcoat would have been disdained by a dandy. After weeks of being cloistered in the halls of government, he was ready for a bit of innocent laughter. He could imagine no place better than this gathering near the end of the Season when he could watch the eager young maidens vie for the attentions of any titled gentleman.

"Lord Brickendon!" called the gaunt dowager. "What an unexpected pleasure to see you still among us! I had heard you intended to return to Essex for the rest of the summer."

Ross bowed his head in her direction, keeping his smile in place when he saw how her younger companion hid giggles behind a lacy fan that matched the yellow silk of her gown. Hadn't the young woman learned by this time in the Season how much most men disliked giggles? "You should have known I wouldn't miss any evening with you as its hostess, Mrs. Averill."

The gray-haired woman laughed, her eyes crinkling in her age-weathered face. "Save your lathering for those who appreciate moonshine, young man. I recall when you were a boisterous lad in short pants and tried to get yourself out of mischief with your wit."

"Ah," he said as she continued to chuckle, "those who regale a man with the tales of his misspent youth are a trial."

"I daresay you have a bit of youth left in you that you haven't squandered."

"But who is truly the younger tonight, Mrs. Averill?" he asked with an arched brow. "Me who feels older than the stones of this house or you who remains so charmingly young at heart?"

"You have been given more than your share of charm," she answered, tapping her fan in her hand, "albeit you have been dealt a full hand of cynicism this evening."

Ross bowed over his hostess's fingers as she smiled, but he looked at the woman next to her. His lips straightened when another collection of giggles clattered from her mouth. The chit had little sense if she thought he was amused by such a shrill sound. Not that she—he guessed her to be Mrs. Averill's niece Darla—was unpleasant to the eyes. The blond curls clustering about her porcelain cheeks were the perfect match for her blue eyes—innocuous eyes, in Ross's opinion.

"I trust you have met my niece," Mrs. Averill said, confirming his thoughts. "Darla, this is Ross Hogarth, Lord Brickendon."

Her niece held her hand almost directly under Ross's nose. She twittered another trill as he bent over it.

"I'm honored, Miss Averill," he said quietly. He released her fingers, which seemed determined to wrap around his. The lasses were becoming more aggressive with every day that passed, he thought. He was sure that, for these young women, ending the Season unbetrothed was the greatest shame they could imagine. "If you'll excuse me . . ."

"My lord—" began Mrs. Averill, her warm voice underscored by the lyrical sound of a violin starting a quadrille. She glanced toward the opposite end of the long room where an orchestra was seated beneath a brass chandelier that matched the one directly over Ross's head. "How can you leave now? I know your reputation for enjoying a dance, and you have spent so little time dancing this Season."

"I would ask you to stand up with me, Mrs. Averille—" He forced a smile for the simpering lass beside his hostess. "—and your niece as well, but I told Franklin I would meet him at the card table long before this, and I do detest being late."

"Sir Wilbur! That fat toad!" The younger woman sniffed. Color climbed her cheeks when her aunt flashed her a silent reprimand.

"Perhaps later then, my lord," Mrs. Averill said.

"I look forward to that time."

Ross locked his hands behind his back and watched as his hostess hurried away, her niece in tow. No doubt, Mrs. Averill would find someone willing to dance with her pretty niece, but it would not be him. Not tonight, at any rate. He had not left his duties behind to be stifled by the conversation of an insipid miss who was scarcely out of the schoolroom. Let Milhouse twirl her about the floor. That chucklehead was looking for a way to pay off his debts. Mrs. Averill's niece surely could be the way.

Cynical—that was what Mrs. Averill had deemed him, and she was quite correct. He was bored with the Season and Town and the endless mesh of government. If he did not find something to entertain him soon, he *would* leave London for grassville.

With the solid heels of his low shoes striking the floor on each step, Ross crossed beneath the bowed ceiling of the expansive room to where an arched doorway opened onto a smaller chamber. Tonight he would spend time with his friends who had wisely remained unattached through the months of the Marriage Mart. It was time to enjoy a bachelor's fare and leave the hapless blocks to their court-promises.

He choked back a curse as a slender form cut him off by almost walking into him. He put out his hands to steady the young woman, but she murmured an apology and rushed past without so much as a proper greeting. Ross watched the brunette disappear into the crowd near the orchestra.

A perplexed frown ruffled his brow. The woman looked familiar, but he could not put a name with the comely face he had caught a glimpse of so briefly. That surprised him, for he had been certain he knew everyone in the small circle of friends Mrs. Averill had brought together that evening.

By all that's blue, he thought, *why are you letting a lass intrude on your evening?* She probably had no more sense than Mrs. Averill's giggling charge.

With a shrug, Ross strode into the room where tables had been set for those who preferred to spend the evening with a hand of books instead of dancing and aimless conversation. He scanned the smoky room. His smile returned as he saw a man motioning at him.

Trust Franklin to be so blasted impatient when Ross was but a few minutes late!

"Where have you been?" Sir Wilbur Franklin called in his rumbling voice. "My pockets are growing hungry for the money I plan to win from you tonight."

"Mrs. Averill was anxious to introduce me to her niece." Ross laughed as he came to stand by the table. "That hornet!"

"Aunt or niece?"

As Sir Wilbur chuckled, Ross clasped his chubby hand. The man's round cheeks grew broader each time Ross saw him. As the buttons strained across Sir Wilbur's black waistcoat with his burst of humor, Ross wondered which one would pop first. It would be worth enduring Franklin's many questions and opinions to see.

"Brickendon, didn't you vow that, at your first opportunity to leave, you would be done with Town?" queried a sharp voice.

Ross was displeased to see Bruce Swinton, for he found the ginger-hackled man's company annoying. A tint of sarcasm edged his retort. "You would be sorry if I said yes, for then whom would you have to lose to at the board of green cloth?"

Swinton's dark eyes narrowed. Sitting at the card table, he whipped out the back of his garish, gold coat. "Your luck was uncommonly good last month, but I shall beat you this time." He stretched his long legs beneath the table, ignoring the baronet's grumbled complaints. "Do sit down, Brickendon, and show us the color of your gold. I trust I shall prove Franklin wrong. *My* pockets are the ones hungry to savor the flavor of your blunt."

"Ever the optimist, aren't you?" Ross pulled out one of the empty chairs. He grimaced as he sat. Apparently—by offering her guests such hard chairs—Mrs. Averill resolved to keep the gentlemen from lingering over their cards. She should know how futile such tactics were. Trying to get more comfortable, he asked, "Do we have a fourth?"

"Rollins." Swinton motioned to a short man who was chatting at the next table.

The balding man stood straighter at the sound of his name. Beneath a bushy mustache that gave him the appearance of a well-fed badger, his smile was nearly hidden. Not that it was often seen, for the man had a dour personality that was compensated only by his skill at cards.

Ross sighed silently. Save for Sir Wilbur—and that was saying little, because the rotund baronet was tiresome at best—the company this evening was worse than he had anticipated. Perhaps he would have been wise to go directly home to Essex, but he had let the thought of the entertainment of the Season draw him to this party. He had pulled the wrong pig by the ear and now was saddled with this dreary company.

He listened to his companions' gossip, but heard nothing new. Taking the cards, he started to ask a question. His first word hung in a sudden silence that smothered the whole room. Curious, he glanced about to see why all conversation had ceased.

A woman waved aside the puffs of cigar smoke and peered around the room, clearly searching for someone. A man next to the door leapt to his feet and spoke to her. The soft sound of her answer did not reach the table where Ross sat.

He struggled not to laugh when he realized his companions were regarding the lady in the doorway with the longing of land-lonely sailors for the shore. As he shuffled the cards, he said, "Do close your mouth, Swinton.

You shan't capture the lady's attention that way—only flies."

"Who . . . ? Who . . . ?"

"Must you sound like an owl? Have you been lost in daisyville, Swinton?" asked Mr. Rollins with obvious disdain. "Surely every gentleman in the Polite World has met Lady Vanessa Wolfe—and been rejected by her."

"Not I!" averred Swinton stoutly. He shook himself and leaned forward to look past Rollins. "By Jove, I didn't realize *she* would be here tonight. She is sweet on the eyes."

"Nor have I been shown the door by the charming lady!" Sir Wilbur laughed and poked Ross with a pudgy elbow. "And you, my friend? Can it be that the marquess's daughter has escaped your attentions? How can that be?"

Ross continued to shuffle the cards, but his gaze strayed again to the lady in question. Like his comrades, he was familiar with this particular lady's situation. Lady Vanessa Wolfe—with her father, the Marquess of Wulfric, dead less than two years before and her brother missing after a heinous battle against the dirty Frogs on the continent—was the apparent heir to a vast fortune as well as Wolfe Abbey in the distant northwest of England. The title had gone to the closest male relative, a cousin, but the estate had never been entailed, so the dirty acres had come into the possession of the late marquess's daughter. Such an heiress was certain to be the center of attention wherever she went, but the thought of that wealth was not what drew his eyes.

Sir Wilbur had—for once—not been exaggerating. Vanessa Wolfe *was* pretty. She was delicately made, but not fragile. It was obvious from the saucy tilt of her gently rounded chin that she was determined to have her way. Definitely the type of woman an astute man gave wide berth to, for she would insist on being the mistress of her home and her husband. Her rose-tinted cheeks were softer than the expression in her gray eyes as her gaze swept the room before she turned—the white silk skirt of her fashionable gown whirling to reveal the lacy work on her stockings—to leave without speaking to anyone else in the card room.

His brows lowered. Lady Vanessa Wolfe was the woman who had nearly collided with him in the main room. If she was always in such a hurry-scurry, that explained why no one had been able to capture her attention. The cards in his hands became motionless as he wondered if she spent the evening in such a rush in order to avoid becoming betrothed, for most men would care little about her high-handed ways when they could claim her father's fortune, or mayhap there was another reason for the young woman's skittishness.

"Beautiful," murmured Sir Wilbur. His voice strengthened. "And 'tis a blasted shame the girl goes unwed when the Season is nigh to its end. If her father were alive, he would have insisted on a match for her before this. I would allow no daughter of mine to make such a mockery of the Season."

"There remains a month." Ross dealt the cards with the ease of much practice. He concealed his smile as he owned to himself that the lass was intriguing. A highly eligible maiden with no interest in marriage might be more entertaining than the women who coveted the chance to share his title. None of his friends could mask their interest in the enticing brunette whose wine-red lips had offered an invitation even as her cool poise kept any interested man at bay. She was an enigma, and Ross disliked puzzles.

He almost laughed aloud. To own the truth, mysteries intrigued him, daring him to unravel them. He understood now why the lady had struck a chord with him;

she possessed a hint of her father's strong features and that created other questions he wished to find answers to.

"Who knows?" he mused aloud. "Perhaps even as we enjoy this game, some chap has won her heart."

Swinton snorted. "Lady Vanessa Wolfe? I doubt there is a heart beating beneath her breast. The old marquess was rumored to be a first-rate rogue who flouted every canon of propriety. Can she be any different?"

"Your eyes fail you," Ross returned, "if you see that lovely woman identical to her grizzled father. I exchanged words with Wulfric once or twice, and I shall forget none of them. He used words like a weapon. His daughter has no need for such a fierce tool, because she can halt a man's heartbeat with a single, cool glance in his direction."

"She *is* beautiful," Sir Wilbur breathed again.

"Are you going to repeat yourself all night?" Rollins demanded.

Clearing his throat, Sir Wilbur gathered his cards and made a show of sorting them. "This bibble-babble is a waste of time. She has shown there's not a man among the *ton* she would consider buckling herself to." His brows rose. "Even you, Brickendon—who has no need to brag about his success with the ladies, for everyone in the Polite World and beyond knows of it—earned no more than a passing glance from that icy lady."

"Yes, she ignored you." Swinton chuckled. "You'd be wise to steer clear of Lady Vanessa; she could destroy your reputation as a rake who has left no woman's heart untouched."

"Or any other part of her?" Sir Wilbur surrendered to a paroxysm of laughter.

Ross let his friend enjoy his sally, but he had no interest in retorting. Any answer would change the course of the conversation, and for the moment, he wished to keep it firmly focused on Lady Vanessa Wolfe.

Looking at his cards, he lowered them to the table. "I see the problem as this, my friends. An heiress with such a sturdy collection of brass should not be left unwed. Anyone among us would know how to handle her fortune."

"And the lady."

Again Ross ignored Sir Wilbur. Looking at the half-empty bottle in the middle of the table, he wondered where the baronet had been drinking before this rout. Such a small serving of wine could not have brought the chubby man to this altogethery state. Sir Wilbur was nearly as drunk as an emperor.

"What do you suggest we do?" asked Swinton, his voice sharp with frustration. He tossed his unplayed cards onto the table. "Once it would have been easy. An unwed maid was swept from her father's house by an eager swain."

Ross allowed himself a slight smile. "I would suggest another, less extreme measure. I fear the late Lord Wulfric would hoist himself from his grave to protect his daughter's honor."

"Egad!" Rollins shook his head. "Why are we gabbling like Old Toughs? The girl has no wish to wed, so leave her be."

"She cut Rollins quite to the quick last month at Almack's," Swinton said, aiming a superior smile at Rollins. "He was trying to ask her to dance, and she left him standing alone."

Ross found listening to this brangle about Lady Vanessa was boring, and he had come to the party hoping for some merriment. Clearly this gathering would not offer it. With a smile, he decided it was up to him to find a way to make the rest of his time in Town enjoyable. "My friends, I have a proposal that may put an end to this discussion so that we might enjoy our cards. I offer you a challenge—a wager, if you wish—to see if one of us can win the lady before the end of the Season."

Sir Wilbur choked, "That's but a few weeks away!"

"I said it would be a challenge."

"A wager?" Swinton leaned one elbow on the table as he lifted his glass. Taking a reflective sip, he smiled. "On the state of the lovely lady's heart? What do you wish to lose, my friend, when I win her favor?"

"A single pound note."

"Are you so sure of losing that you're reluctant to wager more?"

Ross folded his arms over the front of his somber waistcoat. Glancing toward the door where he could see the brunette in conversation with their hostess, he said, "It's a foolish man who bets more on the state of a young woman's fickle heart."

"And the man who wins her hand will have little need for such insignificant gilt, for Wulfric's dirty acres would satisfy even the greediest soul." Swinton laughed and slapped his hands on the table. " 'Tis a grand idea, Brickendon. Worthy of myself, I must say. Are you in, Franklin?"

Sir Wilbur rubbed his double chins between his thumb and forefinger. "I don't know . . ."

"Stay out if the thought of winning such a prize unmans you. Could it be that you have no idea how to deal with such wealth and such a woman?" taunted Swinton.

The shorter man blanched, but squared his shoulders. "I don't wish to be left out. I was thinking only of you, Swinton, and your despair when you lose yet again in an *affaire de coeur.*"

The redhead's cheeks took on the color of his red vest. Ross smiled as his companions chuckled. Bruce Swinton's fervent pursuit of Miss Barbara Masterson had ended when she had wed another admirer less than a fortnight ago.

"I want nothing to do with this." Rollins aimed a glower at each of them. "I'm amazed at you, Brickendon. That Swinton and Franklin wish to make such a distasteful wager is no surprise, but I thought you knew the boundaries of decency in discussing a lady's heart."

"Bah!" Sir Wilbur reached under his coat and pulled out his enameled snuffbox. Opening it with a practiced flick, he pinched some and held it to his nose. He sneezed vehemently, then sighed as he replaced the box. "You would take part if you had a thought you might win."

Rollins mumbled something under his breath and, setting himself on his feet, stamped away.

"That guinea pig is ever a poor loser." Swinton smiled. "However, he shows good sense in not accepting this wager for Lady Vanessa Wolfe. She would crush him with a single, sharp word. So it shall be the three of us." He plucked some coins from beneath his coat and dropped them in the center of the table. "One pound wagered that *I* shall be the victor in this game of hearts."

Sir Wilbur started to do the same, then hesitated. "My friends, there must be some order to this pursuit of the lady. If we all try to woo her at once, I feel she shall be quite right in dismissing all of us."

"Then there's nothing to do but draw to see which one of us shall have the honor of courting her first," Ross replied as he placed his coins next to Swinton's.

"Pray you shall be first, Franklin," the redhead said, "for I would hate to see you lose your money without having a chance to pursue the lady."

"You're so sure you'll win her?" Sir Wilbur fired back.

"My friends," Ross interrupted, "let us begin this wa-

ger as comrades with a single goal, not scratching out
each other's eyes like barn cats." He spread the cards
facedown across the table. "Draw, and highest card goes
first, lowest last. It's that simple." With a magnanimous
wave, he said, "Do draw, Swinton."

The red-haired man flashed him a smile, then selected
a card. Swinton glanced at it and laughed softly. Ross
did not respond as Sir Wilbur made his pick. The
chubby man said nothing.

"My turn," Ross said needlessly, but he had to own
he was relishing the slight excitement of this miniature
drama. Certainly the amusement yet to come would be
even more grand.

He tilted his card toward him. Not allowing even an
arch of an eyebrow or a twitch of his lips to betray his
thoughts at the one he had drawn, he regarded the other
two men. They shifted uneasily in their seats, anxious
and fearful at the same time. Yes, this had been an in-
spired idea, for if they had drawn as he expected, the
next few weeks were going to be most intriguing.

"A nine," said Swinton, placing his card on the table.
"Can either of you beat that?"

"I have a jack," the baronet interjected with an abrupt
laugh as he placed his card atop the other. "I best you,
Swinton. What did you draw, Brickendon?"

"You both top me." He rested his elbow on the table
and said in a conspiratorial voice, "So you have the first
chance to win Lady Vanessa's cold heart, Franklin. If
she fails to consider your suit, then Swinton and I shall
have our opportunity." He put his hand over the money
in the middle of the table. With a smile, he watched as
his friends set their hands over his. "To Lady Vanessa
Wolfe and to our wager to win her for one of us."

They echoed his words, then Sir Wilbur stood. He
pocketed his share of the coins. "I look forward to win-

ning this wager as well as Lady Vanessa's hand. I shall begin courting her on the morrow."

"Not tonight?" asked Swinton, also rising. "Why do you delay?"

Ross watched as the baronet waddled from the room, followed by Swinton who was determined to get an answer. Ross suspected Franklin—quite rightly—wished to be a bit more sober before he presented himself to the marquess's daughter.

He relaxed against the back of his chair and flipped the card he had drawn onto the others. As the queen of diamonds stared back at him, he smiled. The rest of this Season might not be so boring after all.

Chapter Two

Lady Vanessa Wolfe frowned when she heard the clanging from the clock set on the mantel at one side of the drawing room in Mrs. Averill's elegant home. Her fingers clenched at her sides, but she forced them to loosen when her aunt aimed a frown at her. Without a doubt, Aunt Carolyn would give her another scold when they returned to their town house on Grosvenor Square. After months of being chided about her behavior at the round of parties her aunt insisted were essential if Vanessa was to find a husband, Vanessa wished to endure no more of them.

"Do smile at the gentlemen, Vanessa," her aunt had said more often than Vanessa cared to recall. "Speak of gentle subjects such as befits a lady. Laugh when the gentleman makes a sally."

Laugh? If they ever said anything amusing, she might. She had long ago tired of the inane conversation and the posturing. At the beginning, it *had* been amusing to see the gentlemen in their finery parading before the eligible ladies, but that had grown old as the *ton* turned its attention on the marquess's daughter and her chances for marriage.

She did not wish to leg-shackle herself to any of her eager admirers. She shuddered at the thought of having to be pleasant to yet another of the men who preyed on the young women thrust into the Marriage Mart. Every man seemed anxious to find himself a wife with either a title or wealth. As everyone believed she had both foisted on her, she was surrounded by a pesky swarm of men. Once this Season was past, her ears would be rid of their endless compliments and their annoying attempts to woo her with bragging and court-promises that had as little substance as a morning fog.

She glanced again at the clock. Midnight! How much longer must she stay at this eternally long party? She had done as her aunt wished and had spoken prettily to Mrs. Averill and her uppity niece. Otherwise, she had spent the evening seeking out Lord Mendoff. She had been led to believe that the gentleman who was high placed in the government would be in attendance, but her hopes of meeting him had come to naught.

"Here you are! Why are you lurking in a corner?"

At the sharp question in a warm voice, Vanessa forced a smile for her aunt. She did not like being on the outs with her beloved aunt, but Aunt Carolyn must come to accept the truth in Vanessa's heart.

Lady Carolyn Mansfield was no bent dowager. Younger than her brother by more than a decade, the black-haired woman could have been mistaken for Vanessa's older sister. She had wedded well, but been left an ace of spades a year before. The effervescent woman whose slim ankles and bright wit delighted everyone she met showed no interest in marrying again. Vanessa knew it was not from lack of suitors; as many called for her aunt during their Thursday afternoons at home as did for Vanessa. Lord Simstal was particularly anxious to present his suit, but Aunt Carolyn always treated the earl with polite indifference.

"I wasn't lurking," Vanessa replied. "I heard the clock clang and wished to check the time."

Aunt Carolyn put a gloved hand on Vanessa's arm. "Vanessa, I know you are anxious to leave, but you do not want to insult Mrs. Averill by departing early, do you?"

"I'm thinking fondly of my bed."

"You didn't sleep well again last night?"

Vanessa was tempted to reply she had not slept a full night since the horrible tidings had arrived of her brother's disappearance on the continent. Aunt Carolyn— although she grieved for Corey—did not share Vanessa's belief that the current Marquess of Wulfric remained alive. If Vanessa spoke of why she sought her bed late every night, her aunt might fly off in a pelter. Vanessa had witnessed one of her aunt's explosions of temper. She did not want to risk another dressing-down. They did not come often, but the memory lingered of Aunt Carolyn's fury when Vanessa had tried to persuade her to return to Wulfric Abbey before the beginning of the Season.

Aunt Carolyn's tongue had had a sharp edge that day which had been honed by her strong words of "ungrateful chit" and "obligation" and "good fortune." Vanessa had acknowledged without reluctance that she had an obligation to her family, but she found nothing good about the fortune which had taken Corey from her and she could not be grateful to any whim of fate that had led her to this need to find a husband to help her oversee the Abbey. She had said that and been rewarded by another scold. Then Aunt Carolyn had dissolved into tears, and Vanessa had vowed never to distress her dear aunt so again.

Instead she whispered, "I am afraid not."

Aunt Carolyn smiled and took her hand. "Then come, dear, and we shall be sure you get a good night's sleep tonight."

Hope burst within her. "We are leaving?"

"Of course not!" She waved, and a man with a gargantuan mustache hurried toward them. Before he was in earshot, Aunt Carolyn hurried to add, "A bit of dancing will tire you, so you may sleep like a babe in its mother's arms."

"But—"

"You know Mr. Rollins, I believe," Aunt Carolyn interjected with a warning smile.

Vanessa recognized the smile that her aunt gave to her often. It was a silent command to be on her most polished behavior. Not that Vanessa's manners were ever questionable. She simply avoided any meeting she did not wish to suffer through, but Aunt Carolyn was clearly going to be insistent that she endure this one.

"Good evening, Mr. Rollins," she said dutifully.

"My lady." He lifted her hand. His lips were so moist she could feel the dampness through her glove. "May I say what a splendid surprise it was to hear your lovely aunt telling me that you wished to dance this evening?"

"I'm sure you were quite surprised by my aunt's fervor," Vanessa answered. "I always am."

Aunt Carolyn smiled with satisfaction, and Vanessa wondered how she could prove to her aunt *this* was not the way to provide her with good prospects for a husband. Vanessa had already suffered too much of Mr. Rollins's company last month, and she had thought when they last parted that he understood she had no more interest in his company.

Knowing it was useless to argue, Vanessa let Mr. Rollins lead her out onto the dance floor. Inspiration blossomed when she saw the furious glance Darla Averill shot in her direction. Although she could not understand why Miss Averill was anxious for the overly effusive Mr. Rollins's company, Vanessa was ready to take advantage of any opportunity that presented itself.

"Mr. Rollins," she said in a near whisper so he had to

bend his head toward her, "I believe you have broken a lady's heart by asking me to dance."

"Yours?" he gasped, his mustache quivering with emotion.

"Miss Averill's," she answered quickly to avoid laughing at the hair dancing wildly on his lip. "Look if you can without her realizing, and you shall see that she's quite distressed you are dancing with another."

"My lady, I—"

"No need to apologize to me." She smiled, hoping he would not suspect that she knew he had intended to ignore Miss Averill's petulance. She would not let this chance to give him his leave pass by. "A fine gentleman like you knows he must soothe a woman's shattered heart at all costs." She withdrew her fingers from his arm and pressed them to her heart. "Oh, how I admire your chivalry, Mr. Rollins!"

Again Vanessa struggled not to laugh as the pompous man puffed up his chest and bowed over her hand before excusing himself to hurry to Miss Averill's side. She guessed he hoped to win the hearts of two ladies with his singular action. She stepped closer to the black walnut walls and released her laughter.

"May I ask what you find so amusing, Lady Vanessa?" asked a deep voice from the shadows behind her.

Vanessa whirled as a man stepped into the light. He was a half head taller than the other men in the room. His dark hair glistened with bluish fire in the glow from the pair of chandeliers. He must have engaged the services of a competent knight of the needle, for his coat fit him well. His valet should be commended for the diligence given to the glittering buckles on his brightly shined shoes. From his black brows along his aquiline nose to the hint of a cleft in his chin, he possessed an

aura of arrogant self-assuredness she found disconcert-
ing.

"Do I know you?" she asked, shocked to hear her
voice tremble.

"I regret I must be so bold as to introduce myself.
Lord Brickendon, my lady." He took her hand.

She tensed. She had grown exasperated by the parade
of men who insisted on kissing her hand as a prelude to
the silly talk that sounded like nothing-sayings in her
ears. Did none of them have a true thought in their
heads?

When Lord Brickendon bowed over her hand, then
relinquished it, she was amazed. She was about to
smile, then his gaze captured hers. Wanting to look
away, she could not, for she was fascinated by his ebony
eyes. In them, she saw unfettered amusement and other,
stronger emotions she could not decipher. Emotions, she
decided with a shiver of uneasiness, she would be wise
not to decipher.

"I am pleased to meet you, my lord," Vanessa murmured when the suspicion of a smile played on his lips.
Through her head rang Aunt Carolyn's entreaty that she
be pretty-mannered. She would find that easier if she
was not so unsettled by this handsome man.

"If I may be so bold, I would say your words contradict your expression." He glanced at the room. "You
look most displeased with everything around you."

Although she was tempted to fire back that his polished words did not match the glow in his eyes, she said
only, "Anyone who doesn't find the rigors of the Season
fatiguing is stronger than I."

"Odd, for you don't appear to be a frail flower. I
own—even on such a short acquaintance—I cannot
imagine you pining in a corner and watching the world
pass by you."

In spite of herself, Vanessa smiled. The image he created with his words was ludicrous. No Wolfe ever would be willing to sit quietly. "You're quite correct, my lord."

"Then I trust I shall see you in the future at another rout or perhaps in Hyde Park. Mayhap then, my lady, you will share with me the jest that left you laughing this evening." He took her hand.

Again, she tensed. She swallowed her gasp as she realized she was actually anticipating Lord Brickendon's kiss upon her fingers. When he surrendered her hand, unkissed, she was shocked at her disappointment. She must be mad! She murmured a farewell, resolved he would not guess the queer course of her thoughts.

"Until we meet again," Lord Brickendon said with another smile.

"Until we meet again," she whispered. Then, with a sharp, but silent reprimand to herself, she added in a stronger voice, "Good evening, my lord."

Vanessa feared she would hear his laughter as she walked away, but either Lord Brickendon silenced it or he found her peculiar behavior as distasteful as she did. After all, she was no swooning miss to be plied with a few fancy words that would send her head spinning.

But then why was her head as light as if she had been drinking too much wine? She did not like the feeling and vowed she would avoid any chance of suffering from it again. That would be as easy as avoiding the handsome Lord Brickendon.

The house on Grosvenor Square glowed with candles as the carriage slowed before its door. Vanessa thanked the tiger who handed her to the walkway and offered Quigley a smile as the butler held the door open.

The tall man had no spare flesh on his frame. What was left of his hair was the same black as his spotless livery. No matter what hour of the day or night, Quigley stood ready to open the door for her, pausing in his other duties to wish her a good day or good evening. She had no idea if he missed Wolfe Abbey as much as she did, for nothing in his ram-straight posture gave her a clue to his thoughts.

It was wondrous to be home, although this house with its simple foyer and the stairs that swept up from the ground floor in a flow of mahogany only made her nostalgic for Wolfe Abbey's grand oaken hall. She had to admire the delicate art her aunt had chosen to fill the niches along the staircase and the elegantly turned furniture with its pale blue silk upholstery in the parlor on the first floor. This house was splendid, but it was not home. She longed for the thick-legged pieces that were pulled around the huge hearth in the solarium at the Abbey. The furniture had been in the house for centuries; yet Vanessa was sure nothing could be more inviting and comfortable on a wintry night.

Quigley took her wrap and Aunt Carolyn's pelisse. "Lady Vanessa, this was returned."

Vanessa accepted the letter he held out to her. She did not need to look at it. Sending a note to the prime minister had been a desperate move, but she had hoped he would read it, even if he could do nothing else. He had returned it, unopened. With a deep sigh, she put it in her bag.

"A problem, dear?" asked Aunt Carolyn.

"Of course not," she answered, but glanced at Quigley, hoping he would not contradict her words. He must know how much she hated being false with Aunt Carolyn. When he bowed his head and whispered a good night, she released the breath she had not realized she was holding. She would thank Quigley in the morning. He was an unwilling ally in her attempt to discover her brother's whereabouts, but not once had he betrayed her.

"Then come with me a moment."

Vanessa glanced toward the stairs, then sighed. The scold she was due must be coming. The only way to get it over was to sit through it and promise to try harder next time to meet her aunt's expectations. As she followed Aunt Carolyn up the stairs and into the brightly lit parlor, she clenched her hands at her side. Papa had urged her to obey her aunt, but he would be outraged at the rôle she had had to assume to be a part of the Season. Then, with another, much deeper sigh, she wondered if she was forcing her own opinions upon her memories of her father. After all, her mother had been a vibrant part of Society before marrying and moving to Wolfe Abbey.

Vanessa sat on the very edge of a blue-striped chair and watched as Aunt Carolyn paced in front of the white marble mantel. The ruffle on the hem of her aunt's gown fluttered on every furious step.

"My dear Vanessa," Aunt Carolyn began in her strictest tone, "how could you embarrass our family by leaving Mr. Rollins alone on the dance floor?"

"But, Aunt Carolyn, I did not abandon him. Miss Averill wished to dance with him and he with her." Vanessa folded her hands in her lap as she spoke the small lie. She rushed to add, "Papa always implored me to think of others. Do you wish me to do differently here in Town?"

"Don't try to twist things your way, my girl." Wagging her finger at Vanessa, Aunt Carolyn lamented, "What your father wanted was for you to marry a man who could take care of you and Wolfe Abbey. Each time I introduce you to a fine gentleman, you rid yourself of him as quickly as a fox loses the hounds. At first, I thought it was nothing but girlish shyness, but, I fear,

Vanessa, you shall end up on the shelf if you do nothing to change your ways."

"Do leave off," she begged. "I have found Mr. Rollins a disagreeable bore each time he has imposed his company on me. Just like every other man I have had inflicted upon me during this interminable Season."

"Even Lord Brickendon?"

"Lord Brickendon?" she choked, not prepared to hear his name. Her aunt had not mentioned him during the ride home from the rout.

"Do you think me blind? I saw you talking to him." Her aunt shook her head and sat on the white settee. "Not that you spoke to him for very long. Did your acidic wit chase him away, too?"

"I merely exchanged a few pleasantries with him."

"Pleasantries?" Aunt Carolyn's brows rose nearly to the perfect curls across her forehead. "My dear child, *you* exchanged pleasantries? This night should be heralded as a first."

She smiled. "You need not make it sound as if I have no manners, Aunt Carolyn."

"Manners you have, child. Pretty ones, but you use them too sparingly. Dare I believe that you have met a man who doesn't bore you?"

Vanessa hesitated too long, for her aunt's smile widened. She should answer, but she had no answer. Lord Brickendon certainly had not been boring, although she had found some of his comments impertinent. Then, she reminded herself sharply, they had spoken for such a short time. Probably he would become as tedious as the others crowding the Season if she had shared more conversation with him.

She rose and knelt next to her aunt. "I implore you to listen to me. Let us be done with this travesty of finding me a husband. I wish only to return to Wolfe Abbey."

Her aunt's long fingers stroked her hair. "Dear child,

you know your father left you to my care because he was sure I would do the best for you."

"Marrying the wrong man is not the best thing for me."

"Indeed." Standing, Aunt Carolyn assisted Vanessa to her feet. "And that is why we must remain a part in the Season until you find the man who is best for you. Go to bed, child. You have a fitting at Madame deBerg's tomorrow morning."

Vanessa murmured a good night and, giving her aunt a quick kiss on the cheek, hurried up the stairs. As she walked toward her bedroom door, she ignored the grim faces of her ancestors in the portraits hanging in a row over the gold-striped wallpaper. Why were they so dour? They had not had to endure this Marriage Mart!

She laughed ironically. She *was* enjoying parts of the Season. Going to the theater with Aunt Carolyn, strolling through the Park, being with her newfound friends—she loved that part of Town. If only her brother could have been here to laugh with her over the men who were anxious to wed her for the Abbey, it would have been perfect. Of course, those eager suitors would have scanty interest in her then because Corey would possess the Abbey.

Only one lamp lit her bedroom, but Vanessa needed no light. The chamber seemed too cozy after her massive room in the Abbey. She had to own—albeit reluctantly—that this chamber with its light pink walls and chintz curtains had become a welcome sanctuary from the Season's craziness. Here, where she could look out over the green in the middle of the Square, she might imagine, for a moment, she was back in the Abbey and listening for her father's gruff voice and Corey's answer.

Her abigail helped her change into a lacy, muslin nightgown. Leale did not ask if Vanessa had enjoyed her evening, and Vanessa was grateful. The gray-haired woman had accepted Vanessa's lack of interest in the Season. Yet, how surprised Leale would be if Vanessa spoke of the viscount and her reaction to his teasing eyes and strange comments!

Vanessa scowled at the thought. " 'Tis nothing," she reassured Leale quickly to soothe her abigail's dismay.

"You're frowning, Lady Vanessa. Such expressions can freeze into your face." She clucked under her breath. "Then who would wish to marry you?"

"I think it would matter not if I was as ugly as a fish-wife."

"Lady Vanessa!"

"Forgive me," she said, smiling. "I'm just tired."

For once, she thought her abigail would refuse to accept such a nebulous answer. Then the short woman went, mumbling, into the dressing room to hang up Vanessa's gown.

Running her fingers along the polished edge of her dressing table, Vanessa stared at the closed door. It would be most unfortunate if Lord Brickendon was as boring as the other men who had vied for her hand.

She frowned and pushed Lord Brickendon from her head. She must think of only one thing . . . her brother. She went to her chest of drawers and knelt to open the lowest one. Each night she took out the packet that was wrapped in a strip of cambric, and each night she returned it to its cache beneath her small-clothes in the bottommost drawer.

Tears filled her eyes, but she allowed none of them to fall as she unwound the material to reveal a miniature in a circular frame. She pressed her finger to her lips, then to the tiny face. Looking into eyes of the same gray as her own, she sat back on her heels.

"Corey, nothing yet, but don't lose hope. I shan't."

"Lady Vanessa?"

Vanessa hastily wrapped the portrait and hid it. Closing the drawer, she jumped to her feet. Vanessa did not dare to trust even Leale with her hopes. She was unsure if Leale would speak of them to Aunt Carolyn. She did not want her aunt to discover she still clung to the hope her brother was alive on the opposite side of the Channel.

Corey Wolfe, heir to the title of Lord Wulfric, had defied their father's edict and had purchased a commission as an infantry captain. Sent to fight the French, his bravery had brought honor to their family in the tradition of their ancestors who had come from Normandy with William the Conqueror. Then, after a fierce battle during which many of his comrades had been killed, he had vanished. Their bodies had been recovered. His had not.

There was nothing to give her hope yet nothing to let her mourn. She had been offered only empty condolences by an indifferent government.

She was certain Corey must not be dead. He was alive. Somewhere he was alive, perhaps in hiding, perhaps as a prisoner of that horrible Corsican. No one else shared her optimism. Aunt Carolyn refused to listen to her, telling Vanessa that her wish to see her brother would fade with time. Vanessa would come to see the truth when she allowed herself to grieve for Corey. Time and the delight of men vying for her hand during the Season would take her mind from imagining her brother might come home.

The government had proven even less sympathetic. The Prince Regent's ministers had turned as deaf an ear to her entreaties for their assistance in discovering Corey's location. One pompous secretary in the Prime Minister's office had told her coldly that the government would soon be destitute if every relative of every man lost in the war demanded an individual accounting and the return of the corpse. There had been not the least bit of compassion in his voice when he added that some of the dead would never be identified, for there was little left to identify in the wake of cannon fire. She would not give up her dream of seeing him home and safe.

Standing, she said, "I think I'll retire now, Leale."

"Then you don't wish—"

"I'll blow out the candle myself. Good night."

Although her abigail's face held a bewildered expression, Leale left the room. Vanessa waited until the door clicked closed, then slipped to her writing table. Checking that the drapes at the two windows were pulled tight, she lit the small lamp atop the table. She opened a drawer. From it, she took a rosewood box and set it on the desk. Her hands clasped the box, pulling it close to her breast. She sighed and leaned forward until her head rested on the carved lid.

She lifted a chain that hung around her neck. At the end of the glittering gold was a tiny key of a tarnished brass. She slipped it into the box and opened the lid. Taking out the topmost page, she put it on the desk. There was no need to read it, for she had memorized every word of Corey's last missive. His brash courage and his determination to best Napoleon's forces shone from every dim word, but the date at the top reminded her how long it had been since he had penned this note.

Putting it back in the box, she lifted out a piece of clean paper. She opened the ink and bent to her task. She was not sure how long it would take to find her brother, but she would not stop until she had written to everyone who might help her. The vow she had sworn as she stood on the family crest set into stone in the chapel of Wolfe Abbey was sacred. Only when Corey was home in England and had assumed the title of Lord Wulfric would she think of her own life and the future Aunt Carolyn was firm she should have.

Chapter Three

Vanessa would have rather been anywhere else this evening, but she was at Almack's. To her, the Assembly Room epitomized the Season, for here the *ton* thronged to file before one another in gowns that where *à la modality* and in dark coats with the white breeches the patronesses deemed *de rigueur*. The room was filled with the prattle that served in lieu of the stimulating conversation she had shared with her father and brother at Wolfe Abbey.

But, worst of all, it was the place where she had to suffer the eager glances of the ardent men who wished to marry her for her father's fortune. Her few attempts to dissuade Aunt Carolyn from insisting that they attend the Assemblies had met with failure. Her aunt remained resolved that Vanessa would marry before the end of the Season. Nothing less would do.

"After all, *yours* is not the only reputation at stake," Aunt Carolyn had told her the first time Vanessa had complained about her discomfort at Almack's. "Each of your cousins was betrothed within weeks of me firing her off. What would be said if I failed with you?"

"That I was an incurable bluestocking who would as lief see my pretty aunt receiving court-promises than abiding them myself."

Vanessa grimaced as she recalled her aunt's laughter. Such honesty had served her well in Wolfe Abbey, but failed miserably in Town.

So—once again—she sat on one side of the crowded Assembly Room while her thoughts were elsewhere. Quigley might be receiving an answer to her latest query even now. Impatience gnawed at her, but she hid it as she spoke to those who were anxious to lure her into conversation.

Mayhaps, she told herself sternly, you might find an ally here. Surely there was someone who could help her locate her brother. While she had sat in antechambers of a minister's office, she had watched how the gentlemen were greeted with more respect and how easily they were granted an appointment. She had called on nearly every office herself and gained nothing. If she could persuade a gentleman to ask the questions for her, she might obtain the answers she needed.

She cautioned herself to choose her ally with care. Not just any gentleman would do, for the one she selected must be willing to pose her questions to the military and the government without asking *her* too many questions. She needed to find a man who was well-connected with Whitehall, but who did not want to involve himself further with her. Nor could the man be any of the ones in Aunt Carolyn's vast circle of friends. Word of Vanessa's continued search for the truth would then reach her aunt's ears. Certainly among the *ton* there must be a man who fit her needs. If she had to be here to meet this unknown ally, then she would.

She smiled at compliments heaped on her and replied graciously. Leale deserved the lauds for her hair that was piled *à la Sappho* and her white gown which was adorned with a ruffle along its decorous neckline and at its hem. She fought not to play with the ribbons dropping from the high waistline that emphasized the curves of her bodice. When she realized her velvet slippers were tapping restlessly, she halted the motion. No one must guess what she was really thinking.

Aunt Carolyn patted her arm. "My dear, I have never seen you enjoy Almack's so much."

"You were right."

"*I* was right? About you coming to Almack's?" Her aunt chuckled lowly. "What has caused this unexpected change of heart?"

"You said to look at each person as if he or she might be special." Vanessa glanced away, so her aunt would not guess how she was stretching the truth. "So I shall. Who knows whom I might meet?"

"Who, indeed? Look who's arrived!" She snapped her fan open and fluttered it fiercely in front of her face. "Tonight shall be interesting."

Vanessa looked past her aunt, expecting to see one of Aunt Carolyn's bosom-bows. Her eyes widened as a tall man walked toward them. Although she had met him but once, she could not mistake Lord Brickendon. His shining dark hair, his confident stance, the stylish clothes he wore so well, she recalled all that as she stared at him. Swiftly she dropped her gaze before he could discover her gaping at him like a love-sick air-dreamer. Her heart pounded so loudly she feared he would hear it above the bibble-babble of the Assembly.

"Good evening, ladies," the viscount said with a curt nod.

"Good evening, my lord. I—" Vanessa gasped as Lord Brickendon continued past. She blinked, astounded that he would be so rude. He had not rushed to her side, anxious to lather her with compliments, as other men had. She had not expected him to do that, but no one was in such a hurry at Almack's. Everyone stopped to speak politely to those sitting by the edge of the floor.

Everyone but Vanessa Wolfe.

Vanessa flinched at the thought. How many people had she treated as the viscount was treating her? Until now, she had not guessed her cordial coolness might be construed as tactlessness. Talking endlessly of the right *modiste* and who was seen with whom in the Park always filled her with *ennui* when she wanted to ask who might help her find Corey. A flush of dismay flooded her as she wondered if she had—in not much more than a score of words—bored the viscount when she met him at Mrs. Averill's party. What irony that would be when he was the first man she had met since the start of the Season who seemed to have an iota of sense about him.

She clasped her hands in her lap. She should care nothing for his opinions. After all, she had no wish for Lord Brickendon to pay court to her. Such frivolities would demand time she could not squander. She must think only of Corey. She must—

Vanessa's thoughts were cut short when her hand was grasped in one that was as soft as unbaked dough. She gasped as her gaze focused on a bacon-face.

A wide grin matched the sparkle in the man's blue eyes as he rumbled in a surprisingly deep voice, "My lady, I beg you to pardon my impertinence in presenting myself without formal introduction. I am Sir Wilbur Franklin."

"It's my honor to meet you," she said quietly, becoming disconcerted again that his words brought to mind Lord Brickendon's. Seeing her aunt's astonishment at her subdued answer, she averted her eyes. She must not let Aunt Carolyn guess what she was thinking *now.*

"Nay, you're being too kind," the portly man gushed. " 'Tis *my* honor. Forgive me for being so anxious to speak with you that I failed to wait for your dear aunt to introduce us."

"You are forgiven." She refrained from adding that if

he was going to spend the rest of the evening atoning for such a small sin, she would give the brown-haired man his *congé* posthaste. Hating the hypocritical words that burned her tongue, she added, "I must say this meeting is overdue. I have seen you at other gatherings, sir, but I fear circumstances have prevented us from meeting."

Aunt Carolyn said, "How wonderful those circumstances have been dealt with! I trust your sister is better, Sir Wilbur."

"You are most kind to inquire of Ethel. She has risen from her sickbed, so we can hope her situation will continue to improve." He beamed at the older woman, and Vanessa wondered if she had misread his intentions. Sir Wilbur Franklin must be older than Aunt Carolyn by more than a half-dozen years, so he might be eager to turn his eye on her. Such a match would be a good one, bringing together two old families from the north of England. Easily Vanessa could imagine Aunt Carolyn presiding over the baronet's estate in the country with its generous expanse of gardens and its deer park.

Her hopes vanished as Sir Wilbur turned to her again. "Would you give me the honor of standing up with me for the next set of dances?"

"You do *me* an honor, sir. I am delighted to accept." She held out her hand and let him bring her to her feet. As she put her fingers on his arm, she risked a glance at her aunt.

The older woman was staring at her in disbelief, her mouth open. No doubt, Aunt Carolyn had been planning to urge Vanessa to accept the gracious invitation. A mischievous thought tickled Vanessa, and she winked at her aunt. Aunt Carolyn's fan began to flutter furiously, as it did when she was trying to hide her smile.

Vanessa did not hide hers. Things would be fine with Aunt Carolyn now, and Vanessa would not have to explain why she had accepted this invitation. Explaining was the thing she hated most, especially when she doubted if she could explain why she was so bothered by a man she had spoken to only twice. Dancing with Sir Wilbur was sure to be the antidote to her uneasy thoughts of Lord Brickendon.

Even more important, it would offer her the chance to discover if Sir Wilbur was the ally she sought. She knew too little about the pudgy man. It could be he had the very connections she needed to discover Corey's whereabouts. The thought lightened her feet as she thanked him when he bowed to her and stepped back to take his place for the quadrille.

Vanessa quickly discovered her escort had little grace. She forgave him courteously the first dozen times he stepped on her toes in the first dance, then suggested they step out of the set and have something cool to drink.

As deeply as he had to concentrate on the not very intricate steps of the dance, every effort to draw him into conversation had been futile. He seemed as impatient to be done with the dance as she and quickly brought her a glass of lemonade.

"Have you found your first Season to your liking?" Sir Wilbur asked, hooking his thumb in a pocket of his white silk waistcoat. The pose accented the breadth of his belly, which bounced on every word. "Hardly a young girl of my acquaintance has not anticipated her first Season greatly."

She took a half step back, for he stood too close. When he was about to lessen the distance, she turned away, as if she was watching the dancers. She saw his discomposure from the corner of her eye, but said only, "A Season in Town is much as I was led to believe it would be."

"You sound less than pleased."

"Do I?" She faced him again. His insight suggested

there might be more substance to the pudgy baronet than she had conjectured.

"Can it be the Season bores you?"

Vanessa wanted to reply with an affirmative, but she was aware of ears beyond hers and Sir Wilbur's. She must remember how quickly the gabblemongers could take her ill-thought words back to Aunt Carolyn.

"I find," she said, choosing her words carefully, "the Season prohibits me from indulging in other pursuits I once considered an important part of each day."

" 'Tis a strain on all of us." He grinned, reminding her of a sprite from an old folk tale. "However, you must own it has its rewards."

She followed his gaze toward a couple whose heads were bowed toward each other in earnest conversation. Gently she smiled. For those women who sought nothing more than a well-placed marriage, the Season must be a delight.

"You are right," Vanessa said and smiled as Sir Wilbur chuckled, clearly pleased. "It gives us a chance to enjoy a bit of chatter-broth about our fellows. It allows us to admire the flowers in the Park. It exhausts us from evenings of music and gaiety."

"And it gives us gentlemen the chance to be in the company of such lovely ladies."

Vanessa ignored the compliment as she continued, "However, I miss a chance to while away an evening with a fascinating book."

"Book? I should have guessed you would be a kindred soul, my lady. I, too, enjoy the chance to read whenever possible."

Vanessa almost gasped aloud. She *had* been wrong about the baronet. Mayhap—at last—she had found someone who shared the love of literature that had been a part of her life at Wolfe Abbey. Eagerly she asked, "Have you read the new book by—?"

He laughed, interrupting her. "I make it a habit, since my school days, to read only the morning papers. One must be cautious about overstraining one's eyes. So I read only the *Chronicle*. I believe it contains all the information my mind can hold."

So do I, she thought with sudden vexation, but forced her lips to tilt in a smile. That the pudgy man had not read a book since leaving his tutor's supervision told her that her first impression had been accurate. Telling herself she must not be so uncharitable, she said, "I, too, read the newspaper over breakfast every morning."

"Perhaps we can discuss what we have read during a ride in the Park tomorrow. A bit of sunshine might put more color into your face, my lady."

Vanessa wondered if he had any idea how she was struggling not to let her color raise along with her temper. Aunt Carolyn was not the only Wolfe with a fierce disposition. "The Park seems a peculiar venue for such conversation."

His brows lowered as his jovial face wore an uncomfortable frown. "May I ask why? I have always found the Park a pleasant backdrop for a bit of talk. If you prefer to go elsewhere—"

"It is difficult for me to speak of the events on the other side of the Channel when I am surrounded by such gaiety."

"I find the discussion of the war most disturbing," he said with a shudder.

"As do I." Her fingers tightened on her glass. "I believe we must—"

Again he intruded with a laugh. "Your fervor is endearing, my lady. 'Tis charming beyond words to see a young woman taking up the banner her fallen brother once held close to his breast. However, you should not trouble yourself with such thoughts. They could bring on ill-humors to smite you."

Vanessa clenched her hand around the glass of lemonade. She had been a complete block to think this man would do anything but speak platitudes. She was not endearing, nor was her determination to see Corey brought home unscathed charming. Snapping back a retort would be useless. Sir Wilbur thought he was complimenting her. Obviously Sir Wilbur Franklin was not the ally she sought. Was he even within this room? Despair pricked her. Mayhap he did not even exist. No, she could not let gloom overtake her. Corey was alive, and she must do all she could to help bring him home, even if she had to let every man in the Polite World torture her toes with his dancing.

"However," he went on, "I prefer not to muddy my day with thoughts of that unfortunate situation. As I can do nothing about the war, I watch my health by thinking only of pleasant things. On that note, I would as lief enjoy the chance to dance again with you, my lady, for that would be highly pleasant."

"Thank you," she answered automatically. Anything else she said would be futile, for this man's very existence was no wider than his stomach. She would dance once more with him, then excuse herself as tactfully as possible.

Sir Wilbur did not take the hand she held out to him, but instead said, in an oddly strained voice, "I did not expect to see you here tonight."

Vanessa turned to see a red-haired man standing beside the baronet. His intense eyes caught hers, but she did not lower hers. He blinked at her forthright stare.

"May I introduce Bruce Swinton?" The tension remained in Sir Wilbur's voice.

The tall man folded in the center to bow over her hand. As he started to raise it to his lips, she withdrew her fingers. She saw a spark of irritation in his eyes, but he was gentleman enough to offer her a smile. Dismay scored her. She should not include Mr. Swinton in her exasperation with the baronet. Did Sir Wilbur fear Mr. Swinton would be more entertaining and turn her attention from him? She almost laughed. No one could be more boring than the baronet with his closed mind and open mouth.

She chided herself. Such childish petulance would only add to her distaste with the whole evening.

"And another friend," Sir Wilbur was saying. "Lord—"

"I have had the pleasure of making Lady Vanessa Wolfe's acquaintance," interrupted a warm voice. Lord Brickendon nodded toward her, but did not take her hand. A smile spread across his lips.

She started to return it, then noticed—as the previous time they had met—his good humor did not reach his eyes. For a moment, she was aware of nothing but how the dark emotions there slowly gentled to amusement. She looked away as she fought her annoyance. How dare he mock her! She could not accuse him of any wrongdoing when he was outwardly polite. He was not the only one who could use manners to turn a conversation to his advantage.

"Yes, I believe we have met," Vanessa drawled, tapping her fan against her fingers. "I am sorry I cannot recall where, my lord."

"You must have a very full life, my lady, if you cannot recall our recent meeting at Mrs. Averill's rout." He tipped his head to her.

She recognized the challenge in his eyes. Letting a slow smile flit across her lips, she said, "I did think you looked familiar when you passed my aunt Carolyn and me a while back."

"So you do remember that? How kind of you, my lady."

Vanessa flinched as his sharp words pricked her. She had been fat-skulled to let him have the opportunity to

retort. Although his smile did not waver, she sensed his
satisfaction with his well-spoken answer.

With irritation in his voice, Mr. Swinton interjected,
"As I was saying, Brickendon. . . . My lady, we were
speaking of the recent events in Hanover Square." He
chuckled lowly as he glanced across the room. "Do you
think the lady had any delusions of keeping such an *affaire* secret?"

"If you will excuse me," Vanessa said as she took a
step away from the three men. She had no interest in
their gossip. If she was to find someone to help her, she
guessed she must look beyond this threesome.

Instantly Sir Wilbur's smile plummeted into a plead-
ing pout as he stared at her like a stuck pig. "My dear
lady, I implore you to grace us a while longer with your
company."

"I must beg your indulgence, but my aunt shall become anxious when I have been gone so long."

Sir Wilbur glanced uneasily at his companions. Vanessa followed his gaze. Mr. Swinton was grinning
broadly. She was tempted to do the same, for Sir
Wilbur's puppyish attempts to beguile her were so obvious. Her urge to smile vanished when she looked at
Lord Brickendon. His face held no more emotion than a
statue.

Abrupt and astounding compassion filled her as she
realized that her hurry to depart had humiliated Sir
Wilbur in front of his friends. Although she regretted
the words as soon as she spoke them to the chubby
man, she said, "I believe my aunt would be delighted to
have more time to talk with you."

"How grand! I shall have the company of two lovely
ladies this evening. I will, without question, be the envy
of every man here." He flashed a victorious smile at his
companions.

Having no choice but to allow him to draw her hand

into his arm, Vanessa whispered a good evening to Mr. Swinton and the viscount. She was glad to leave them behind, for she found their company disquieting. Yet, the alternative of being forced to tolerate more of the baronet's company was nearly as unpalatable.

Her plan to give the baronet a hasty excuse was ruined by her aunt's enthusiasm at his company. Aunt Carolyn could not hide her happiness that Vanessa had not given the baronet his leave.

"I enjoyed watching you dance together," Aunt Carolyn said. "Vanessa is such a lovely dancer, but she seldom finds a partner to match her skill."

Sir Wilbur replied, "You are being too kind to me, my lady. However, I must say Lady Vanessa possesses a grace that draws every eye. She is much the wiser for keeping a slim figure. Better for the health, I hear."

"How kind of you to say that! Isn't he kind, Vanessa?" Aunt Carolyn gave her no chance to answer as she gushed, "You must join us tomorrow evening." She wafted her painted silk fan in front of her face. "Vanessa and I are having an intimate party for no more than a score of our dearest acquaintances. An evening of cards."

"It sounds like a delightful evening."

"I believe you are right." Aunt Carolyn turned to Vanessa and added, "Don't you think so?"

Vanessa kept her smile in place. Any evening with Sir Wilbur Franklin was sure to be interminable. Yet it might not be the worst of circumstances. The portly man was so eager to impress her that she could keep him from pressing his suit too heavily by showing him a mere frown. Such a suitor could work to her advantage because it would keep the other, more demanding swains from calling.

Quietly she said, "I think it shall be an interesting evening for all of us."

* * *

Aunt Carolyn followed Vanessa up two flights of stairs to her bedchamber. Dismissing Leale after the abigail had helped Vanessa undress, she sat on Vanessa's bed and laughed. "I daresay you have gained an incredibly avid suitor, my dear child. Sir Wilbur Franklin could not be dislodged from your side this evening. Not a soul in the Assembly Room missed his eager attention to you."

"I shall have to disabuse him as gently as possible of the notion of courting me." Vanessa winced as her hairbrush caught in a snarl. Putting the brush on her cherry dressing table, she looked at her aunt's reflection in the glass. "He isn't as intolerable as some of the other men I have met, but I daresay that too much time in his company would drive me quite mad. He speaks endlessly of his sister's precarious health and his determination to avoid enduring the same."

"The Franklin family is a well-to-do one."

She lowered the brush to her lap. "Money to ensure my comfortable future is not an issue for me. As the many men hovering around me prove, my father's fortune is more considerable than most." She sighed and stared at her high color in the glass. The vexation she had not been able to show at Almack's was visible now. "I thank heaven every day I am not a wretchedly poor woman who has no choice but to accept a husband from among those anxious to buy a bride."

"Vanessa!"

"Don't sound so scandalized! After all, I have heard you say much the same yourself."

Aunt Carolyn laughed softly. "That is true, but, Vanessa, you must own that Sir Wilbur would do anything for you. You could see that in the way he acquiesces to your wishes."

"Capitulates, you mean." Going to the bed, she leaned her cheek against the carved upright. "Dear Aunt Carolyn, don't try to convince me to buckle myself to a man who would bore me quite to tears. Do you know he's proud to own to never reading a book?"

"A wise woman finds a husband whose interests aren't her own."

She laughed at her aunt's ironic grin. "A man who's not as intelligent as her. Is that what you mean? In that case, Sir Wilbur Franklin would be the perfect match for any woman at Almack's tonight."

"There were others you spoke to this evening. Mr. Swinton and Lord Brickendon, I believe."

"Your eyes are as crafty as a hawk's!"

"You are my responsibility." Taking her niece's hand, Aunt Carolyn brought Vanessa to sit next to her on the white coverlet. "Dear child, it gladdens my heart to see you the center of such attention, but the Season draws to a close. You must decide soon."

"Between that trio?" She laughed. "None of those confirmed chuckleheads urges me to offer him more than a polite greeting."

At that, Aunt Carolyn showed her infamous temper. Vanessa was glad her aunt scolded her at length for her outspoken retort, for the pulse of guilt flashing through her was a sharp reminder she was not speaking the truth. She wished she could have conversed at length with Lord Brickendon. Even though he was sure to put her in a bad skin with his sharp tongue and outrageously amused stares, she enjoyed his company. Surely he would not be so proudly unread and so resolved not to have any opinions as Sir Wilbur was! Telling herself, that if she spent more than a few moments in his company, she was sure to find him as insufferable as his comrades, she murmured an apology to her aunt and promised to treat Sir Wilbur with kindness when he arrived at the *soirée*.

She nodded as her aunt kissed her cheek before leaving. She stared at the door for a moment, then turned to her writing desk. In the midst of the preparations for the party tomorrow evening, surely her aunt would not notice Vanessa arranging with Quigley to send one of the maids with a letter to be delivered to Lord Mendoff who might have some influence with one of the Regent's ministers.

Her fingers trembled as she reached for a sheet of paper. If having Aunt Carolyn all a-blither about Sir Wilbur Franklin kept her from noticing that Vanessa still sought information about Corey, even marrying the boring baronet would not be too much to pay in return for having her brother safe once more.

Chapter Four

"This is going to be better than I thought," Ross crowed as he set the newspaper down on the table. Reaching for a muffin from among the warm ones in a basket near his cup of coffee, he smiled.

"I am pleased, my lord."

His grin widened as he looked to where his valet was coming into the breakfast parlor with Ross's coat. "Pott, you have no idea what I'm talking about."

The man, who was nearly as short and as round as Franklin, chuckled. "I find it always is wise to agree with you, my lord."

"That is arrant nonsense! You enjoy a brangle as much as the next man."

"Not if you are the next man."

Ross stood and took the coat from his man. The sleeves still held the warmth from being pressed. He was grateful that Pott kept his clothes in such a good state. Otherwise, he would have been sure to run off to some meeting at Whitehall with his coat wrinkled from being tossed on the back of a chair.

"You seem in an excellent temper this morning," Pott said with a sigh.

"Rightly so." He was amused at his valet's observation. Pott could not hide his eagerness to return home to

Essex and to be away from the crowded city, but he would never speak a word of complaint. Not a *word,* although he made his feelings clear with every motion. Ross picked up the newspaper and grinned. "Listen to this: 'It was noted at Almack's last evening that Sir Wilbur Franklin partnered with Lady Vanessa Wolfe for several dances.' "

"That is nice, my lord."

"Nice?" He laughed and threw the paper back on the table. "Last night was one of the best times I have had since this blasted Season began. Franklin was nearly blithering with his excitement at being in the exulted lady's company, and Swinton could barely tolerate being forced to watch."

"And you, my lord?"

"I enjoyed the whole."

"And the lady?" Pott toyed with one of the buttons on his waistcoat. "Did she enjoy the whole?"

Ross's smile vanished. Blast! He did not wish to think of Lady Vanessa Wolfe. If he did, he might let his mind linger on the warmth of her smile, which he had seen so seldom, or the soft glow of her eyes or the gentle curves that drew his eyes even from across the crowded floor of Almack's. She was a lovely, enticing woman, and he had no need for a lovely, enticing woman cluttering up his head.

"What lady doesn't enjoy having suitors eager for her hand?" he retorted shortly.

Pott turned toward the door, a frown on his full face. "I have heard talk that the maquess's daughter is not like any other woman."

"All women are the same. They think only of playing coy with a man's heart until they twist it so tightly that there is no escape." Taking a bite of the muffin, he frowned when crumbs dropped along the front of his coat. He brushed them aside. "If we match them at their own sport, who is to say nay?"

Pott shook his head as he plucked another crumb off the coat. "Not I, my lord, although I urge you to show caution in this game. What if the young woman develops a true affection for one of you?"

"If she is caper-witted enough to have a *tendre* for Franklin or Swinton, she deserves the life she has chosen with her ardent suitor."

"And if her heart turns to you, my lord?"

"I aim only to win this wager, Pott, not the lady's heart."

Pott frowned. "This is an unwise course, my lord. You trespass on dangerous ground when you play with a woman's heart."

"I have my reasons for what I am doing."

"To chance breaking a lady's heart should put a halt to a gentleman's actions, not be the cause of them."

Ross chuckled. "I have no intention of hurting the lady. Simply I wish to win this wager."

"There are other things to bet on, my lord."

"None as interesting as watching Franklin and Swinton falling over each other to vie for the lady's attentions." He laughed again. "No one shall be injured. I would not have embarked on this attempt to assuage my *ennui*, if I had thought that would be so."

Pott still frowned. "I would be less concerned if the lady knew you meant this wager only as a jest."

"You have heard the gossip as frequently as I, Pott. Mayhap more often, if the truth be told. Lady Vanessa Wolfe has no wish to leg-buckle herself to any man, but I intend to prove it is in her best interests to accept my suit . . . at least temporarily."

"Temporarily?" Amazement widened Pott's eyes.

"Long enough to enjoy the rest of this otherwise ignoble Season and to collect on this wager from those two pig-widgeons."

"I still urge you to be careful."

His grin returned. "A creed I live by, Pott, for I have no more wish to be wed by this Season's end than I did when it began."

A tall-case clock ticked contentedly to itself in one corner of the antechamber in the house on Hanover Square. Sifted by the thickening clouds and the stained glass in the window, the feeble sunshine edged along the Persian rug to mark the slow movement of time.

The room was empty except for Vanessa. When she had arrived, an imperious man had been sitting behind the massive desk in front of the door leading into a private chamber. Nearly as hairless as his mahogany desk, the man had introduced himself curtly as Mr. Dennis, secretary to Lord Mendoff. She had requested an interview with the earl for this morning, and Mr. Dennis had promised to convey her request. That was the last she had seen of his gangly height. Almost an hour had passed since his disappearance, and she wondered if he would ever return.

She resisted rising and going to the tall, gilt mirror by the door. She knew she looked her best for this call. Her straw hat was tied beneath her chin with a ribbon to match the light yellow ribbons at the bodice and along the long sleeves of her gown. The white sarconet muslin rose beneath her chin in a small ruff. Her fingers clasped in her gloves of lemon kid. She must sit quietly and wait, she reminded herself.

This call was too important to let her impatience ruin everything. Lord Mendoff might be the perfect person to assist her in finding information on Corey. Vanessa was not sure when she might be able to come back if she left now, since Aunt Carolyn kept a close eye on her.

Oh, why couldn't Aunt Carolyn share her faith that Corey was still alive? It would be so much easier if they joined their rather formidable forces to demand an answer from the government. Instead, Aunt Carolyn had mourned for her nephew and had become even more determined to find a match for her niece.

Mayhap it was as simple as the fact that Aunt Carolyn had nothing to regret about Corey's leaving. How many times had Vanessa relived that last conversation with her brother? How many times had the anger come back to haunt her? If she could live those moments over again. . . . She was not sure if anything would be different, and, if Corey never returned, she would never know if the pain between them could be healed.

She stood, unable to sit any longer. Her rebellious feet paced across the room. How much longer could she be kept waiting? She would wait, even if she trod a path in the carpet with her pacing.

Her steps faltered when she caught her reflection in the mirror. She did look presentable, save for her frown. Forcing a feigned smile, she let it fall away instantly. It appeared as false as a thumper. How long had she been wearing a face as long as a fiddle? She could not recall the last time she had worn a genuine smile. No wonder she had obtained no help. In her dismals, she had offended everyone about her with her melancholy. She must make an effort to disguise her dreary spirits and be as charming as if she could talk the hind legs off a bird. Then she might find the help she needed for Corey . . . and for her own happiness.

Sitting again, she tried another smile. It still was as uncomfortable as someone else's boots, but she must remember how to smile. She must.

Vanessa looked up as the door behind the desk opened. She slowly stood, deciding exactly how she would make Mr. Dennis aware of her impatience at how slowly he had related her message to the earl.

Instead of the thin secretary, another tall man entered the room. He carried more flesh on his broad frame than Mr. Dennis and the lines of many more years upon his face. Thick, gray hair was brushed forward to edge the high collar he wore beneath a floor-length dressing gown of emerald silk. Felt slippers emerged from it to whisper against the rug as he walked toward her.

"Lord Mendoff?" Vanessa dared to ask, although she was sure the man who was dressed so casually in this town house could be no one else.

"Have I kept you waiting long?" He smiled, ironing the wrinkles out of his cheeks as others crinkled around his eyes. "I beg your indulgence."

"You do not need to make excuses," she answered, returning his smile. She decided her long wait must be all the doing of that insufferable Mr. Dennis. The earl was charming, and she would be no less. For the first time in longer than she wished to remember, she began to hope someone might be willing to listen to her petition on Corey's behalf. She had heard Lord Mendoff had the ear of the Prime Minister. She must find out if that was true and, if it was, if he would assist her.

"Do come in." The earl glanced around the antechamber and grimaced. "This room is intolerably formal. I have no idea why Dennis would insist on you waiting here. I prefer to offer my special guests welcome in a more cozy setting. I trust you will find it more comfortable than that hard bench."

"Thank you, my lord."

Stepping aside, he held the door open for her. She understood the earl's grumbles when she entered the smaller room beyond the door. Two settees, covered in pale blue silk, flanked the black marble hearth and faced each other to make for comfortable conversation. The drapes had been drawn to shut out the dreary half-light hanging over the Square, and a trio of lamps brightened the corners and lit the portrait over the mahogany mantel. She recognized the man as a younger Lord Mendoff and guessed the slight woman at his side was his wife. The elegant rug was a twin of the one in the other room, and her slippers sank into its lush nap.

"Please sit down, young lady," he said with a low chuckle. "I think you shall find this settee much more to your liking."

Sitting on the settee closer to the door, Vanessa said, "I appreciate you giving me this time, my lord."

He rumbled a laugh as broad as his stomach. "And I appreciate your company . . ."

"Vanessa," she supplied when he paused expectantly. "Vanessa Wol—"

"Vanessa! What a charming name!"

"Vanessa Wol—" she tried again.

"There is no need for more than the amity of given names between us. Don't you think so?" He gave her no time to add more as he went to a table where a bottle of wine sat between two glasses. "I trust you like Madeira."

"Yes . . . thank you." Vanessa folded her hands in her lap. This was nothing like what she had envisioned after her long wait in the outer room. Lord Mendoff must regret delaying her interview so long and wished to atone by making her feel welcome. She hoped that longing would become a desire to help her in finding Corey.

"I do own to being surprised you are here so early."

"Early? I—"

Again he intruded with a laugh. "Rest assured, Vanessa, I admire your fervor." His dressing gown stroked the rug as he walked toward her.

Vanessa took the glass he held out, but did not raise it to her lips as he sat next to her. He tapped his crystal goblet to hers with a sparkling clink and urged her, with a wide smile, to taste the wine. His gaze tried to hold hers, but she shifted her eyes toward the hearth. Uneasiness oozed through her as she noticed his arm slipping along the settee's carved back. His fingers grazed her shoulder.

She moved away, trying to make the motion seem unhurried. "My lord, I wish to speak to you of a very important matter."

"You must not be so formal. You may call me Josiah." When she hesitated, his smile wavered. "I do insist on that, my dear. Do humor me on this very *unimportant* matter."

Taking a quick sip of her wine allowed her a moment to compose her thoughts which he sent into a tangle with every puzzling word. "As you wish, Josiah. What I wish to speak to you about concerns a matter very close to my heart."

"An excellent place to begin."

"I wish this more than anything else in the world." Her fingers gripped the goblet's stem as she whispered, "If you could help me, I would be indebted to you beyond anything mere words could convey."

Lord Mendoff emptied his glass, then stretched past her to put it on the table behind her. She gasped when his other arm slipped around her waist. "Debts need not be spoken of between dear friends."

"Lord Mendoff!" she gasped and pulled away. Standing, she edged around the settee. Had the man taken a knock in the cradle to think he could treat her so? "My lord, I believe you are mistaking my offer for another."

He set himself on his feet and lessened the distance between them. Backing toward the door, Vanessa winced when she bumped into a table. She inched past it. Where was the door? Had it vanished?

The earl chuckled. "This is amusing, Vanessa." He motioned toward where she had been sitting. "Come back to the settee. Our business—how delightfully droll of you to term it thus—can be best dealt with there."

"No, my lord, I think it would be wiser if I left post-haste."

His eyes narrowed, and the twinges of despair within her became dismay. She had angered him. But why? She should be the one infuriated by his coarse treatment. Staying to argue would be jobbernowl. She took another step backward. The raised panels of the door were sharp against her back. Groping for the latch, unable to find it, she choked back a shriek when the earl stepped forward and put one hand on either side of her head, imprisoning her between his broad arms, the sleeves of his wrapper flapping like dark wings around her.

"Leave?" he asked in a deceptively calm voice. "Is this a ploy to wrench a bit more gilt from my pockets?"

"My lord, I beg you to let me go. I shall take my business to another."

"To another?"

"You clearly are not interested in—"

"But I am interested, Vanessa. Most interested." A smile returned, thinning his lips. "You need not play the shrinking virgin with me any longer, my dear Vanessa. I prize you already for your loveliness. Reward me, pretty one."

His face descended toward hers. Her stomach cramped. He was going to kiss her! Was he totally deranged? She wanted to shriek, but her voice was lost beneath the clog in her throat.

Suddenly the door opened, and she stumbled backward into the antechamber. She struck something hard.

Hands steadied her, but pulled away as the scream burst from her. Her knees nearly buckled, but the strong hands caught her again. She shuddered as she drew away and put her hand on the door to steady herself. How furious Aunt Carolyn would be! Not only had Vanessa continued her quest, but she might have destroyed every shred of reputation by being discovered in such a compromising situation.

The earl stared past her. Vanessa saw dismay, fury, and embarrassment flash across his face before he growled, "What are you doing here?"

"I thought to call upon you, Uncle, while I was driving past Hanover Square," said a deep voice behind her.

Vanessa whirled. Her eyes widened in horror as she raised her gaze along a pale blue waistcoat worn beneath a gray coat and past a high collar closed with a sedate white tie to meet ebony eyes in a sternly sculptured face. Taken aback, she gasped, "Lord Brickendon!"

"You remember me today?" He dipped his head toward her, but the motion did not hide his grin as he reminded her of her cold words at Almack's. "I am honored, my lady."

"My lady?" demanded Lord Mendoff.

Lord Brickendon's smile grew wider as his eyes twinkled with amusement. "Uncle, I am surprised you have not met Lady Vanessa Wolfe before this."

"You are Lady Vanessa Wolfe?" the earl sputtered. "Lord Wulfric's daughter? Why didn't you say so?"

Before Vanessa could remind him that she had tried to enlighten him about her name more than once, Lord Brickendon laughed. The older man glowered at him, and Vanessa wished she had never considered asking the earl to help her. If his actions today were representative of his character, Lord Mendoff would have very little influence with the present government.

"Uncle, you have made an incredible mistake by

playing the duddering rake with a marquess's heir."
Lord Brickendon's eyes glittered as he added to Vanessa, "I assume you wish to depart, my lady."

"Yes." She was grateful for his gracious attempt to
remedy the situation. "My business is done here."

Lord Brickendon's chuckle sent more heat clamping
around her. "I see that it is." He stepped aside and motioned for her to join him in the antechamber. "I shall
knock upon my return, Uncle," he added, "in case you
have another caller with you."

He closed the door to shut off the old man's grumbled
curse. Vanessa was relieved not to hear her name muttered, but the earl's courtesy was belated.

"How are you doing, my lady?" asked Lord Brickendon as he led her across the grand antechamber.

She was pleased he did not offer her his arm. She did
not want to touch or be touched by any man at that moment. She whispered, "That man is your uncle?"

"It is said that every family has a black sheep or two
in their midst." He smiled. "It is my family's misfortune
to have a full flock of them."

Vanessa did not return his smile. Shivers rolled along
her, but she would not let him guess how unsettled she
was. A word of this spoken into the wrong ear would
spread the tale throughout the Polite World. Her shame
did not bother her, but she knew how it would reflect on
her aunt.

As Lord Brickendon hurried her down the stairs and
through the empty hallway a slight, feminine form appeared.

"I believe this is yours," Lord Brickendon said as the
maid held out a rose-colored spencer.

Vanessa reached for it, but her fingers trembled. Lord
Brickendon said nothing as he took it and settled it over
her shoulders. She whispered her thanks, but wished she

could find the words to ask him to conceal this whole predicament.

When they reached the walkway, Lord Brickendon said, "I would venture a guess that Lord Mendoff mistook you for another—shall we be generous and say lady?—he hoped to have join him this morning. Accept my apology in lieu of the one he may be too mortified to send to you."

Vanessa was sure her color was as bright as his waistcoat, but she kept her head high. "That is generous of you, my lord."

"Nonsense." He waved aside the tiger and opened her carriage door himself. Handing her in, he smiled as she settled herself on the leather seat. He closed the door behind her. Through the window, he asked, "A word of counsel if I may?"

"Of course."

"Choose your calls more carefully in the future, my lady. My uncle may be a doddering dunce, but a lady as comely as you inspires ideas in even the most opaque head." His eyes twinkled as he added, "Not only my uncle, but my friend Sir Wilbur, for example. His prattling about your charms last evening was endless. I know how he eagerly anticipates your gathering this evening."

She pressed her hand to her bodice, but clasped her fingers in her lap when she noticed Lord Brickendon's gaze following every motion. "That is kind of you to say."

"What were you doing here?"

"I had thought to call on Lord Mendoff on a concern for my father's estate." She nearly stumbled on each word of the half-truth, knowing that he was gauging everything she said. "I had no idea such an innocent visit would turn so dark. Whatever will Aunt Carolyn say?"

"You needn't worry about that fine lady or any other person learning of this day's misadventure." He folded his arms on the open window. "I shall convince my uncle of the good sense of saying nothing of the matter, which I am sure he will be eager to keep as quiet as you would wish."

"Thank you again for . . ." She was not sure what she could say without adding more fire to her suddenly burning face.

"My pleasure, but one I hope I need never repeat." He slapped his hand on the side of the carriage to let her driver know she was ready to leave.

Vanessa whispered, "I hope so, too."

She leaned back against the seat. Closing her eyes, she was amazed when Lord Brickendon's uncompromising features filled her mind. She shivered. It was likely she would meet the devilishly handsome viscount again during the flurry of entertainments at the Season's end. She hoped, by then, she would have devised something to say to him without setting her cheeks to flame again . . . or her heart to pounding with pleasure.

Chapter Five

Penelope Downing prided herself on being a creature of habit. Every morning, she rose exactly at the stroke of ten. She enjoyed her breakfast in her breakfast-parlor with its enchanting view of the tiny garden behind her Grosvenor Square town house. Her housekeeper received Penelope's instructions each day at precisely thirty minutes before noon. For the next hour daily, Penelope gave her complete attention to the abigail's ministrations to her light brown hair and her vast wardrobe. Before the church bells chimed two, she was about on her calls or receiving on the days she was at home. She always was waiting to greet her husband when he returned from his ride about the Park just as the clock on the mantel chimed six. With him, she enjoyed an evening of entertainment with the *ton*.

That exacting schedule explained Lady Carolyn Mansfield's nearly speechless incredulity when Penelope was shown into her small blue sitting room before one the next afternoon. With her beribboned poke bonnet positively quivering with agitation, Penelope offered Carolyn a swift smile as she crossed the flowered rug and sat on the white silk chair next to where Carolyn was ringing hastily for refreshments.

"Dear Penelope, whatever is distressing you?" Carolyn asked, unable to curb her curiosity. She would sooner have expected Napoleon to come calling than Penelope arriving before two.

"Not distress, but happiness." Her full lips rounded into a moue, which countermanded her words. With a sigh, she bent her full form to pick a piece of straw from the hem of her sedate yellow gown. The ribbons dropping from her bodice would have better suited a girl half her age.

Carolyn laughed. "Mr. Porter is ever a doting husband. Now that his wife has given him a son, there shall be no end to his overindulgence. I fear everyone on the Square will be driving over straw for weeks to come."

"I appreciate the respite from the clatter of carriage wheels as much as the new mother." Penelope's usual smile appeared as a maid approached with a tray of sweetmeats and a steaming pot of tea. "I was saying to dear Samuel just last evening how pleasant it was not to be bothered by the passage of carriages under our window. He suggested that the straw might be a permanent addition to the Square, but I do believe he was jesting."

Carolyn resisted laughing and busied herself straightening the sprigged linen of her gown. Penelope Downing had no more sense of humor than the pink flowers on Carolyn's dress, but her heart was nearly as large as her broad shelf of bosom and her intentions well-meant. Carolyn doubted she could find a more pleasant neighbor, although, in secret, she often wished she might pass the afternoon with someone with a bit more wit.

Pouring tea, she held out a porcelain cup to her guest. "Penelope," she said as she stirred sugar into her own cup, "you have yet to answer my question. What brings you calling at this hour? Not that I'm not always pleased to see you. It's just that you're all a-quiver."

"As you should be, my dear."

"Me?" Carolyn set her cup back on the table. Her

neighbor's words could mean anything . . . or nothing. It was not easy to tell with Penelope.

"Yes, you! What a coup! You must be delighted about sweet Vanessa's triumph last evening at Almack's. How I wish I could have witnessed that myself."

Carolyn raised her cup to hide her growing amusement. She loved her niece with all her heart, but never could she imagine calling the headstrong girl sweet. "I own that I had thought Vanessa would be one of the first married out of this Season. She is pretty, well-spoken, and not lacking in either family connections or wealth. Oh, how deliriously high my hopes were when I fired her off."

"But, my dear Carolyn, your hopes are at long last coming to fruition. The Franklin family is quite plump in the pockets."

Carolyn offered her neighbor a smile. "Something that my niece needn't worry her head about, for my brother left her without that concern."

"Poo! A woman needs always to think of such things. Not just for herself, but for her children. I had begun to despair that Vanessa would fail her obligation to her late father." Penelope shuddered. "I know he was your brother, Carolyn, but I vow I never met a more disagreeable man."

"Or a more endearing one. I see more of him in Vanessa every day."

Penelope took a hasty sip of tea and clumsily changed the conversation back to the topic that had brought her to the sunny parlor overlooking the Square. "I believe you shall soon be announcing your niece's betrothal."

"I have harbored such hopes before, and they have come to naught." Carolyn leaned back against the settee. "Forgive me if I seem indifferent, but Vanessa's heart will be a hard-won prize. She is so serious about so many things, but not about finding a suitable husband." She sighed. "Or to own the truth, any husband at all."

"You must speak honestly with her." Both of Penelope's chins jiggled with her fervor. "A young miss needs to be made aware of what she must do to plan for her future. Not that you would ever be remiss in such tuition, Carolyn, but it is a young woman's place to be grateful for any man who pays her heed."

Carolyn almost laughed. How incensed Vanessa would be to hear Penelope speak so! Raised, as all the Wolfes had been, to know her own mind and to speak it, Vanessa would not assent submissively to an offer of marriage from a man her aunt had chosen. Not that Carolyn would have been so much a block as to suggest such a thing, since she was a Wolfe as well.

Quietly, to hide her thoughts, Carolyn said, "Perhaps we shall be given a greater clue into Vanessa's mind this evening. I shall be certain that she sits with Sir Wilbur Franklin when we play cards. Then I must trust he will know the proper court-promises to delight her."

"What a fitting watchdog you are! When my sister Agatha's youngest comes out next Season, I would dearly love to have you sponsor her."

Carolyn toyed with a sweetmeat, then dropped it back into the dish. Wiping her fingers delicately on a linen napkin, she glanced at the clock on the mantel. Vanessa should have returned from the *modiste* more than fifteen minutes ago. The girl had developed an uncomely habit of being late when some task she disliked faced her. Carolyn had suspected the attention they must give to overseeing the final plans for this evening's entertainment would slow Vanessa's return.

Vanessa was so like her father. Grant Wolfe had exhibited a single-minded determination to do what he thought was right. Although that manner had lost him a few friends on occasion and gained him more than a few enemies, he had remained steadfast to those who understood his ways. Vanessa was in good pax with only a handful among the *élite,* but she held those friendships dear.

Despite herself, Carolyn's eyes rose to a painting set in prominence on the chimney-piece. Even in the portrait, her sister-in-law Julianna appeared a frail wraith, for she had succumbed to a fever in less than a year after the painting was completed. Carolyn's gaze settled on the other faces in it. Dear Grant, his eyes burning with the ideals he had not lived to see come to consummation. Sitting next to him was Vanessa, a younger version of her mother's beauty, but with a set of her shoulders that suggested her father's strength. Lastly, Carolyn looked at the lad with his hand on his father's shoulder. Corey Wolfe had inherited a large share of the Wolfe stubbornness and indifference to others' opinions. That had led to his death on a distant battlefield.

A pulse of the sorrow she had tried to set aside coursed through her. So much grief this family had suffered. Only Vanessa remained, and Carolyn repeated her silent pledge that the last of the Wolfes would not come to disaster as the others had. If only Vanessa could learn to compromise, she might escape the pain and failure that had haunted her family.

"We shall speak of bringing out your niece once I have Vanessa settled with a good match." Carolyn smiled sadly. "My brother's final wish was that I would see to his only surviving child's future. That must be my sole concern."

"And of your own future?"

Her smile became warmer. "Vanessa is both my present and my future concern at this time. Perhaps—when she is happily married with a husband who dotes on her—I can turn my mind to more personal matters."

"If you are putting your life aside until she is wed, then, my dear Carolyn, you should make certain that Vanessa is given more opportunities to meet suitable men."

"Exactly why I invited the baronet to join us this evening." Carolyn reached for her cup. "I also have extended an invitation to others of my acquaintance so the party shall have a merry air."

Penelope tapped her finger against her chins, then nodded. "That should work. Allow Vanessa to see the differences among the gentlemen who join you this evening, so that she might appreciate Sir Wilbur Franklin's noble mien."

Carolyn doubted that anyone save Penelope, whose generous spirit was well known, would use the word noble to describe the baronet. Yet her neighbor's advice was sound. A bit of competition for Vanessa's attention might urge the baronet to present his suit in short order. She smiled. Who would have thought that Penelope would give her the idea that was sure to turn this evening from a quiet party into a chance to resolve Vanessa's future once and for all?

Carolyn raised her cup in a silent salute to her own thoughts. This could be the solution she had sought all Season.

Vanessa settled her bonnet more securely on her head as the tiger assisted her from the carriage in front of the house on Grosvenor Square. Leale followed. Vanessa was in a bang as she went toward the steps, bracing herself for having her ears boxed with her aunt's dismay. Not only had Madame deBerg, the *modiste,* been eternally slow, but Leale had been in a fidget over waiting at the *modiste*'s shop for hours. The abigail had been furious that Vanessa did not explain exactly what had delayed her, but Vanessa had been in no mood to talk.

How could she tell dear Leale about her foolish call on Lord Mendoff? And how Lord Brickendon had come to her rescue? She hoped she could trust the viscount and his uncle to hold their tongues on this. She did not want to break Aunt Carolyn's heart.

And now she must begin the search again to find someone to help her. Too many doors had been closed to her, and the only one that had opened. . . . She shuddered again. She must not stop now. She was sure she was close to discovering the truth about her brother. She wondered why her own government was so reluctant to release the information to her, but that answer was as impossible to find as Corey.

The front door opened just as she reached it. Quigley stood inside, his face naked of emotion as always. Leale nodded to him, then rushed up the steps to set out Vanessa's gown for the gathering this evening. She turned, a warning frown on her face, but Vanessa pretended she had not seen her abigail's fierce expression. She needed to speak to Quigley first.

The butler took Vanessa's spencer. As he held it carefully, he said, "Lady Mansfield requested that you join her and Mrs. Downing in the blue sitting room upon your return."

"Mrs. Downing? Is it so late?" Vanessa understood Leale's distress if they were that dilatory in returning to the Square. She looked at the tall-case clock standing in one angle of the octagonal foyer. "It's not yet two." Dismay swept her. "What is wrong, Quigley?"

"My lady, to suggest that I would eavesdrop on your aunt's conversation—"

Vanessa interrupted, with a smile, for they had come to points like this on more than one occasion at Wolfe Abbey, "Quigley, you are an excellent butler. Nothing happens in this house that you aren't privy to. Is there something wrong at the Downing house?"

"I would as lief," he said, drawing himself up to his lanky height, "say that Mrs. Downing is eager to determine what is taking place with your life, my lady. I did hear her mention Almack's."

"Oh, bother." Vanessa grimaced as she looked at the stairs. "I should have guessed Penelope could not resist the chance to enjoy a bit of gossip at my expense." She took a step toward the stairs, then paused. Facing the butler, she asked, "Has anything been delivered for me today?"

"No, my lady. Not yet." She was unsure if it was her imagination or if his shoulders slumped a hairbreadth. The timber of his voice had not changed, but she knew he also missed her brother. Whether he also believed Corey was alive was something she had never asked him. She was afraid of what he might say. She did not want to be the only one who kept the hope from dying.

A knock halted her from asking that Quigley send any letters to her immediately. The butler grumbled something under his breath as he opened the door.

Vanessa's eyes widened when she met Lord Brickendon's. Their dark depths were as shuttered as Quigley's face when he asked, "Is Lady Vanessa Wolfe in?"

"Whom may I say is calling?" Quigley returned as if Vanessa was not viewing the exchange.

Taking off his beaver, the viscount held it in one hand as he offered the butler a *carte des visites*. It was the same tan as his riding coat and buckskins. "Lord Brickendon. I have a message for her, which I would appreciate delivering in person."

Vanessa did not wait for Quigley to turn to ask her if she wished to speak with the viscount. She had no interest in the canons of Society this afternoon. She must learn why Lord Brickendon was calling after saying goodbye to her less than an hour past.

"I would be delighted to speak with you, Lord Brickendon."

The viscount's Hessian boots marked each step as he crossed the harlequin pattern of the foyer floor. "I trust you will excuse this intrusion."

"You must excuse *me,* my lord. I am just returned from my errands."

A smile crept across his lips. "May I say that you look very well in the wake of your *errands?*"

She faltered, unsure what to say. No one else made her lose her wits as he did. As Quigley stepped back into the shadows, she said, "My aunt will be delighted with your call."

"I have not come to give you a look-in." He reached beneath his light brown coat and pulled out a folded sheet. "As I informed your man, I wanted to deliver this to you personally. I thought you might wish to know that my uncle has left Town, so he is unable to respond to your invitation."

Vanessa struggled to keep her fingers from quivering as she reached for the letter she had labored to write last night after her visit to Almack's. "Thank you," she said softly.

"My lady, I can see that I have disturbed you greatly when all I wished was to let you know that my uncle did not intentionally ignore this missive."

His deep voice, as he spoke the lies much more easily than she could have, contained such compassion that she raised her eyes before she realized her error. With her eyes caught by his gaze, which no longer was bereft of emotion, she feared he might be able to read her feelings more clearly than she could his.

"I ask again," he continued when she said nothing,

"to be forgiven for intruding on you. I had considered giving the letter to Sir Wilbur Franklin, so he could deliver it to you this evening, but the obligation to see that it was put in your hands was mine."

"I truly appreciate your thoughtfulness." She saw a flash of amusement in his eyes at her trite answer. "The baronet might not have appreciated its import."

Lord Brickendon's smile stole some of the harsh edge from his face. "You are the one who is thoughtful, my lady, to be so generous with your compliments to Franklin. It did not take keen eyes to note how uncomfortable you were last evening. He can be stifling to any lady he has set his heart upon."

"I thought he was your friend."

Lord Brickendon laughed so lowly that the sound would not climb the stairs to her aunt's ears. "I accept the faults of my friends, as they accept mine, for I need not worry that I might have to buckle myself to one of them."

When she smiled at his sally, Vanessa was astonished. She should not be smiling. In her hand, she held the proof that yet another route was closed to her. She should have been down-pinned, but she was not. Lord Brickendon's teasing lightened her spirits.

Knowing that she was being bold as brass, she asked, "Might you do me a favor, my lord?"

"Another?" When she flushed, he added, "Of course, if it is within my power." His eyes sparkled with the laughter in his voice. "What do you wish? A dragon slain? A castle stormed? A prisoner freed from a tower? I would do most anything to rid myself of the boredom of the endless rounds expected of one while in Town."

Vanessa almost told him what she really needed, because his jesting came so close to the truth. Lord Mendoff was well connected with the government, so mayhap his nephew might know of a way to help her. She shrugged aside that tempting thought. Despite his honorable behavior this morning, she knew too little about Lord Brickendon to trust him. Others had laughed at her assertion that Corey was alive. She had vowed that never again would she suffer that mortification. Somehow she would find her answers herself.

"If it is not too much of an imposition, my lord, would you consider joining us this evening for a few hands of whist?" She heard voices coming toward the stairs and added in a rush, "I know my aunt would appreciate your company."

"And I could stand as a buffer between you and Franklin's attentions?"

His insight did not astonish her. He had revealed it every time they had spoken. She wished she could be as honest. "My lord, I had hoped that—in the presence of one he keeps in with—I might be able to see more clearly some of the fine attributes my aunt tells me he possesses."

"To be offered the chance to allow you to see Franklin's finer points is an appealing invitation." He set his hat on his dark hair. "I would be a sap to turn it down. I look forward to speaking with you . . . and with Franklin this evening. For now, I suspect—although you are too polite to say—I am keeping you from other guests. Good afternoon, my lady."

Vanessa did not move as Quigley abruptly appeared to open the door and close it behind the viscount. She pressed the letter to her bodice as she tried to settle her mind, which was telling her that she had wanted for sense to ask the viscount to return this evening. Lord Brickendon might be a stranger, but he treated her with the friendly indifference and respect she had enjoyed from her brother's tie-mates. She appreciated not having to guard every word she spoke, because she feared he might take it as an invitation to dangle after her.

Lost in her musings, she was jolted back to herself when she heard her aunt telling Penelope to call again soon. Vanessa managed to say something in farewell to the dumpling-like woman. Her aunt's face, which was set in lines of disapproval, warned Vanessa that her words had not been properly polished.

With rare meekness, she let Aunt Carolyn herd her up the stairs to the blue room. She deserved to be given the rough side of her aunt's tongue. She would stand silently for the admonition and then retreat to her private room where she would try to think of someone else who might help her find Corey.

Aunt Carolyn sat prettily on the settee. Instead of flying out at Vanessa, she asked, "Do you have an excuse for being gone so long?"

"I was delayed."

"At Madame deBerg's?"

"Yes."

"You were delayed only at the *modiste*'s shop?"

"No."

"Then where?"

She glanced away, not wanting to lie, but knowing she must never speak the truth.

Her hesitation betrayed her to her aunt's perceptive ears. "Vanessa, I have told you that you must give up this nonsense of looking for your brother. You shall ruin your reputation by lingering outside a minister's door like a Cyprian plying her trade in Covent Garden."

"Aunt Carolyn!" She bit back the rest of her retort. She must not let her aunt guess how closely her words came to the truth.

Carolyn wagged her finger under Vanessa's nose. "You

should sound shocked. You should *be* shocked. Not by my plainspoken words, but by your own acts. When will you see the futility of your efforts? If there was any news of the whereabouts of Corey's remains, do you think the government would fail to share it with you?"

"I'm beginning to believe they would."

"Vanessa!" she returned in the same appalled tone Vanessa had used. "I fear you have taken a maggot into your head over this whole *affaire*. You are throwing away your first Season to chase a dream that is dead." Her voice gentled when tears bubbled into Vanessa's eyes. "My dear child, you must stop being so fanciful! You need to put this pain behind you and look to your future."

"How can I when I think of Corey so often?"

Rising and putting her arms around her niece, Aunt Carolyn whispered, "Then think of what he would wish you to do. He chose the path he did so you could have the life you deserve, the life your dear, late father wished you to have. Both of them, in their own ways, entrusted you to my care. If you honor their memories, and I know you do, you must listen to me and put aside this impossible quest. You must settle yourself into the life they would want you to have. You have the responsibility to oversee Wolfe Abbey and be sure the legacy your father left in your hands is well taken care of."

"But it is Corey's legacy."

"Not now when he is dead."

"He cannot be dead!"

"He can."

Vanessa shook her head. She would not listen to these heartless words. If only Aunt Carolyn could believe as she did. Wiping tears from her icy cheeks, she whispered, "I shall never accept that until it is proven to me.

I know Corey is still alive. Why won't anyone listen to my plea to find out where he is?"

"You mustn't be as stubborn as your father. It will gain you nothing."

"Nor must you." She gathered her skirts and ran out of the room, although she knew she could never escape the anguish.

Carolyn sighed as her niece went up the stairs at a frantic pace. There must be a way to convince Vanessa to resign herself to the dual tragedy in their lives. So easily she could share Vanessa's grief and her dreams of having Corey return home alive, but Carolyn had become a pragmatist in the years since she had left her father's house. Dreams were for the young and the foolish. Clear-headed thinking was the only way to achieve one's ends.

Hearing the housekeeper's voice in the other room as Mrs. Sturgis directed the staff in setting up the tables for cards, Carolyn listened as well to her memory. It urged her to recall the advice Penelope had given her. She had allotted Vanessa several months to find a husband among those loitering about the edges of the Marriage Mart. The young woman had made no decision, so it was up to Carolyn to persuade her niece to do so.

It would not be easy, but Carolyn Wolfe Mansfield never shrank from a difficult task. With a smile, she raised her chin and went to the writing table near the hearth. Selecting a sheet of her finest stationery, she drew out a bottle of ink. She faltered for only a moment before she began to write the note she had been composing in her mind during her conversation with Penelope.

"Lady Carolyn Mansfield is pleased to invite Lord Brickendon to . . ."

* * *

". . . an evening of cards and conversation among dear friends. I am sure your presence would both surprise and delight my niece, Lady Vanessa Wolfe."

Ross tossed the invitation onto a table in his comfortable book-room. It was his favorite place in the elegant town house on Berkeley Square. In the chamber set on an upper floor of the house, he could shut out the hubbub while he enjoyed reading the newspaper. None of the fancy furniture that filled the other rooms on the first floor had invaded this room where a man could feel comfortable enough to untie his cravat, toss aside his collar and boots, and sit with his stockinged feet on a footstool.

Light splashed from a single window onto the dark green rug as Ross stretched for the bellpull. He gave it a sharp tug. He owed Lady Mansfield an answer to her generous invitation, which was to more than the evening's party. Lady Mansfield was urging him to pay court on her lovely niece.

That would surprise the lovely Lady Vanessa Wolfe . . . if he had been silly enough to consider courting her for anything other than a silly wager. Setting himself on his feet, he went to the window and looked out at the street through the steady patter of rain. He laughed lowly.

The wording of the invitation suggested Lady Mansfield did not know that her niece already had asked him to attend the gathering this evening. Had Swinton been honored with an invitation as well because he had spoken with the marquess's daughter last night? This would not please Franklin, but nothing in their wager would prohibit any of them from attending Lady Carolyn Mansfield's card party this evening.

After all, hadn't he suggested this wager in the hopes of finding some entertainment amid the otherwise dreary end of the Season? What better way to be enter-

tained than to watch his inept friend try to win the hand
of a woman who clearly wished to leg-shackle herself to
no man?

This evening was certain to be exactly the entertainment he had hoped for.

Chapter Six

Vanessa scowled at her reflection in the glass. She was wearing her second best gown. Aunt Carolyn had urged her to don her best, but a recalcitrant streak had coaxed Vanessa to show her vexation with the evening's arrangements by choosing this gown. The pink lace along the rounded collar of the white silk dress matched the normal color of her cheeks. Tonight, however, her cheeks were fiery with her high emotions.

And where was the smile she had vowed she would wear to disguise her true feelings? This was the first time she had to live by that pledge to seek her lost happiness at the same time she looked for Corey. She could not turn her back on her troth so quickly. Not when everything might depend on her ability to be fetching and agreeable tonight. Until she had dismissed Sir Wilbur Franklin from her list of possible sources of help, she needed to treat him with every bit of charm she possessed. Who could know where this might lead? The pompous man might be able to offer the very assistance she sought.

Leale pinned flowers in Vanessa's upswept hair. "Do sit still. Otherwise I suspect I shall stab you." The abigail's voice strained past the hairpins she held between her lips. Her forehead puckered beneath her silver-gray hair as she put each pin carefully in place.

"I fear the wound would need to be mortal for me to avoid this gathering."

"Don't grumble, my lady. Your aunt is only concerned with your well-being."

Vanessa rolled her eyes. Leale must have seen, because the older woman began to chuckle.

Standing, Vanessa heeded her abigail's plea not to upset the roses in her hair. Her voice was as prickly as the thorns along their stems. "Leale, I'm tired of everyone debating which man Lady Vanessa Wolfe will marry. Look what happened when I was little more than pleasant to the baronet. Now I must endure listening to him air his vocabulary all evening."

"Fortune and title have brought you a fame you do not wish."

"No one would care a rap about me if Corey was here."

Leale's voice gentled. "But he is not, and you have an obligation you must not ignore. Think of what your sainted father would say if you are unwed at the Season's end."

"My father was no saint, Leale. And what do you think he would have said if I had leapt at the first proposal offered to me?" she asked bitingly. "Do you wish me to be a complete block?"

"Of course not. I wish you to be as happy as you deserve to be. You have been too serious for too long."

"You sound just like Aunt Carolyn."

"Mayhap you should heed the advice of two people who care deeply for you."

"If you cared deeply for me, you would leave me to live my life as I see fit." Vanessa sighed as she saw tears glistening in her abigail's eyes. This night was doomed to be a complete disaster if she started it by causing Leale to weep. "By the elevens, Leale, I'm nearly ready to cross the Channel myself to find Corey. That's the only way I can see to rid myself of these unwanted suitors. I daresay they would not traipse after me into Boney's dominion."

Leale abruptly laughed. "Most young women would envy your predicament. They long for a suitor they can give their heart to."

"As I do." She drew on her silk slippers and tied the ribbons over her stockings. When Leale did not answer, Vanessa discovered her abigail regarding her with puzzlement. "Do not look so taken aback. Of course, I yearn to meet a man I can love, but he has not appeared yet among the *ton.*"

"I know what kind of man you want," Leale said with a sniff. "You want a mixture of your father's obsession and your brother's misguided courage and the heroes in the books you read. Such a paragon doesn't exist. Even if he did, you would ignore him, because you think only of finding your brother."

"I must think of Corey before my own happiness. Certainly he would do the same for me."

"Would he?" Leale picked up a pair of shoes. "Did he think of your happiness when he beat hoof to France to win glory for himself?"

"He—"

"Never said a word to you after that last argument you had. I remember your shock when you read the note he left behind for you. Don't be a moonling just because he was."

The abigail stamped out to leave Vanessa staring after her, for once at an utter loss for a reply.

* * *

"My dear lady, how radiant you look! Where is Sir Wilbur? I had hoped to greet both of you upon my arrival."

Vanessa's smile felt like a smirk, but she kept it on her face as she greeted Penelope Downing, who was accompanied by her dour husband who seldom said more than a single word. Not that poor Mr. Downing had a chance. Penelope filled every silence with her own chatter. Her neighbor was not the first to ask with little subtlety about Sir Wilbur. As she had to those who had preceded Penelope, Vanessa said, "The baronet has yet to arrive. I know my aunt is anxious for his arrival."

"I am sure he is eager to spend the evening with you."

"I am sure."

Penelope turned to gush a greeting to Aunt Carolyn. When they put their heads together, clearly conspiring, Vanessa restrained her chuckle. Next Season, when Penelope fired off her sister's daughter, the activity on Grosvenor Square would reach a new high in a whirl of parties and flirtations. Vanessa liked the idea of someone else being the center of their intrigues. It was regrettable that the girl was still in the classroom *this* year.

"Good evening," came a rich voice from her left.

Vanessa's smile became sincere when she saw a striking, muted blue uniform that stood out among the drab, evening wear worn of the other gentlemen. The guinea-gold haired man, who touted a bushy mustache, was tall enough to wear the uniform with dignity. His black boots shone so brightly in the lamplight that Vanessa had to avoid looking at them.

A multitude of buttons on his coat rattled as he bent over her hand. "My lady, it is, as always, a delight to be in your company."

"Captain Hudson, I thought you were in garrison." She smiled. She was accustomed to his effusive compliments. He had teased her since she was little more than a child, and she always enjoyed replying in kind.

"Even an old soldier is allowed a bit of leave."

"You are hardly old, Captain."

He touched his temple where silver glittered among the pale strands. "Old enough to remember you with scraped knees and a black eye from trying to get your cat down from a gnarled tree in your father's orchard. What a gawney I was not to ask you to marry me while I was down on my knees to bandage yours!"

"I fear I would have made you a poor wife at the exasperating age of nine." She laughed and added, "Aunt Carolyn, I believe you know Captain Victor Hudson."

Carolyn offered her hand. Vanessa was certain she had never seen her aunt look so lovely. Dressed in white silk, Aunt Carolyn had left a tendril of hair loose to drape across the unblemished skin of her shoulder. A single strand of pearls was her only decoration. "We have met, but it has been several years since I last had the pleasure of your company, Captain. I am so delighted you could join us this evening."

"It may have been several years, but those were years that have had no effect on you, my lady."

"You were always a jester."

"But never have I minced on the truth."

Vanessa hid her smile behind her fan, which was the same pink silk as her gown. Aunt Carolyn should flirt with handsome men more often. Her dark eyes glittered like twin stars, and her lips offered a warm smile. Aunt Carolyn should not be wasting her life trying to find her reluctant niece a husband.

Vanessa's smile dwindled as another guest approached the parlor. Sir Wilbur Franklin should have instructed his man to select another waistcoat for him, because this bright red one strained too tightly across his broad corporation. When he wore it with a forest

green jacket, he could have been an oversized lepre-
chaun from the far side of the Irish Sea.

She looked past him, but saw no sign of Lord Brickendon. Irritation pricked her. The viscount had told her
he would be here. Chagrin followed that unbecoming
thought. Lord Brickendon was not at fault for her discomfort. She had let Sir Wilbur think there could be
friendship between them. Now she must be a good hostess. Perhaps there were intriguing depths to be found in
the fubsey baronet. She could always hold onto that
hope . . . faint though it might be.

"Horrible night," Sir Wilbur said in lieu of a greeting,
and her hopes waned. "Have you closed your windows,
my lady? It would not do for you to take a chill. It
would not do a bit. My sister often complains of the
damp weather here in Town. One look at you, and I can
say it is not fit weather for a delicate lady like you."

"Why don't you come into the parlor?" she asked to
halt the advice spilling from his mouth. "The windows
are latched, and I think you shall find the room overly
warm."

" 'Tis not me I fear for, but your health."

"You are most kind to think of me." Commonplaces
served her best with him, but they tasted acrid on her
tongue. She preferred Captain Hudson's candid teasing.

"Not kindness, but *my* pleasure."

Vanessa fought a grimace. She must not reveal her
distaste with his blatant attempts to woo her. Wishing someone would interrupt their conversation, she
realized—with a quick glance about the room—that everyone was anxious to watch the baronet pour the blar-
ney over her. She tried to listen to his prattle, but an
ache between her eyes threatened to overtake her whole
head. How long could a man be all jaw with no head?
He spoke without pausing for so much as a comment
from her. She wondered if he would notice if she simply

walked away. When Sir Wilbur abruptly stopped and asked if she would like a glass of wine, she nodded, glad for the respite on her ears.

She saved her sigh of relief until Sir Wilbur was pushing his way past the other guests. Being false was difficult for her at best, and tonight she was not at her best. Again she looked about the room for Lord Brickendon. She had thought he would be faithful to his promise to attend this evening. Dismay flooded her. He had vowed, too, to say nothing of the day's events. If he had not been honest about coming tonight . . .

"I assume," Aunt Carolyn said softly, intruding on her horrifying thoughts, "you said nothing to convince the good baronet to leave your side."

Vanessa was about to reply with rare heat, then saw her aunt's eyes sparkling with good humor. Her frustration faded. No matter how much her aunt might try to persuade her to give the baronet consideration as a future husband, Aunt Carolyn would never force her to enter a marriage that was doomed to unhappiness.

"Mayhap I am the one who should take insult," Vanessa whispered, "for he was anxious to trade my company for that of a bottle of wine."

"He seems shockingly attentive." Aunt Carolyn chuckled, and Vanessa was glad they could laugh together in the way that had been customary at Wolfe Abbey.

"From the way he chastens me on the slightest thing and worries constantly about the state of my health, I believe he wishes to replace my father."

Instead of the rebuke Vanessa expected, her aunt mused, "I had not considered he might have such an interest in you."

"I would as lief he found someone more in need of a parent than me."

"Vanessa, do curb that tongue of yours before it gets you into trouble this evening."

"Too late." She laughed, delighted with the sound. Perhaps Leale was correct. She had become too obsessed with her yearning to find Corey. She needed to laugh more.

Aunt Carolyn started to retort, but halted as a deeper voice said, "I hope you haven't been avoiding me, Lady Mansfield." Captain Hudson offered them a scintillating smile. "I would be heart-wrenched if I thought I could not steal your company for a few moments of catching up on all those *years* since we have last talked."

"I can assure you, Captain, that I had no intention of distressing you," Aunt Carolyn answered with a laugh as full of music as a lark's song. "The rôle of hostess can be an exacting one."

He offered his arm. "Then allow me to reminisce with you while I escort you about your duties."

"Do go," Vanessa urged when she saw her aunt hesitate. "I shall not be alone. I see the baronet coming with my wine."

Whether the idea suffering Sir Wilbur's company or the glitter in the captain's eyes weighed more heavily in her decision, Aunt Carolyn placed her hand on the captain's arm and went with him to where another guest was entering the parlor. They were, Vanessa decided, an uncommonly handsome couple.

"Here, my lady. A bit of wine will—"

Vanessa gasped as wine splattered her gown. She looked from the spots all along the front of it to Sir Wilbur's distraught face.

"Oh, no!" He reached under his coat for a handkerchief and dabbed at the wine. When she pulled back, he colored as red as the wine. "My lady, I'm sorry. Don't think me a souse-crown. I would never drink myself blind in your company, for I would as lief drink in your bewitching beauty. I—"

"It's nothing," Vanessa said to hault his babbling which was drawing the attention of everyone in the room.

"Your lovely gown. I fear for the ribbons, and the lace . . ." Again he reached toward her. "It must be cleaned posthaste."

"Sir Wilbur!" She blocked his fingers only inches from her breast. If he thought an overturned glass allowed him *carte blanche* to touch her bodice, he must be set to rights immediately.

He backed away. "My lady, you should know I only wish to help."

"If you wish to help," she answered, fearing it was impossible to talk sense with him, "please convey to my aunt that I shall return as quickly as possible. I must remove the wine from the silk before it is ruined."

"Ruined?" He put his hand on her arm, but pulled it back when she glared at him. "My lady, you must allow me to replace this exquisite dress."

"Sir, I could not accept such a gift under any circumstances." Her voice thawed when she saw consternation lengthening his full face. "Certainly I could not accept such a gift when the spill was an accident."

"Yes, yes," he said, bobbing like an overweight bird. "That is what it was. An accident. I shall tell your aunt of this unfortunate *accident.*"

Vanessa bit her lip to still her laughter. What a pompous shuttle-head! He had latched onto her excuse as if it was his own. Her urge to laugh disappeared as he continued.

"You must be more careful, my lady."

More careful? Her? Vanessa clenched her damp gown. Slipping past the guests before someone else took note of her disheveled state, Vanessa wondered what the baronet would say to her aunt. No doubt, he would lambast Aunt Carolyn for failing to teach her niece a lady's graces.

By the elevens! This evening was even worse than she had feared it would be.

"Good evening, my lady."

The voice, which was more sonorous than Captain Hudson's, halted her in midstep. Vanessa whirled to face Lord Brickendon.

"Where have you been?" she asked, knowing she was being outrageous, but—at the moment—not caring.

"I realize I came by lame post, but I thought you would wish me to appear in prime twig to assist in your nonconquest of the baronet." He laughed and put his hand on the newel post of the second-floor stairs.

She had to own that the cut of his navy coat was the rage. It was unbuttoned to reveal the sheen of his white waistcoat. A cascade of starched ruffles dropped from his high collar and peeked from his cuffs. Breeches of the same immaculate shade as his snowy cravat were a sedate contrast to the shining buckles on his shoes. As he bowed over her fingers, recalcitrant locks of ebony hair drifted toward the strong line of his cheekbones.

His elegant clothes reminded her of the state of her own. Setting her face into a serene expression to cover her tumult, she said, "Lord Brickendon, I must ask you to excuse me while I repair the damage to my gown. My aunt—" She halted herself. She had not told Aunt Carolyn she had invited the viscount.

He chuckled as he boldly eyed her from the flowers in her hair to the tip of her wine-spotted slippers. Warmth slapped her cheeks. He must have noticed her high color, but said only, "Your appearance and your sharp greeting give me no doubt that Franklin has preceded me this evening."

Vanessa started to laugh, then clamped her lips

closed. She should give this man no encouragement to speak so coarsely.

"Oh, blast it!" he went on. "I haven't enjoyed your hospitality for a minute before I have clearly insulted you. What can I do to beg your forgiveness, my lady?"

"Introduce the baronet to some other eligible woman while I am changing into something he has not bedecked with wine."

Lord Brickendon's smile lightened her dreary spirits, and she laughed as he said, " 'Tis a high price to pay for a few badly spoken words, but a knave deserves to be given his oatmeal. Do hurry, for even a hapless knave should not have to suffer interminably." As she put her foot on the first stair, his hand settled on hers on the railing. "My lady, I am not hoaxing you when I say you look lovely tonight."

Delight swirled through her as his fingers stroked hers so lightly the potent sensation could have come from her sweetest dream. Odd how swiftly she found a sincere smile when she spoke with Lord Brickendon, for she doubted if much of what he said and did was with sincerity. He seemed to be delighted to observe the foibles of others and hid the truth of his thoughts with a dexterity that awed her. Yet when they stood this close and the warmth of his breath brushed her face and his hand covered hers, she yearned to believe his easy grin was real. With her eyes level with his, she saw golden sparks dancing there. As they crinkled, she slowly drew her hand from beneath his. He said no more as she climbed the stairs.

She did not look back until she had rounded the top, then watched until he had disappeared into the parlor. The glorious warmth left by his fingers did not fade quickly. Nor did the happiness bubbling within her as she thought of Lord Brickendon's smile. Seeing it gave her the courage to face what she must do tonight. Sir

Wilbur must not clutter up her life any longer. She began to plot how she could rid her life of him.

She grinned. She could always dump a glass of wine on *him!*

". . . and that is why Ethel is still feeling ill. Did you ever hear of such foolishness, my lady?"

Vanessa considered answering that every word from Sir Wilbur's mouth was as cockle-brained. The gabble-grinder had been talking endless nonsense all evening. Even through supper, while he explained in gruesome minutia how his father had suffered from the gout, his words had rained nonstop on her ears.

"Franklin, I must admire your rare intelligence in monopolizing our hostess's company this evening," Lord Brickendon interjected, "but I have come to put an end to that."

"I thought I would have the first chance alone to . . ." The baronet swallowed so roughly Vanessa could hear his gulp.

"I noticed the lady looking longingly at the sideboard and thought she might be thirsty." Lord Brickendon smiled as he handed Vanessa a glass of wine. "White, my lady. To match the color of your gown."

She smiled at his impertinent answer. She wondered if the viscount was serious about anything, then silenced that thought. He had been appropriately somber when he returned the note to her this afternoon.

She had no chance to thank him for the wine or for saving her ears from more of Sir Wilbur's prattle, because Aunt Carolyn joined them, saying, "My friends, the card tables await our skill. Lord Brickendon, would you join Miss Averill, Captain Hudson, and me? The Downings hope you'll play against them with Sir Wilbur, Vanessa."

Vanessa glanced at Lord Brickendon. He gave a sardonic shrug as he offered his arm to her aunt. Seeing his wry grin, she smiled. Aunt Carolyn had arranged things so well that even the viscount could not be counted on to help her suffer through an evening with the baronet.

And suffer is what Vanessa did. Not only her ears, which were beaten with more of Sir Wilbur's tiresome tales of woe and Penelope's nothing-sayings, but her pockets. The baronet seemed to have no head for the simplest game. Even when she explained the rules to him over and over, he made the same mistakes. Yet he refused to let the game end, even when the other guests began to depart in the hours past midnight.

More than once, Vanessa saw Lord Brickendon look in her direction with a sympathetic smile. She smiled back and resisted laughing at the game they were playing. He could not help her, and she could not escape, but surely the night would come to an eventual end. When the viscount rose to take his leave, he came to where Vanessa was listening to Penelope and Sir Wilbur struggling through yet another debate about a rule of the game.

"Thank you for your invitation, my lady," Lord Brickendon said as he bowed over her hand. "The evening has provided all the entertainment I would have wished." With a nod to the others, he added, "Good evening, sir, madam. I assume I shall see you at Brooks's tomorrow evening, Franklin."

The baronet raised his eyes from his cards and arched his eyebrows. Patting Vanessa's hand possessively, he replied, "Do not assume anything, Brickendon."

"I never do. Leaving things to chance is the road to defeat." Smiling as Sir Wilbur sputtered at Lord Brickendon's words, which must have meant more to him than they did to Vanessa, he turned on his heel and left.

Vanessa lowered her cards to the table as a strange, forlorn sensation washed through her, leaving fatigue in its wake. She wished the night would come to its conclusion, but Penelope and the baronet had already resumed their disagreement. Only when the Downings excused themselves did Sir Wilbur accept that the game had come to a close.

Vanessa bid the Downings good evening and watched as Aunt Carolyn escorted them down the stairs to the front door. She was not surprised when Captain Hudson accompanied them. The captain had been as attentive to her aunt as Sir Wilbur had been to her. With a grimace at the thought, she went to where Sir Wilbur was rising from the table.

"My lady, you have been so patient with my bumbling this evening." He poured himself another glass of her aunt's best port. He glanced around the room, which was empty save for himself and Vanessa. His smile was one of a man who had crept into favor with himself. "I learn these new card games slowly, but I have found that kindness and patience are the reward of a gentle teacher."

Vanessa almost retorted that she had no interest in being kind and that her patience had become as thin as an anatomy's shadow. Walking to the door, so that he would have to acknowledge that the time to leave had long since passed, she said, "My aunt and I are pleased you were able to join us this evening. I am sure she will tell you so herself when she returns."

"That may be a while." He chuckled and drained the glass. Putting it on the table, he wobbled across the room, clearly worse for the wine he had been drinking. "Captain Hudson won a lion's share of her time this evening."

"Our families are friends of long standing."

"As I hope you and I shall be able to say some day."

His smile faded when she continued toward the stairs. "I shudder at the thought of you ladies living alone. These times are not without peril."

"I can reassure you. The staff comes from Wolfe Abbey. My father accepted no one in his household but the most competent." She smiled, because she knew several ears—the most important belonging to Quigley—would be listening on Aunt Carolyn's orders. Her fingers slid along the silken wood of the bannister. Glancing at the shadowed foyer below, she saw no one. That astonished her. She had thought Aunt Carolyn would be waiting there to say good night to their final guest.

When they reached the octagonal foyer, she surreptitiously looked out the half-opened door. Quigley stood on the walkway, a discreet distance from where Aunt Carolyn was admiring Captain Hudson's horse. Vanessa smiled at the light sound of her aunt's voice.

The baronet said, "You need someone to look after you. Your aunt seems to have found someone. So should you."

"I can take care of myself."

His full face broadened with a smile. "My lady, I mean no insult, but you are unaccustomed to the ways of Town, for you have spent most of your life in grassville. You need someone to guide you."

"Aunt Carolyn—"

"Can be as naïve as you if she allows you to ride about Town unchaperoned."

"Leale is always with me." When he put his hands on her shoulders, she took a step back. "Sir, I fear you have pulled the pig by the ear if you confuse the hospitality of this house for something else."

"You need never fear anything with me. I wish only to safeguard you."

The temptation to laugh tickled her as she tried to envision the baronet as a dashing knight bustling his round form across the castle moat to save his lady fair. She flinched as she thought of Lord Brickendon's words. She could imagine him coming to her rescue over the corpse of a fire-breathing dragon.

Hastily she set him from her thoughts. Right now, she must think only of convincing Sir Wilbur to bid her a good evening. "I assure you once more that neither my aunt nor I are incapable of taking care of ourselves."

"No?"

Vanessa's answer became a gasp when he gripped her arms and pulled her to him. The flaccid heat of his lips pressed on her mouth. She shoved against his full chest and heard him grunt as she escaped his harsh embrace. Horror filled her. First Lord Mendoff, now Sir Wilbur. . . . She did not want either of them to touch her ever again.

Victory filled his narrowed eyes in his porcine face. "As you can see, you need someone to protect you, my lady."

"From you." She locked her trembling hands together as she fought to keep her voice even. "I must ask you not to call again."

"Not to call?" His florid face bleached to a sickly shade of gray. "My dear lady, I implore you—"

"I implore *you* to refrain from making a scene that we both shall rue." She raised her hands as he stepped toward her again. Did the man have no sense of propriety? Or could he think only of his designs on her virtue?

"My lady, my heart is filled with warmth for you. I would not have been so presumptuous if I had not intended to ask you to be my wife."

"I fear that is quite impossible. We are little more than strangers." She turned away. "Good night and goodbye."

He stepped in front of her. "My lady, I urge you to

reconsider. Haven't I proven my concern for you this evening? Let me prove that I am heart-smitten for you."

She tried to push his chubby hands aside, but he grasped her arm and drew her closer. Suddenly his fingers fell away. She pressed her hands to her mouth as she saw a shadowed form take the baronet by the collar and waist. Quigley kicked aside the half-opened door and propelled the baronet out of the house. Sir Wilbur's yelp rang across the Square as he fell onto the straw-covered cobbles.

Aunt Carolyn rushed into the house. "Vanessa, what is the meaning of this?"

"Quigley is helping me say good evening to the baronet in a manner *his* manners deemed appropriate. As they are better suited for a sty than a house, let him wallow in the straw."

"Dear me!" Aunt Carolyn glanced toward the door Quigley was closing. "I suppose I should send someone to be sure he isn't hurt."

The butler shook his head. "Rest easily, my lady. I aimed him at a thick pile." He peeked through the window by the door. "You will be glad to hear that Captain Hudson is assisting him. The baronet is picking straw out of his posterior now."

Vanessa knew she was wrong to laugh, but she could not silence the sound. Guiltily she looked at Aunt Carolyn. Suddenly her aunt began to laugh, clutching her side. She wagged her finger at Vanessa, but only laughed.

When she had regained her breath, Aunt Carolyn said, "I guess you had no choice."

"None."

"Just make me one promise."

"Of course, Aunt Carolyn."

"Promise me that you shall not treat your next admirer this way, Vanessa."

She linked arms with her aunt as they climbed the stairs. "I hope I shall not need to." Only to herself did she add, "But I will if I must."

Chapter Seven

Rumor had a way of spreading quickly through Town, rattling on the tongue of every gossipmonger. Among the *ton,* tales were repeated at every look-in. Truth or fallacy, each story was carried from house to house, from square to square. A proposal whispered in a moonlit garden was known throughout the Polite World before the end of the next afternoon. An *affaire d'amour* was kept secret only from the capricornified spouse, for the intimate particulars were exchanged over tea and in the clubs.

Although she had known how impossible it was to be close as wax among the *élite,* Vanessa clung to her hopes that Sir Wilbur would be too mortified to repeat the story of his dismissal from her aunt's house. She hoped as well that Captain Hudson cared enough about Aunt Carolyn's reputation as a hostess to restrain himself from telling the amusing anecdote of the finale to the card party. Nothing had been said last night about her call on Lord Mendoff, so she dared to have hope about this.

Vanessa noticed no curious glances as she was driven along Bond Street. Beside her, Leale was a trifle quieter than usual, but Vanessa knew her abigail's reticence came from their disagreement before the party instead of Sir Wilbur's unexpectedly forceful departure.

"Leale, I shall not be long at Madame deBerg's shop," she said, wanting to patch the rent between them.

"After you cut your visit short yesterday, you owe *Madame* as much of your time as she requires."

"Which will not be much. The dress is nearly done." She smiled. "If you wish to visit the apothecary, you shall have time. Mr. MacGregor may have received a shipment of that liniment you prefer for your knees."

"They have been creaking like two old frogs down in the Abbey pond, haven't they?"

"I miss that music from the pond, but I would as lief you could move with more ease."

"The dampness will pass."

"When we return to Wolfe Abbey," she said hastily. Leale's dolorous words brought the dreary Sir Wilbur and his endless warnings about guarding his health to mind.

No note from the baronet had been waiting among the thank-you letters from their other guests. Vanessa had expected Sir Wilbur would again fail to obey the canons of propriety and fail to thank her aunt properly for the evening's diversion, but she cared not a rush if he disappeared completely from her life.

Even Lord Brickendon, despite his sometimes quoz ways, had had a note delivered. A smile pulled at her lips as she recalled reading it at the table in the breakfast-parlor.

My dear Lady Vanessa,

Your party of the evening past was most enjoyable. Please convey my thanks to Lady Mansfield for her generous welcome into your home. I trust, as I saw no announcement of your impending nuptials in this morning's paper, that you succeeded

*in your strategy with Sir Wilbur Franklin. I look
forward to speaking with you at Swinton's fête tomorrow evening. Do not think me ill-mannered to
mention this, for you should have received his invitation by this time.*

Vanessa had discovered the invitation, printed on light
green vellum, in the pile of mail on the breakfast table.
She and her aunt were cordially bid to attend a musicale
at the home of Bruce Swinton, not many blocks from
St. James. Putting aside the invitation, she had finished
the note from Lord Brickendon.

*Just remember that if you ever find yourself need-
ing the services of a brave knight (or a knave who
is a quarter flash and three-parts foolish), you
need only call upon*
                                        Your humble servant,

Lord Brickendon's signature had been as bold as his
flashing eyes, but she appreciated his humor even more
in the clear light of the morning. She could imagine his
volley of laughs if he chanced to learn of Sir Wilbur's
precipitous expulsion from the house. As she looked out
at the shops on Bond Street, she wondered what lay behind that humor. Yesterday, she had learned there
clearly was more to the viscount than his quips.

When the carriage stopped in front of the *couturière*'s
shop, Vanessa waited for Leale to alight onto the
walkway under the creaking sign with Madame
deBerg's name. Gently she asked, "Leale, why don't
you go to the apothecary now?"

"My lady, you should not be out by yourself. If your
aunt heard of such a thing—"

"Eveline Clarke is here." She pointed to a carriage
waiting on the far side of the street. "She must have re-

covered from the sniffles that kept her home last night. You know she will not allow me to leave Madame deBerg's without a full accounting of who attended the party and what was said. That will not be done quickly."

Leale nodded reluctantly, but said, "You must not leave until I return for you."

"I suspect you shall be waiting quite a while for *me.*"

"Do not leave!"

"I shall not."

Vanessa was unsure if Leale would take her word, for the abigail looked back over her shoulder as she walked along the street. Leale's sudden lack of trust would make it even more difficult to hide her determination to find Corey.

But she would.

How many times had Papa told them that they must depend on each other? *Even if no one else in the world will not stand with you, stand together.* His words in her memory were as clear as if he had just spoken them.

She and Corey had heeded his advice until the night before Corey left for the continent and the battle where he had disappeared. If she had listened to what Corey tried to tell her that night . . . if he had listened to her . . . It might have been easier now, for what had been said in anger would not be tormenting her as the words rang through her mind.

Corey, I never meant what I said. You know that, don't you? How she longed to speak those words to him, and she must, or she would never be able to free her heart from the weight of her guilt.

Vanessa opened the door of the small shop. The scent of roses rushed out at her. Madame deBerg kept her shop filled with as many bouquets as could be perched on the tables and sills. After the less pleasant scents of the streets, it was welcome, even though it was smoth-

ering. Bolts of material were stacked against a wall, and
white silk trailed along the floor.

A girl in a simple gown of muslin ushered Vanessa
into the back where Madame deBerg had her finest
books of fashion plates. Vanessa paused by a curtained
door and ignored the girl who was urging her to go into
the next room.

"Is Miss Clarke in here?" Vanessa asked.

"Yes, my lady."

"Do check with her and with Madame. I would like
to join them."

The girl's blue eyes filled with bafflement at the
change in the usual routine, but she slipped through the
curtains. Vanessa heard her chirping voice. Gazing
along the hall, she saw a bundle of material set in a
shadowed corner. No one asked how Madame deBerg
obtained the lovely fabrics that were woven on the opposite side of the Channel. The war had not lessened the
yearning of Society to dress *à la française* or halted the
owls from bringing cloth from France.

Interlopers! Vanessa asked herself why she had not
considered them before. She wondered if it was possible
to have a letter smuggled into France, mayhap even to
the highest reaches of that government. Perhaps one of
Boney's ministers might be willing to assist her . . . for
a price. She sighed. Such a bribe—assuming she could
get it to the right person—would beggar even her father's estate.

She was given no more time to ponder how she might
accomplish the impossible when the girl returned to announce Vanessa was welcome to go into the fitting
room. The lass stepped aside, holding the curtain out of
the way.

"Vanessa, just the one I wanted to see!" Eveline
Clarke's enthusiastic welcome matched her brilliant
smile and the rich wealth of her auburn hair.

Eveline was an incredible beauty with a figure that frequently propelled Madame deBerg into her native language to find words to praise it. Eveline would have been wed long before except for the unfortunate shadow cast over all the Clarkes because her mother had had the audacity to try to divorce her father. Mrs. Clarke had died in the arms of her lover, leaving a pall to haunt the rest of the family. None of that mattered to Vanessa, who had known Eveline since childhood, for their fathers had been schoolmates in their own youths.

Vanessa untied the checkered ribbons of her high-brimmed hat and set it on the table. Sitting next to the table, so she had a good view of Eveline, who was perched on a small platform, and the *modiste,* Vanessa said, "You look as if you are feeling quite well."

"I am fine." Eveline raised her hands with exasperation, then lowered them quickly on Madame deBerg's order. "If Papa hadn't been so afraid a mere cough might be deadly, I would have attended your *soirée* last night. I was able to convince him to let me come out this morning, but only because he insists we return to Berkshire before the week is over. Can you believe that?" She gestured her irritation, but stood still again when the *couturière* mumbled.

"The Season has only a handful of weeks to go. Why would he want you to leave now?"

Eveline's pretty smile grew dim with sadness. "He feels that if you are unable to find a match, I have little hope. Town fills him with *ennui,* so he is using any excuse to return to the country." She raised her hand to wipe a single tear from her cheek.

Madame deBerg glanced at Vanessa, clearly upset that one of her patrons was weeping. Vanessa hurried to ask, "Do you think your father would allow *you* to remain in Town? Aunt Carolyn and I would be thrilled to have you stay with us."

"Would you?" She clapped her hands, laughing as Madame deBerg shook her head in resignation. "I do so want to stay. I have met the most charming man. Edward Grey."

"Lord Greybrooke?"

"One and the same." She smiled. "The earl is so sweet. I have seen him several times in the Park, and he never fails to take a moment to speak with me."

Vanessa hid her own smile. She found the earl as boring as Eveline's father found the whirl of the Season—as she found the whirl of the Season—but Eveline's heart clearly had discerned something Vanessa had failed to see. She would hear every facet of the meetings in the Park because Eveline held onto a secret no longer than a gambler kept a losing hand.

"We shall plan on having you be our guest for the rest of the Season," Vanessa said. "All you need to do is send word of when you will join us."

Bouncing from the dais, Eveline flung her arms around Vanessa. "Oh, thank you. I did not know what I would do when Papa insisted we leave."

"You needed only to call. You know our house is always open to you."

"I had thought to give you a look-in this afternoon." She stepped back up on the low platform and offered the *modiste* an apologetic grin. "I was anxious to talk to you about many things, but I feared your aunt might be at home."

Vanessa regarded her with bafflement. "You didn't want to call on Aunt Carolyn?"

"Would you be willing to give me all the luscious details if Lady Mansfield was present?"

"Of the party?"

Eveline giggled as she peered over the top of the *modiste*'s head. "You need not pretend with me. Is it true

what Mrs. Garber told me? Did you really have Sir
Wilbur Franklin tossed out onto the Square?"

"Do stand still!" implored Madame deBerg. "The
hem will be askew, Miss Clarke, if you continue to wig-
gle and jump about the room like a crazed rabbit."

"Is it the truth?" continued Eveline, irrepressible. Her
cheeks dimpled. "Oh, Vanessa, say that it is! It is too
amusing!"

Vanessa was torn between embarrassment and laughter. She chose the latter. If Eveline had heard the news,
it must have spread completely throughout the Polite
World. "I wish you had been feeling more like yourself,
Eveline. I swear that Quigley nearly smiled when he
sent the baronet flying through the door."

"Quigley? Smiled? No!" She grimaced as Madame
deBerg muttered another warning. "And Lady Mansfield? Surely she must be distressed."

"Aunt Carolyn has owned that the baronet must have
been born at Hogs Norton, because his manners are so
intolerable." Vanessa could not bring herself to speak
Sir Wilbur's name. With a shudder, she stood. "But that
contemptible situation is over, for I doubt that even he
would be foolish enough to present himself at our door
again in the wake of his dismissal."

"It shan't be over until you betroth yourself." Eveline
stepped down from the low pedestal and turned toward
the dressing room. Looking over her shoulder, she
added, with a sly smile, "I heard as well that Lord
Brickendon attended the party last night. Oh, how I
wish I had been able to be there! He is quite in dash."
Her smile vanished. "But you must be careful, Vanessa.
He is a rogue of the first stare with his *à suivie* flirtations. I wish you would allow me to introduce you to
Mr. Symmes. He is the dearest man. I know you would
like him. Besides, he belongs to the same club as Lord
Greybrooke. I understand they are good friends. We

could go to the Park together to meet them next week. With your aunt to chaperone us, we—"

"Enough," she interrupted with a laugh. "I have no need of your matchmaking. Aunt Carolyn batters my ears every day with her determination to find me a husband. Do be a friend, and leave off with this."

Eveline shook her head, sending her ruddy curls cascading along her neck. "And right your aunt is! You need to find a man to marry. You are too kind and sweet to be left on the shelf. I shall speak with my brother Edgar the next time I see him. He is coming to Town before the end of the week. Mayhap a dear friend he has met during his studies in Cambridge will touch your heart."

"Eveline, please don't do that."

"Nonsense." Ignoring Madame deBerg, who was picking up scraps of lace and pins from the floor, Eveline rushed to Vanessa. She took Vanessa's hands in hers. Tears filled her olive eyes. "I fear you have forgotten how to be happy. It behooves me, as your dearest bosom-bow, to lighten your heart and help you forget your grief."

"I do not want to forget my grief. Not for a moment!" Vanessa saw Eveline's dismay, and, although she wished everyone would let her lead her life as she wanted, she remembered her vow. Smiling with Eveline usually was not a task, but today it was. She loathed being false with Eveline, but did not want to burden her bosom-bow with the truth. Dear Eveline had enough heartache of her own. "Forgive my outburst, Eveline. The truth is that I shall forget my grief when the time is right."

"Forget it now, and tell me all about last night."

Vanessa smiled. Eveline was quite the opposite of her dour father, so it was little wonder that prospective matches worried she would be as hedonistic as her mother. As Eveline redressed and Vanessa tried on a dark crimson riding habit Madame deBerg had nearly complete, Vanessa answered the barrage of questions from Eveline and made plans for Eveline's visit.

Leale's arrival and pursed lips silenced Eveline's laughter. The comb-brush said nothing until she was seated next to Vanessa in the carriage again, but then chided Vanessa all the way back to Grosvenor Square for her amusement at Sir Wilbur's expense.

"I shall say no more," Vanessa vowed, although she continued to smile. "I hope the baronet has been cut for the simples and will recognize the futility of paying a *visite de digestion* on our household."

"He behaved abominably, I grant you, but he did profess a true affection for you."

Vanessa walked through the door Quigley held open. "Leale, I cannot find myself tacked together with him simply because I have sympathy for his unrequited love."

"I would think not." The abigail unbent enough to shake her finger in Vanessa's direction. "Don't forget that I am well-accustomed to how you twist words as facilely as the old gentleman in black himself. I doubt if you have much sympathy for him."

"I would have if he hadn't—" Vanessa shuddered and hastily changed the subject so she did not have to think how her first kiss had been so loathesome. For so many years, she has wondered what it would be like to have a man draw her into his arms and brush her lips with his. Sir Wilbur had destroyed that fantasy. "Aunt Carolyn and I have received an invitation to Mr. Swinton's musicale tomorrow night. I would like to wear my white crêpe with the blue silk ruffle."

Leale nodded. "I shall have it ready."

As the abigail climbed the stairs, Quigley cleared his throat lowly. Vanessa tried to contain her excitement as he held out a folded sheet to her, hoping that Leale did not guess *this* was the reason Vanessa had remained in the foyer.

"It was delivered but five minutes ago," the butler said in a strained voice.

Overmastered by Quigley's reaction, Vanessa took the letter. As she turned it over to see the unfamiliar seal, her fingers quivered, and her stomach did an abbreviated leap toward her throat. This was not her own letter being returned unanswered. Someone had responded—at last. Could this be the information she had prayed for?

"Thank you, Quigley," she whispered.

As she turned to follow Leale up the stairs, the butler said, "I hope it is the news you have sought, my lady."

"If it is, you shall be the first to know. Whatever it says, thank you, Quigley, for all you have done and all you have kept to yourself." She stood on tiptoe to kiss his sallow cheek.

"Well, well," he said, blushing. She had never seen him as flustered.

Vanessa hurried up the steps before she embarrassed the butler more. She paused at the top of the stairs. If she went to her room, Leale would be there. Going to the blue sitting room, she saw her aunt working on the embroidery she enjoyed. Vanessa inched away. She wanted to savor this moment alone.

On the second floor, she went to a window seat overlooking the small garden. Taking a deep breath and whispering a short, fervent prayer, she broke the sealing wax and unfolded the sheet.

The answer was terse. His lordship could not offer her any assistance in locating the body of her brother. Many brave men had died far from their native land. She must take solace in knowing that the French gave their enemies a decent burial.

She lowered the page to her lap and closed her eyes.

Tears oozed through her lashes and along her cheeks. Struggling to keep Eveline's cheery voice out of her head, she failed miserably, for she could hear Eveline prattling about how successful her brother was at Cambridge and how he would be coming to Town for a visit. She was a wicked person for begrudging Eveline her happiness.

She bit her lip and shuddered as her sobs thudded against her heart. *A hero.* That was what Corey had aspired to be. That was what he was, but had he given even one thought to the misery his heroics would cause for those who loved him?

A hand settled on her shoulder, and Vanessa wiped her eyes as she looked up. Puzzlement and sympathy aged Aunt Carolyn's face.

"My dear Vanessa," she whispered, "why are you piping your eyes? Did someone speak horribly of last night's party while you were out on your errands?" Her hands tightened into fists by the sides of her pale gold dressing gown. "By all that's blue, I wish I had never asked Sir Wilbur to our home!"

Vanessa put her hand over her aunt's. "Don't worry about him. If you ask Leale, she will reassure you that, when I met Eveline at Madame deBerg's, all our words about the baronet were mixed with laughter."

Dabbing a handkerchief against her niece's damp cheek, she asked, "Then why these tears?"

She stood and faced her aunt. Silently she held out the letter. Waiting for her aunt to read its few words, she bit her lower lip to keep more sobs from oozing forth.

Aunt Carolyn said nothing as she put the letter back on the window seat. Sitting next to it, she folded her hands in her lap. Her gaze rose to Vanessa's, and she whispered, "I thought I asked you, weeks ago, to put an end to this odious correspondence."

"You did."

"You chose not to obey?"

"No, I could not."

"This." She touched the letter. "This is what I hoped to spare you from suffering. Vanessa, why are you doing this? You must accept the truth."

Vanessa knelt next to her aunt and folded the older woman's hands between hers. "Aunt Carolyn, I accept the only truth I know. The truth within my heart. It tells me Corey is still alive."

"No!" Aunt Carolyn set herself on her feet. Taking two steps along the corridor, she turned to affix Vanessa with a furious glare. "I shall not let you waste your life hoping for what we both know is preposterous." She picked up the letter.

Vanessa gasped as her aunt tore it in half. "But, Aunt Carolyn, if I don't keep the hope alive, what will happen to Corey?"

"Nothing." Her voice softened as she threw the pieces of paper onto the floor. "There is nothing we can do to help him, but there is something I can do to help you."

"I know. I need to find a man to wed, so that Wolfe Abbey is not left without a family to tend it. Don't you see?" Tears burned in her eyes again. "We are a family. You and me and—"

"I will hear no more of this out-of-hand talk." Aunt Carolyn cupped Vanessa's chin in her slender fingers. "I have let you have your head during this Season, but I long for the days when you smiled easily. I fear you have forgotten how to have fun."

"You tell me my brother is put to bed with a shovel, but ask me to smile."

Aunt Carolyn shook her head sadly. "If you would mourn for your brother as is right, you could forget the lies your heart whispers to you. I know you think your heart is trying to protect you. You are wrong. You cannot change what has happened. You must think only of what is to come."

"I do. I think often of Corey's homecoming."

"Which may never happen, and I fear never as you wish." She sighed once more as she released Vanessa. "I did not want to say this, but you leave me no choice. If you do not find yourself a husband before this Season comes to an end, I vow to you, Vanessa, although it goes against every grain within me, that I shall spend the next Season arranging for a husband who you will marry slap-bang."

"Aunt Carolyn!" Disbelief tainted her voice.

Lady Mansfield was silent as she walked away. Then she paused and came back to gather the shreds of the letter. Sorrow drew unfamiliar lines on her face as she handed Vanessa a lacy handkerchief. She left Vanessa knowing that—although it would have seemed inconceivable the day before—her aunt meant to do exactly as she had threatened.

Chapter Eight

Ross told himself he should have known better than to accept the invitation to this evening's musicale. Bruce Swinton was tolerable company at the table of green cloth, but he was the *ton*'s most inept host. If Swinton had any taste in music, the orchestra playing at one end of the ballroom gave no clue to it. Ross grimaced as another drum roll careered across the room. The selection was better suited to a parade ground than a London town house.

He crossed the room beneath the friezes edging the high walls. The ceiling was painted in a mural meant to represent heaven. Tastefully draped cherubs played among rose-colored clouds. The scene was broken by a pair of bronze chandeliers and scores of candles. Below them, the floor glittered past the green Kidderminster rug. Flowers sat on rosewood tables along the sides of the room, their fragrance nearly choking in the crowded room. A hint of a summery breeze, as soft as baby's fingers, touched his cheek, and Ross saw a set of French windows open at the far end of the room. This chamber was the perfect setting for an evening's entertainment, but he was not entertained.

He reminded himself of the real reason he was here tonight. With Franklin acting like a beaten cur, it was

Swinton's chance to try to turn Lady Vanessa's head. Ross was not going to miss witnessing this.

"Blast!" he muttered, adding a pair of earthy curses. Nothing eased the agony of his ears when the musical piece reached its crescendo. Fitful applause followed the end.

Taking a glass from a passing servant, Ross sipped the wine. His smile returned. Swinton might be tone-deaf, but he had cultivated his palate.

Greeting other guests he passed, he paused when Swinton scampered past him toward the door. Ross chuckled. That level of anticipation could herald the arrival of only one person. With Franklin's abrupt announcement that he had cut himself out and would as lief pay the pound for the wager than call on Lady Vanessa again, Swinton must be calculating how best to win the lady's hand.

Now *this* could be entertaining. Ross set his glass on a table as a slender form entered the room.

Lady Vanessa was wearing white, like most of the women. It was a shame, he decided. The pink she had worn at her aunt's home had complemented her delicate coloring, which gave no hint to the steel within her. He could not halt his grin as he thought of the various versions he had heard of Franklin's last moments in Lady Mansfield's house ... and on the street in front of it. Promising himself that one day he would learn the truth of what had happened from Lady Vanessa herself, he watched his host.

The red-haired man recalled his manners in time to bow over Lady Mansfield's hand, but his attention focused on the younger woman, who was giving her Indian shawl to a maid. When he raised Lady Vanessa's hand to his lips, a wide grin on his lips, a peculiar tightness cramped Ross's stomach. He frowned. Perhaps the wine had not been as excellent as he had thought.

He walked to where Swinton was stumbling over his words in his eagerness to impress the two ladies. Tapping his host on the shoulder, Ross smiled at Swinton's sharp glance. He resisted retorting that he could not enjoy this if he watched from halfway across the room.

"Good evening, my lady," Ross said to Lady Mansfield, then he added, "and to you, my lady."

"My lord," Lady Vanessa answered tersely.

He saw her glance at her aunt, then quickly away. He could not guess what message had passed between them. When Lady Vanessa gave Swinton a smile and accepted his offer of a glass of wine, he watched them walk toward where chairs were set for the abominable performance ahead of them.

Lady Mansfield mused, "Not an impossible match."

"Not impossible," Ross agreed.

She looked at him, a smile lilting at the corners of her lips. "You sound distressed, my lord. You need not look the sad scamp. Vanessa has given no more than her ear to Mr. Swinton at this point."

"My lady, you mistake a bit of queasiness from soured wine for heart-sickness." He held out his arm. When she put her fingers on it, he led her toward the chairs. "I consider it a point of honor never to have more than a casual *amitié* with a lady my friend has expressed an interest in."

"So Mr. Swinton is interested in Vanessa?"

Ross nearly laughed. *This* was what Lady Mansfield had hoped to discover. "I can assure you that Bruce Swinton would find winning your niece's heart very worthwhile."

"I have few doubts about that," she replied dryly, then chuckled. "You play with words as readily as Vanessa. I own to being astounded that you stand back while Mr. Swinton commands her attention. Your sense of honor is exemplary."

"No, my lady, only my determination to enjoy others' pursuits of matrimony."

"Something you do not wish for yourself?"

"Mayhap someday, when I am senile enough not to know better."

Across the room, Vanessa heard her aunt's light laugh. Looking back, she saw the amazing sight of her aunt on Lord Brickendon's arm. Their heads were bent toward each other in earnest conversation. When Captain Hudson strode toward them, she heard what sounded like a snort from beside her.

"Mr. Swinton?" she asked pointedly.

The red-haired man seated her in the front row of chairs, the tails of his black evening coat flapping about his legs. "Excuse me, my lady, but I cannot help being amused about the collection of admirers your aunt is gathering."

"You can't?"

Mr. Swinton smiled and sat next to her. "You are misreading my words. I meant no slight to your charming aunt. You Wolfe ladies should be named for the perfect flower, for you intrigue a gentleman into thinking of gentleness instead of the feral temper of your family's namesake."

"You are the one mistaken." Vanessa relaxed, for Mr. Swinton was trying to be agreeable company. Just because she had been in the dismals since her aunt's ultimatum did not grant her the right to inflict her low spirits on him. "The Wolfe women are not sacrosanct from our family's many faults."

"May I say you and your aunt have shown rare aplomb in light of the distasteful escapade of earlier this week?"

" 'Twas no escapade, Mr. Swinton. It was—"

"Intolerable of Franklin," he supplied, his smile broadening. "Franklin can be a boor when sober. When blind as Chloë, the man is a knight and barrow pig and loses every manner he ever possessed. I must offer my abject condolences for your discomfort at the hands of my friend."

"You cannot be held responsible for the behavior of your friend. I am, I must own, just glad to be shut of him."

"I am pleased to hear that you do not judge a man by the cup and can he enjoys at his club. I have found that those companions, who are boon about the card table, can be an embarrassment when we are amid the fairest blossoms of the Polite World."

Vanessa was about to reply, but the orchestra began playing even more loudly again. Rising, for she was certain her ears could not abide the noise for long, she saw her motion had set up Mr. Swinton's bristles. His brown eyes, which were not as dark as Lord Brickendon's, were wide with dismay.

And dismay was what *she* felt as she found herself comparing Mr. Swinton to the viscount. In spite of herself, she looked across the room. Lord Brickendon was no longer talking with Aunt Carolyn, and she had no chance to discover where he was, as Mr. Swinton asked if she would like to see the painting that he recently had had commissioned.

"Yes," she answered. At that moment, she was eager to agree to just about anything to escape the crash of the music and her thoughts of the equally disquieting viscount.

Vanessa breathed a sigh of relief when they emerged from the ballroom into a small alcove.

"They are thunderous," Mr. Swinton said with an apologetic smile. "I must speak with them before the beginning of the musicale. The selections for that are much more serene." He pointed to an ornate, gilt frame. "This is the painting, my lady."

A gasp of admiration burst from her lips as she stepped to where she could better see the canvas, which was more than her height and twice the length of the mahogany library table beneath it. Rolling hills of spring's freshest green provided the backdrop for almost life-size figures of riders in their pinks mounted upon fine horses. About the steeds' feet, dogs pranced, eager for the hunt across the stone walls and through fields stroked with the first gray light of morning.

"See the dog in front of the lead rider?" Mr. Swinton asked with undeniable pride. "He is of the Swinton Park kennels. The white patch just above the dog's forepaws marks my kennels' distinctive marking."

"They look like excellent dogs. I can imagine them flushing the fox from its hold in no time."

"You sound as if you enjoy the hunt, my lady."

"I do. We often rode out at Wolfe Abbey before . . ." Her voice nearly broke as she thought of the halcyon days before Corey left for the continent and while her father had still overseen Wolfe Abbey. The longing for those simple diversions, for mornings chasing the fox across a dew-dappled field, for evenings when they sat by the hearth and shared a hot drink and read from the books they all adored, swarmed over her, as stinging and fierce as a hive of bees.

"My lady?"

She smiled, although she feared her expression would appear as feigned as it felt. "Forgive me. I lost myself in thoughts of hunts past."

"And of hunts future?"

"I fear there is little worth hunting in Town."

"If one isn't seeking a spouse on the Marriage Mart?"

Thoughts of the past evaporated as Vanessa's smile became genuine. "Those words could be considered blasphemous by certain parties."

"I find the desperate search for a whither-ye-go can

stand in the way of friendships." He took her hand and held it between his. "Why should we not become friends? We share a love of the hunt and a dislike of that cacophonous music."

"I would like that." Guilt pinched her, for Mr. Swinton's offer gave her the best opportunity to please Aunt Carolyn. Mr. Swinton was honest enough to say he was not setting his cap on her. She appreciated that and the fact that she could be seen enough in his company to discourage the insipid men she had met during the Season. She wanted little to do with any of them, save . . . Lord Brickendon, she had to own to herself, who was not in the least insipid. Yet, by appearing to live in Mr. Swinton's pocket, she could avoid the viscount's touch, which had been so unsettling. So deliriously unsettling.

She glanced back at the ballroom. She saw Lord Brickendon as clearly as if no one else stood within the huge room. He looked over his shoulder, and their gazes touched, as intimate and eager as a caress. As her fingers clenched in the silk of her dress, she fought the craving to surrender herself to the passions in his dark gaze. So easily she could have walked to him, drawn to him in a spellbound rapture.

Mr. Swinton's pleasant tenor intruded, and she flinched. "Is something wrong, my lady?" he asked.

"No—no, I am fine."

Puzzlement furrowed his forehead, but he said, "I would be honored if you and your aunt would join a small party I have arranged at Swinton Park this weekend. My master of the hunt has informed me that the dogs are anxious to be put to the scent, and I wish to oblige both him and them by setting them after the fox. Do join us."

"I wish we were able to," Vanessa said with regret. After months of being confined amid cobbles and mar-

ble, she longed to exult in the commonplace wonders of
the country. Also—and perhaps more importantly—she
would be far from Lord Brickendon. "Your invitation is
generous, Mr. Swinton. However, I have promised a
friend to be her hostess for the remainder of the Season.
I could not be so remiss as to leave her right after we
had opened our house to her."

"Of course not." A smile blossomed across his thin
face. "I have just the dandy. Our party is small. Please
offer your friend an invitation to join us in our hunt."

Vanessa put her hand on his arm as they walked toward the ballroom. Her voice trembled when she saw
Lord Brickendon talking again to her aunt. Getting out
of London now would be prudent. A few days away,
while she talked Aunt Carolyn into seeing sense, and
she would have a better perspective on everything in
Town. "That is generous of you, Mr. Swinton. I would
be delighted to," she said with a smile. She was glad
she could be honest when she said, "I can't imagine
anything I would enjoy more."

"Nor I, my lady." His eyes glistened. "Nor I."

Opening her parasol, Vanessa took a deep breath of
the fresh air as she stepped out onto a small terrace
overlooking the gardens of Swinton Park.

"To think," said Eveline with a soft laugh, "that I
threatened to fling out of the house when Papa said we
would be going to daisyville. Now here I am." She
wrapped her arms around herself beneath the bright col-
ors of her fringed shawl. "This shall be so much fun, although I look forward to the hunt with dread."

Vanessa tilted her head, so she could see past the
wide brim of her green Oldenburg bonnet. She smiled
as the wind pulled at Eveline's Scottish-style bonnet and
twisted the plume attached to one side. "You need not

dread anything. You can stay here in the house. Few women ride to catch the fox."

"But you do."

"Papa and Corey insisted that I ride as they did." She laughed at Eveline's gasp of shock. "Don't worry. I shall not shame you or Aunt Carolyn by riding astride tomorrow. Everything I do or say shall be *comme il faut.*"

"As I am sure you always are, my lady," answered Mr. Swinton as he climbed the trio of stone steps to the terrace. "I am delighted to see you have arrived here in such good humor. The journey from London can be tiring." His eyes widened as he looked at Eveline. "Miss Clarke, this is a surprise."

"For me as well," Eveline answered as she offered his hand. When he bowed over it, dimples pocked her cheeks. "I was delighted with the invitation you asked Vanessa to present to me."

"So you are staying with the Wolfe ladies."

"We are dear friends." She squeezed Vanessa's hand, then added, "I must ask you to excuse me, Mr. Swinton. I make it a habit, any time I travel, to be certain that my abigail has unpacked my fripperies properly."

"Eveline—"

"I shall be but a minute, Vanessa." She walked toward the double doors opening into the book-room, pausing only long enough to wink brazenly at Vanessa.

Smiling, Vanessa walked with Mr. Swinton in the opposite direction. Trust Eveline to try to give her an unchaperoned moment with their host. She resisted the urge to be honest with her dear friend. Eveline would be sure to let the secret slip, and Aunt Carolyn soon would be looking for another suitor for her.

For now, everything was better than she had dared to hope. Coming to the country had been a grand idea. She would have fun with her bosom-bow and keep in with

Mr. Swinton. Aunt Carolyn had been quite the prattle-box on the journey to Swinton Park, and Vanessa had said nothing to disabuse her of her notion that Vanessa and their host would soon be coming to a permanent understanding.

Vanessa walked with Mr. Swinton in companionable silence across the eider soft grass toward a rose garden, which was surrounded by a waist-high stone wall. Within it, the rose vines contorted as if mad with a fever. She was surprised to see that little pruning had been done to keep the vines blooming longer.

"They must have been lovely," Vanessa said.

A smile widened Mr. Swinton's thin face. "I need only look at the beautiful blush in your cheeks, and I can understand why they surrendered before your loveliness."

"Mr. Swinton, you flatter me needlessly."

"I speak the truth. Isn't that the obligation of friends? To be honest with each other?"

Vanessa walked along the low wall to hide the truth. She was honest with too few people now. "It is so quiet here after the clatter of Town."

As if to make her words false, the furious clucking of chickens and the sharp sound of hoofbeats splintered the afternoon. She laughed, but stopped when she perceived Mr. Swinton was not sharing her merriment.

"My lady, I hesitate to say this, but I feel I must." His voice was funereal.

"Didn't you just say that friends owe each the duty of honesty?" She leaned against the wall and set the parasol on her shoulder, so she could more easily see his face. It was set in somber lines.

"Then I shall not insult you by lathering you with goose's gazettes. My lady, I own to a great consternation at discovering that the friend you brought with you to Swinton Park is Eveline Clarke."

Vanessa's smile fell. Telling herself she should have expected this as soon as he faltered on his greeting to Eveline, she straightened. Her fingers bit into her gloved palm as she clutched her parasol more tightly. "Mr. Swinton, Eveline and I have been oars first with each other since our childhood. I know well what is said of her family, but I know Eveline. She has been grossly misjudged, for her heart is as warm as this sunshine and as large as the sea."

"You are misunderstanding me again. I do not condemn your friendship. Quite the opposite. I laud faithfulness in the face of scorn. However, you must see the truth. You may believe Miss Clarke to be an angel, but she is her mother's daughter. As her friend, you may be considered of the same ilk."

"I do not judge you by your friends, Mr. Swinton!"

He caught her hand. "As your friend, I think only of your place in Society, my lady. If you want to safeguard that, you must rethink your friendship with Miss Clarke."

Vanessa blinked back tears that blurred Mr. Swinton's face in front of her. "I thought you were my friend."

"I am. That is why I speak of this." He stepped toward her. "My lady, I am concerned that your gentle heart is ruling you, blinding you to the disaster awaiting you if you do not put Miss Clarke from your life."

"Although you can do Eveline no harm in my eyes, I find your words hurtful."

"Nonsense! Words cannot hurt you, especially when they are the truth."

Settling her parasol on her shoulder, she whispered, "Excuse me, Mr. Swinton. I would like to take a walk. Alone."

"My lady, you must not ignore my advice. If—"

"Please, Mr. Swinton. If you are truly my friend, please understand I wish to be alone now." She did not look at him. She could not bear to see his sincerity when she lied as she went on, "I shall think about what you have said."

He nodded. "As you wish, my lady."

Vanessa struggled to keep her pace slow as she left the rose garden. To perdition with the good intentions of the misguided! Mr. Swinton's hope of preventing her from being hurt had deeply wounded her soul. Putting her hand to her bodice, she felt the crinkle of Corey's letter. She could not bear to be parted from it, not even for a short journey into the country. As she touched it, she whispered a vow that she would never allow Eveline to learn of this conversation. She did not want her dear friend to feel the pain she suffered every day.

The sun was reaching toward the western horizon when Vanessa realized she had been walking aimlessly for most of the afternoon. Seeing a gazebo shaped like a bright yellow Chinese pagoda, she peeked inside. Shadowed benches offered a chance to rest her feet. She stepped over the droppings left by squirrels that had gnawed holes about the base of the gazebo.

Sitting on a hard bench, she leaned back against the latticed walls and closed her parasol. She hoped the rest of the sojourn at Swinton Park would go better than its beginning. She sighed.

"Such a sigh!"

Vanessa could not ignore the pulse of pleasure pounding through her as she recognized Lord Brickendon's voice. Turning, she saw him in the door of the gazebo. The small space fit him poorly, and she saw him glance about with candid distaste as he sat on the bench across from her. She was so grateful he did not crowd his attentions on her as Sir Wilbur had that she almost thanked him. That would label her as ill-mannered as Aunt Carolyn had suggested.

"Am I disturbing you, my lady?" he continued in his

lush, deep voice that was appropriate amid the cool shadows. "If so, I will leave."

"You are disturbing me," she said, adding hastily when his eyes narrowed, "but I find I would like other company than my thoughts."

"I was unsure if I would find a welcome. You seemed very displeased at the idea of my company at the musicale."

She managed a slight smile. Again amazement filled her. She found it so simple to be straightforward with Lord Brickendon. With him, she never felt obligated to produce a false smile. She could be honest about her feelings, whether they were joyous or bleak. "You must forgive me for any curt words that night. I was not myself."

"May I say that I find yourself more captivating when you are smiling?"

Warmth coursed through her, but she said only, "I had not guessed you to be a part of the hunting party."

"I always accept an invitation to poaching country, even though Swinton is not at his best as a host." His smile did nothing to ease the strength of his jaw. "However, he does set a good table, so we should not have a wolf in our stomachs while we are here."

"I am not sure we shall be staying for supper."

"No? You are thinking of returning to London when you have only just arrived?"

Vanessa's exasperation burst forth before she could halt it. "Mr. Swinton took great pains to tell me that he finds my friendships distasteful. He thinks he can blow coals between me and my bosom-bow."

"With Miss Clarke? I can understand that."

She leapt to her feet. "Can you? I had thought you more open to thought than that, my lord." Grasping the handle of her parasol, she pointed its tip at him. "I see you are as shortsighted as our host."

Astonishment wiped the smile from his face as he slowly stood. He pushed the parasol aside. "You need not brandish such a weapon against me, my lady."

"No," she said, hating the fire climbing her cheeks, "I need not. Nor do you need to speak to me again. I shall not listen to my dearest friend being derided by you as well."

When he put his hand on her arm as she was about to storm out of the gazebo, she quivered. Not just with her rage, but with a sweeter, potent emotion that seared her. She did not resist when he turned her to face him. She was not sure she could have.

Bending, so his eyes were even with hers, he whispered, "What a shame you were not born heir to your father's title! You would have been another Marquess of Wulfric who is ready to battle with a broadsword or a bunch of fives."

"Don't mock me."

"I'm not." He smiled as he lifted her parasol. "I wouldn't think of jesting a woman who was ready to spear me with a summer-cabbage." Before she could retort, he went on, "I meant no disparagement on your bosom-bow. I was only acknowledging that it is no surprise that Swinton would act so coarsely, although I am astounded he would risk your burgeoning friendship with such an attack on Miss Clarke."

"Perhaps he feels so strongly that he had to tell me."

"Are you defending him?"

Vanessa started to give him an answer, then realized she had none. When she began to laugh wryly, Lord Brickendon led her out of the gazebo. He waited while she opened her parasol.

"That's better," he said as he drew her hand into his arm. "You should laugh more often, my lady. I find a good laugh keeps me from taking myself too seriously."

"Something I tend to do."

"Than I must change that. Would you like to walk down to the pond? On the way here, Swinton mentioned something about ducklings that have recently hatched." He reached under his coat and pulled out a small pouch. "I purloined some bread from the kitchen. A habit left over from my unruly youth, I fear, but I will ease my guilty conscience by allowing you to share in feeding the ducklings."

"And implicate me in your crime?" she asked.

"You see through my ploy, my lady."

Vanessa's heart fluttered like a butterfly she had cupped in her hands. She was grateful that the lace dropping from her parasol and her broad bonnet hid her face, for she was unsure what it might have revealed as they walked across the garden to where a small pond glistened emerald bright in the sunshine.

Voices from the house were muted as they climbed down a steep hill to the pond. She was grateful that Lord Brickendon did not caution her to worry about getting her feet wet as Sir Wilbur would have. Instead, he guided her around a clump of reeds and pointed out the nest hidden inside. She smiled as she saw a quartet of ducklings swimming near the edge of the water.

The duckling were just a few days old, little more than balls of fine feathers. As she tossed bits of bread to them, Vanessa watched Lord Brickendon trying to coax the drake out of the pond to where he was sitting on a white cast-iron bench beneath a stand of oak. The testy black duck snapped at him, and the viscount chuckled. He threw a handful of bread on the ground in front of the drake. As the bird came out of the water and began to eat it, keeping a suspicious eye on the viscount, his mate joined him.

Lord Brickendon wiped crumbs from his hands as he walked back to where Vanessa was standing. "I admire any beast that knows its own mind."

"You make two of a kind."

"I would as lief say we were three of a kind." He leaned against one of the thin trees bordering the pond. For the first time, she noticed he was wearing the riding coat and buckskins that he had worn the day he returned the letter she had sent to his uncle. His high riding boots accented the strength of his legs and were as black as his tall beaver.

She laughed to cover the deliciously unsettled feeling in her stomach as she admired how his coat flattered his shoulders. "Is that so?"

"You seem admirably aware of what you want, my lady. Even a dolt like Franklin must be aware of your intentions to let no one but yourself plot the course of your future."

"You are correct again. We Wolfes have what others perceive as a nasty habit of being single-minded in our pursuits." She threw the last of her bread crumbs to the quacking ducklings. When Lord Brickendon smiled devilishly and poured more into her hand, she said, "You are well prepared, my lord."

"A skill I have found necessary amid the halls of government."

Bread crumbs dropped, unnoticed, through her fingers. Words fell out of her mind but did not reach her mouth.

"My lady, are you well? You look quite gray." He put his hand on her arm and drew her to sit on the cast-iron bench.

"Forgive me," she whispered, not sure she could speak louder.

Kneeling in front of her, he said, "I should be asking you to forgive me, for clearly I have said or done something to unsettle you."

She was astonished at her yearning to smooth the worried lines from his forehead. Clasping her hands in her lap to keep them from reaching out to him, she said, "No, you have done nothing."

Softly he said, "Perhaps it is nothing more than fatigue from your journey."

"Yes," she whispered, glad for the excuse, for she was truly exhausted, "perhaps it is that." Taking a deep breath, she added in a stronger voice, "Lord Brickendon, I must ask you to excuse me. I fear I have left my aunt and Eveline alone too long."

"You can rest easily, my lady. I spoke with Lady Mansfield before I decided to wander through Swinton's gardens." He stood as she did. "I believe she is quite happily occupied with Captain Hudson, who arrived shortly after you did."

"Captain Hudson is here?" Surprise sent other thoughts from her head. Aunt Carolyn had mentioned nothing about the captain joining them this weekend, which was indeed curious.

"Yes, and, if my rudely eavesdropping ears garnered their words correctly, they are planning to be partners at the card table this evening."

Vanessa put her hand on the arm Lord Brickendon offered. She must not think about asking him for help to find Corey until they reached Town. Then she would make a few inquiries to discover exactly what connections he had . . . and if she could trust him not to laugh at her quest. Until then, she must keep her yearning to be open with him to herself.

In a cheerful voice to prevent him from guessing what she was thinking, she said, "Eavesdropping is a deplorable habit, my lord."

"But one that can garner much valid information."

"Or invalid, but I'm not surprised Aunt Carolyn is looking forward to an evening of cards."

"Does that mean you have changed your mind about returning to Town tonight?"

PRESENTING AN IRRESISTIBLE OFFERING ON YOUR KIND OF ROMANCE.

Receive 4 Zebra Regency Romance Novels (A $16.47 value) *Free*

Journey back to the romantic Regent Era with the world's finest romance authors. Zebra Regency Romance novels place you amongst the English *ton* of a distant past with witty dialogue, and stories of courtship so real, you feel that you're living them!

Experience it all through 4 FREE Zebra Regency Romance novels...yours just for the asking. When you join *the only book club dedicated to Regency Romance readers,* additional Regency Romances can be yours to preview FREE each month, with no obligation to buy anything, ever.

Regency Subscribers Get First-Class Savings.

After your initial package of 4 FREE books, you'll begin to receive monthly shipments of new Zebra Regency titles. These all new novels will be delivered direct to your home as soon as they are published...sometimes even before the bookstores get them! Each monthly shipment of 4 books will be yours to examine for 10 days. Then, if you decide to keep the books, you'll pay the preferred subscriber's price of just $3.30 per title. That's $13.20 for all 4 books...a savings of over $3 off the publisher's price! What's more, $13.20 is your <u>total</u> price...there's no additional charge for shipping and handling.

No Minimum Purchase, and a Generous Return Privilege.

We're so sure that you'll appreciate the money-saving convenience of home delivery that we <u>guarantee</u> your complete satisfaction. You may return any shipment...for any reason...within 10 days and pay nothing that month. And if you want us to stop sending books, just say the word. There is no minimum number of books you must buy.

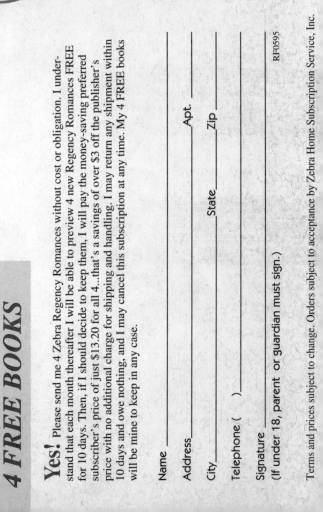

A $16.47
value.
FREE!
No obligation
to buy
anything, ever.

ZEBRA HOME SUBSCRIPTION SERVICE, INC.

120 BRIGHTON ROAD

P.O. BOX 5214

CLIFTON, NEW JERSEY 07015-5214

"I doubt if Aunt Carolyn could be budged right now. There is nothing my aunt enjoys more than a friendly wager."

His smile was the most genuine she had ever seen on his face. "I can assure you, my lady, that I understand that well."

Chapter Nine

Eveline liked Mr. Swinton's book-room with its rows of bookshelves and comfortable chairs. Not, she had to own, for the reason Vanessa would have enjoyed it, for Eveline did not share her friend's delight in reading. She had chosen this room because it was deserted. Mr. Swinton's guests were engrossed in card games or had already retired. When she had left, Vanessa had been caught up in conversation with their host, and Eveline had wanted to avoid interfering.

No one else but Vanessa and Lady Mansfield had spoken to her. She was accustomed to that, although she had seen Vanessa's despair at the cool treatment. Later, she vowed, she would take her bosom-bow aside and ask her not to worry. Censure no longer bothered her. Not since she had met Lord Greybrooke. His genuine acceptance of her, in spite of her family's shame, convinced her that Vanessa was not the only kind member of the *ton*.

Eveline smiled as she looked at the sheet of paper on her lap desk. Just writing Lord Greybrooke's name made her feel as if she was going to heaven in a string. Running her fingers over his name, she read what she had written before her thoughts had wandered to Vanessa.

Dear Lord Greybrooke,

You may have heard that Papa has closed our London house. I write this from the country, but not from my family's home. I am tonight, as I shall be until the Season's close, a guest of Lady Vanessa Wolfe. She has urged me to run tame through her home and to welcome you to call on Wednesday afternoons when I shall be at home.

Pray do not think me presumptuous to write you. I remember your invitation to let you know when we might talk. I hope that opportunity shall come shortly after we return to Town. I look forward to that moment.

Eveline frowned. How should she sign the letter? She must not be too bold, nor must she be cool. She smiled. Perhaps she was being overly cautious. With her family's reputation, the earl might expect her to be a bit brazen. Yet her fingers balked when she tried to sign the note "Yours." Maybe if she wrote—

Her hand froze as she heard voices. Concealed as she was by the shelves of books, the others—she guessed there might be two or three by the sound of their footfalls—would not see her. She stood and was about to announce herself when she heard her name mentioned bitterly.

"Lady Vanessa should know better!" Mr. Swinton grumbled. "Not only does she besmirch her own name, but she threatens to damage my household's reputation with Miss Clarke's presence here."

"Calm yourself." Eveline's eyes widened at Captain Hudson's voice. She was surprised he had torn himself from Lady Mansfield's side for even a moment. "Lady Vanessa has a kind heart and a strong will. She shall not have her opinions formed for her by the rest of the Polite World."

"Well, I can tell you Miss Clarke shall find no welcome under our roof again."

" 'Our roof'?" Captain Hudson laughed. "You presume much. Or have you already asked Lady Vanessa to marry up with you?"

"Not yet." Eveline could almost see the sly smile on Mr. Swinton's pasty face. "She thinks I wish no more than friendship from her, but any man would be a muff not to be drawn to her loveliness."

"And wealth?"

"It is a consideration."

Eveline heard a layer of anger beneath Captain Hudson's voice. "I had guessed you to be a man of more sense."

"Sense?"

"To see that the lady is a fair prize even without the blunt."

Mr. Swinton did not answer immediately, but his voice was steady when he said, "Here is the book you wanted, Hudson, although I find it peculiar that you are interested in reading maudlin poetry."

"Carolyn enjoys it. I thought we might share some tomorrow in a quiet moment." His hand struck the cover of the book. "I bid you good night, Swinton, and wish you good luck on the morrow with your pursuit."

"Of the fox?"

Again Captain Hudson laughed. "With the pursuit of whatever you wish to capture. If you hunt other than the fox, you shall need every bit of good luck you can gather. Your chase may be a long, fruitless one as others have discovered."

As their laughter receded, Eveline released the breath searing her throat. She put the letter into her lap desk and edged out from around the bookcases.

She hurried up the stairs and knocked on the door of

Vanessa's bedchamber. When Leale opened it, Eveline said, "I must speak with Vanessa."

"My lady has retired."

"Leale, please!"

The abigail hesitated, then stepped back. Eveline rushed in as Vanessa rose from a chair. Seeing her friend hold a sheet of paper, Eveline wondered if Vanessa had been writing a letter, too.

"Eveline, whatever is amiss?" Vanessa asked, staring at the pallor of her friend's face.

"Forgive me for querying you about what may be none of my bread and butter, but do you have a true *tendre* for Mr. Swinton?"

Vanessa put Corey's letter in the pocket of her dressing gown. Curiosity pierced her. If Mr. Swinton had spoken of his prejudices to Eveline ... She took the lap desk her friend was carrying. Setting it on a rosewood bookcase, she clasped Eveline's hands in hers.

"My dear Eveline," she said as she drew her friend, who was trembling, to sit, "you have yourself in quite a state over something that is of the least significance."

Eveline's green eyes were flooded with tears. "Do you have a cupboard love for him? I saw how earnestly he spoke to you tonight."

Vanessa sank to a chair. Noting Leale in the shadows, she guarded her words. Eveline must never guess how Vanessa had struggled to be pleasant to their host after his crude words this afternoon. Only the fact that the other men seemed to accept Mr. Swinton's claim on her attentions had kept her from sending him from her side at the evening's beginning. She did not want to have to deflate their interest in her as well. "Do not confuse friendship for more."

"But he said—"

"He spoke to you of this?" Vanessa gasped, shocked that Mr. Swinton would speak of a personal matter to

Eveline, when he had professed such a strong dislike for the Clarkes. Her composure splintered as she wondered if *she* was the only one truly strung on by her tactic of pretending to accept Mr. Swinton's attentions.

"No, but I overheard him speaking to Captain Hudson."

"And he told the captain he wished to have more than friendship with me?"

Eveline lowered her eyes. "Not in so many words. He said—oh, thunder! I wish I could recall his exact words."

"No need." Vanessa rose and hugged her friend. "Mr. Swinton and I have spoken only this afternoon. You must have misunderstood our host."

"But, Vanessa, I am sure I heard him say he wishes to take you as his wife."

"Eavesdropping is a deplorable habit," she answered, then winced. She had said the same to Lord Brickendon by the duck pond. "I am sure you misheard Mr. Swinton."

"Perhaps," Eveline said reluctantly. She stood and gripped Vanessa's hands. "Forgive me for disturbing you. Good night."

"There is nothing you need to be forgiven for." She hugged Eveline again. "Will you change your mind and join us for the hunt in the morning?"

Eveline picked up her lap desk and smiled. "I think not. I have a letter I must finish."

"Then I shall see you at nuncheon." Vanessa smiled wryly as her friend left.

Leale came forward. "My lady, perhaps you should give Miss Clarke's words more credence."

"Why?"

"There is talk belowstairs of what the house will be like when you are overseeing it. They are very eager to speak to me, because I know you well."

Vanessa opened her mouth, then closed it. If the servants were speaking openly of Mr. Swinton's plans to marry her, they must see them as a *fait accompli*. Bother! Mr. Swinton had been honest with her . . . hadn't he? Bother again! She could not be sure of anything any longer.

A yawn flowed into her mouth. Freeing it, she slid her dressing gown off, then took Corey's letter from the pocket. Putting the note in her bodice, she vowed to confront Mr. Swinton during the hunt and demand him to be honest with her. Then the matter of these rumors, which were as discomforting for her friends as for her, would be put to rest. She had too much to concern herself with to be embroiled in such silly intrigues.

"On the morrow, you shall see how mistaken Eveline was."

Leale said nothing, but her frown proclaimed she did not share Vanessa's expectations.

Clouds hung low over the stone house as Vanessa emerged into the eager crowd waiting for the hunt to begin. The wind brushed her face, offering an invitation to ride at *ventre-à-terre* across the meadow, which was still drenched with morning dew. Holding the skirt of her new crimson riding habit over her arm, Vanessa saw the other women glancing enviously at the bobbish scarlet plume in her cocked hat. With a smile, she recalled Madam deBerg's delight when she first had shown the feather to Vanessa and suggested it would complement her new habit.

Hearing her name, she smiled as she went to where her aunt was waiting by a gray russet mount. Vanessa was not astonished to see Captain Hudson next to Aunt Carolyn.

"Good morning," he said with a tip of his beaver.

Without his uniform, he was not as imposing, but he still was an undeniably handsome man.

Aunt Carolyn smiled as she left his side to take Vanessa's hands. "My dear, you look lovely. I swear your color is nearly as rich as the shade of your habit. How long has it been since we have ridden together to the hunt?"

"Since the week before Corey's seventeenth birthday," she answered, then wished she had remained silent when she saw sorrow in her aunt's expressive eyes. She had not intended to ruin Aunt Carolyn's day. Forcing a smile, she added, "I agree that another ride together is long overdue, and we shall rectify that today."

"Are you enjoying your visit to Swinton Park?" the captain asked as he took the reins of the brown horse a stable boy brought to him.

"It is always pleasant to feel a cushion of dirt beneath one's boots," Vanessa replied.

"But not inside the house." Aunt Carolyn's nose wrinkled with distaste. "This house needs the light touch of a feminine hand. Think of the fun it would be to put it in apple-pie order, Vanessa."

"You know you have more skills in that direction than I do."

"You need not be shy with me. Mr. Swinton follows you like a shadow. He is undoubtedly taken with you."

"I think we shall be friends for a long time," Vanessa answered carefully. She did not want to disabuse Aunt Carolyn of her misapprehensions now.

When Captain Hudson offered to throw Aunt Carolyn up in the saddle, Vanessa excused herself to find her mount. She grimaced as the hem of her habit dropped to the ground. The accursed thing was the proper length for riding, but not for walking halfway to the stables to find a lazy stable boy.

A shout pierced the morning. She whirled to see a

horse rearing, its ironclad hoofs inches from her head. A woman screamed. Something struck Vanessa. She crashed to the soft ground, a weight over her knocking the breath out of her. She cringed as hoofs hit the earth, spraying her with dirt.

The frightened shouts surrounded her when she heard, much closer to her ear, "Are you hurt, my lady?"

She opened her eyes to see Lord Brickendon's face only a shadow's breadth away. His kohl-colored eyes were filled with fear, and gray tinged his healthy coloring. Feeling her cheeks burning as she realized how intimately they lay amid Mr. Swinton's fearful guests, she whispered, "I am unharmed."

Standing, he easily drew her to her feet. He was about to release her hand when she wobbled. His arm encircled her waist, and she rested her head against his chest. Contentment, unlike any she had ever known, sent warmth through her useless limbs.

"I fear you were being overly optimistic," Lord Brickendon murmured, and she was fascinated by the resonance of his words beneath her ear. To someone else, he added, "She can barely stand."

Vanessa grudgingly raised her head when she heard Aunt Carolyn's sob. She edged away. As Lord Brickendon drew his arm from her waist, he kept his hands out to catch her if she collapsed.

"I am fine," Vanessa asserted with more strength. Putting her arms around her quivering aunt, she realized her words were true. "Hush, Aunt Carolyn. Lord Brickendon saved me."

Looking past her aunt, she again saw the unfamiliar, somber expression on the viscount's face. Even as she watched, his smile returned. She whispered her thanks, but he dismissed her words with a wave of his hand.

"Nothing any dashing knight would not have hesitated to do." He bent to collect the dirty hem of her skirt and hand it to her.

Mr. Swinton pushed past his guests. "Oh, my lady, that fat-pated stable boy will be turned off before day's end."

"It was an accident." Hearing the echo of her words to Sir Wilbur, she pasted a smile on her lips. "The hounds must be eager to be on their way. Shall we take to the chase?"

Aunt Carolyn murmured, "Vanessa, I think it would be wise if you returned to your chamber and rested until your head is settled upon your shoulders."

"I am unhurt," she repeated, offering her aunt a smile. "Let's ride after the fox."

Mr. Swinton said, "Lady Mansfield, fear not. I shall not allow your niece out of my sight during the hunt."

"Kind of you," Captain Hudson replied, a hint of sarcasm in his voice.

Vanessa was sure she heard a muffled laugh behind her, but Lord Brickendon was busy talking with a stable boy, who held the reins of a black horse. She frowned. Someone had laughed, but who?

A lad came forward, leading a chestnut horse. Vanessa smiled. "Mr. Swinton, this is an excellent mount."

"I had thought you would appreciate him, my lady." Mr. Swinton stepped between her and Lord Brickendon. "If you are certain you feel strong enough to ride—"

"I do."

"—allow me to assist you into the saddle."

Vanessa accepted his help. Settling herself comfortably in the saddle, she waited for the others to mount. Bafflement threaded her forehead when she realized Lord Brickendon had not mounted his horse.

"You aren't joining us, my lord?" she asked. Dismay struck her. "Are *you* hurt?"

He put his hand over hers. The motion—which

should have been friendly—consumed her in succulent warmth. "Your consideration is as entrancing as you are, my lady. The truth is that just before that horse went wild, I learned Maestro had picked up a stone. I must remain to be sure it is tended to properly." His gaze led hers to where his fingertip grazed her longest finger, then touched the next as lightly. "Perhaps we can ride together another time."

"In Town?" she asked before her good sense could silence her words.

"Perhaps." The yapping of the hounds halted his next words. He stepped back and nodded to her.

Vanessa urged her horse forward, reminding herself that she could not ask Lord Brickendon for his help to find Corey until she was sure he *could* help her. She had no chance to look back, because Mr. Swinton was riding toward her. He clearly intended to keep the pledge he had made to her aunt. She vowed not to slow him, so he could follow close on the heels of his prized hounds.

With a shrill call of the master of the hunt's horn, the dogs raced from the hole in the hedgerow to chase down the fleeing fox. Vanessa slapped the reins and let the horse have its head. She glanced back to see Mr. Swinton's surprise, but he sent his horse at top speed after hers.

The bumpy ride revealed aches Vanessa had not noticed before, but she gamely continued. Her discomfort must have been visible because Mr. Swinton signaled to her to slow her horse. With regret, she watched the other riders race past.

"Perhaps we might be wise to take this hunt at an egg-trot," Mr. Swinton said when he maneuvered his horse closer.

"I cannot tolerate riding at a snail's gallop. I would as lief follow the hunt."

"If you will not pause for your own good, then pause while I express words that demand to be spoken."

"Mr. Swinton," she said, torn between exasperation at being left behind and gratitude for his concern, "nothing needs to be said between us. The horse's actions were not your doing."

"There is much to be said."

"If this is about Eveline—"

"No!"

His vehemence astounded her. "Mr. Swinton, we must ride if we wish to catch up with the others."

His hand on hers halted her from slapping the reins on the horse's neck. She jerked her hands back when she saw the glitter in his eyes. Once again Sir Wilbur Franklin sprang to mind along with Eveline's cautions the night before.

"My lady . . . Vanessa, if I may be bold—"

"I wish you would not."

He blinked at her stiff words. "It is such a small indulgence for someone who would give you his heart in return."

"Mr. Swinton, you said—"

"Bruce," he interrupted with a smile.

Vanessa could not return it. If she had had any idea she would have to suffer this discomfort, she would have remained at the house. She heard the excited baying of the dogs and looked past him.

"We must hurry," she said. "I do not want to miss the fox's capture."

"I have just the jolly. If I can prove to you that—"

"You need prove nothing to me, sir."

"On the contrary," he said with another grin showing his good humour, "I wish to prove to you that I am worthy of your heartfelt affection. How better than to bring you, like a cavalier of old, a token of my admiration!"

She laughed. Perhaps she could defuse his ardor with

mirth. She must put an end to this before she was smothered by his solicitousness. "You wish to bring me the carcass of the fox to show the affection of friends? You have a peculiar sense of what a lady finds a proper gift."

"I realize the beast is nothing but the lowest vermin, my lady. Nor is it mere friendship I—"

Again Vanessa interrupted him. "Mr. Swinton, 'tis not the creature I find offensive, but the idea you think I cannot play a part in running the fox to earth myself."

"My lady, I never meant to suggest such a thing."

"Then leave off!" She touched her horse's flank with her whip.

The mount leapt forward. Vanessa turned the horse to take a shortcut through the field to reach the other riders. Hearing hoofbeats, she knew Mr. Swinton was riding after her. Abruptly she had sympathy for the fox.

When a horse cut in front of hers, Vanessa choked back a scream. She reined in. Her horse pranced on its hind feet, frightened. She steadied him and aimed a scowl at Mr. Swinton as he drew his horse next to hers again.

"Are you bereft of the sense God gave a goose?" she snapped.

"I want for wits whenever you are near, Vanessa."

"Mr. Swinton, I asked you not to—"

He gripped her elbows and tugged her toward him. In disbelief and horror, she realized he intended to kiss her. Her small whip struck him soundly on the shoulders. He pulled back in shock.

"Leave off!" Vanessa said icily. "If this is your conception of friendship, it does not gibe with mine."

"We can be friends even after we are wed."

"You are wrong. We cannot remain friends, and we never shall be wed."

He sneered, "You wish to be a thornback forever waiting on a shelf."

"What I wish is not your concern."

"You need to marry. Your father's fortune—"

"Belongs to my brother."

"Your *dead* brother has no claim on it." He edged his horse nearer again. "Vanessa, my dear, such talk will lead people to believe you are unsettled in your head. Can't you see that you need someone to guard you from your own impulsive behavior? Someone who will watch over you so you bring no dishonor to your family's legacy with your jobbernowl ideas?"

"Like believing my brother is alive?"

"Exactly!" He grinned triumphantly.

"And being loyal to my bosom-bow?"

His lip curled into a caricature of a smile. "You know I do not approve of your unfortunate friendship with Miss Clarke."

"You are right. I do need to guard myself against my impulsive behavior." She swallowed her fury as his grin widened. "I should be flogged for ever believing one of your bigoted bashers."

"Vanessa—"

She gave him no chance to finish. Turning her steed toward the house, she laid the small whip to its flank. It raced at top speed across the meadow.

At a shout, she turned to see Mr. Swinton riding neck-or-nothing after her. All thoughts of the scoundrel vanished when she saw a brambled hedgerow in front of her. There was no time to turn.

She held her breath as the horse gathered its feet beneath it. They rose from the earth. Flying, the wind screeching in her ears and scoring her face, she gripped the reins. The beast's muscles contracted in the moment before they struck the ground on the far side of the briars. The jolt sent new agony along her bruised body.

Behind her, Mr. Swinton shouted to his horse to follow. The horse balked. He screeched as he flew over its head to land squarely in the middle of the briars.

"Mr. Swinton!" Her fears for his life vanished when he pushed his way out of the copse and glared at her as he plucked a pricker from the back of his riding breeches.

"Are you mad?" he demanded. He shook his head, and small sticks fell from his hair. "No wonder your aunt is so eager to get you wed before anyone discovers you are all about in your head."

"Haven't you said that I suffer from impulsive behaviors?" she fired back. Any sympathy she might have had for this pig-sconce was smothered beneath contempt. "Perhaps you should think again. You were the one who put your horse to a hedge it could not take."

"Forget the damned horse!" He rubbed his hip. "You are more worried about the beast than about me."

"You worry enough about yourself, Mr. Swinton." She tilted her hat back. "You clearly wish to think only of yourself, so let me inform you that you needn't worry about me any longer. I thank you for your hospitality, but, as soon as I collect my aunt and my friend, we shall infringe on you no more."

His scowl disappeared. Limping toward her, he said, "Vanessa—my lady—you must stay and allow me to apologize for—"

"Mr. Swinton, I have no time to listen to all the apologies you owe me and my friends."

When she raised her whip, he cried, "You aren't going to leave me here, are you?"

She smiled icily. "You are only a short distance from your house, Mr. Swinton. I trust even a singleton like you can find your way back."

"I'm hurt." He pulled another briar from his buckskins.

"By my words, Mr. Swinton?" She widened her eyes and raised her chin. "You should recall your own words that words can't harm you. Only stones and sticks." Touching her whip to her horse's flank, she added, "I bid you *adieu.*"

Chapter Ten

No letters waited for Vanessa among the stack of invitations when she returned to Grosvenor Square. Tears threatened to betray her silly hopes that she would arrive home to find the answer to seeking Corey, but she refused to let Aunt Carolyn see them. She did not wish to suffer another chastisement. Vanessa had endured enough of a scold during the carriage ride back to Town.

Eveline had not gloated over being correct about Mr. Swinton's intentions. Like Vanessa, she had sat in silence while Aunt Carolyn reprimanded her niece for her quick words that had cost her another suitor. Only when they were behind the closed doors of Vanessa's bedchamber with Leale down in the kitchen catching up on the gossip with the other servants did Eveline reveal her true feelings.

"Vanessa," she said, sitting in a chair by the window with a glorious view of the Square, "I do not fault you for putting the high and mighty Mr. Swinton aside. I think you were wise to see him as the cur he truly is."

"Don't you mean finally?"

"As long as you saw the truth before you buckled your heart to him, it matters little. And," she said, her green eyes twinkling merrily as she held a piece of paper over her heart, "I am glad to be back in Town."

"I'm not," she said as she put Corey's letter in the small box in the lowest drawer. She straightened and laughed. "I suspect, by this time, Aunt Carolyn has already set her sights on another man who will be 'perfect' for me and Wolfe Abbey." Going to the window, she looked out at the carriages driving around the Square. "I wonder which addle cove I shall have to deal with next."

Eveline grabbed her hand. "Forget that."

"I would love to, but Aunt Carolyn shall not."

"Vanessa, you are going to down-pin me, too, if you keep on. Listen to this. Even before I had a chance to let Lord Greybrooke know I was your guest, he has sent me a note. He would like to invite all of us to accompany him to the theater tomorrow evening. Do say you will come, Vanessa."

"How could I say no?" she asked, although she had looked forward to several quiet evenings of writing letters. She felt no more than a twinge of remorse at disobeying her aunt and continuing her search for Corey. Aunt Carolyn would forgive her when Corey was home. And she owed Eveline this favor, for her friend was unswervingly loyal, even when Vanessa was in the depths of her melancholy. After all, it was senseless for both of them to be miserable. "Of course, you must ask Aunt Carolyn. She may have planned something else."

"I have already asked her." She laughed at Vanessa's amazement. "It seems Captain Hudson already had proposed a similar outing to her. I wonder how long it will be before he proposes something else. Not long, I wager."

"Nor do I," Vanessa said as she sat on the edge of her bed. "Aunt Carolyn has been so anxious to have a betrothal party here. Wouldn't it be amusing if it was her own?"

"Better than if it was yours?"

She laughed. "Unless I find someone who is more interested in me than my father's fortune, I think I shall dance at Aunt Carolyn's betrothal party before my own."

Lord Greybrooke was nothing as Vanessa had feared. His smile was not dimmed by signs of dissipation, warning that his reputation was so sullied that his attentions were unwelcome by any decent woman. Nor was he bracket-faced or as round as a pig. His tongue was not sharp with acrimony. In every facet, he appeared to be a charming gentleman, who was willing to overlook Eveline's family's shame. His black hair was thinning, but his face was unlined. Dressed elegantly in a navy coat over his white waistcoat and black breeches, he offered Eveline a well-spoken compliment as he greeted her in the foyer.

As he should, Vanessa decided, for her friend was the epitome of grace and beauty in the incredibly lovely dress Madame deBerg had finished only a few hours before. Gold lamé flashed along the hem as she turned to introduce the earl to Aunt Carolyn. Ribbons of the same brilliant shade were woven through the long sleeves of white crêpe and along the curved neckline of the high bodice. A hint of her ribbed stockings was revealed as she stepped back to let Lord Greybrooke bow over Lady Mansfield's hand.

"And my dearest bosom-bow," Eveline said as she gestured for Vanessa to join them. "Lord Greybrooke, this is Lady Vanessa Wolfe."

"This is a long overdue pleasure," Vanessa remarked, noting how the earl held her hand only for the briefest moment. He clearly could not wait to return his gaze to Eveline. For the first time, Vanessa considered how wonderful it would be to have someone that devoted to her. She shoved that thought out of her head. She had someone to devote herself to now. Until her brother was safely home, she must think only of him.

Aunt Carolyn left Eveline to talk to the earl while she came to fuss at her niece. She straightened Vanessa's white lace gown. It was pulled back to expose her rose satin slip. Pleats dropped from the high waist to the base of the skirt, which was ringed with silk flowers matching the ones on her full-brimmed bonnet. It was her very best dress, and Aunt Carolyn had insisted that Vanessa wear it this evening, although Vanessa had no idea why.

"What do you think of the earl?" Aunt Carolyn asked softly.

"He seems a fine gentleman."

"I agree." She sighed, and Vanessa needed no key to unlock her aunt's thoughts. Aunt Carolyn could not understand how her niece, who possessed both wealth and an immaculate reputation, could not find such a suitable match when Eveline had with ease.

When Captain Hudson was ushered into the foyer by a stone-faced Quigley, Aunt Carolyn brightened. Again the captain wore his military uniform, and, as they walked to the open carriage parked in front of the house, he told them he had spent the day with his superiors at the ministry.

Vanessa said nothing as the others chatted amiably. So fervently she wished she could ask Captain Hudson to help her in her search, but he would mention her request to her aunt. She must find another way.

The street in front of the Theater Royal on Bow Street was jammed with carriages and urchins, who were eager to run errands or do a trick for a farthing or two. Vanessa thanked Lord Greybrooke as he assisted her from the carriage. She stood aside to let him offer his arm to Eveline. A sad smile pulled at Vanessa's lips as she walked behind the two couples up the few steps to the portico beneath the tall columns. The unfamiliar stab of envy pricked her again. Trying to ignore it was futile. She would have delighted in having a gentleman regard her with the adoration enjoyed by her aunt and Eveline, but she had not met the right man yet. Maybe Leale was right. Maybe the man of her dreams could never exist.

The foyer of the theater was as crowded as the street, and heavy clouds of perfume threatened to strangle Vanessa. She glanced toward the elegant staircase to one side, but it was overrun with people. There was no choice but to struggle every inch to the box Lord Greybrooke had engaged halfway up the five tiers above the floor of the theater.

An elbow jabbed her arm. Vanessa glared at it, then raised her eyes to the face above. Lord Brickendon! She snapped her fan open to conceal her astonishment . . . and her admiration of how his black coat accented his lean strength.

"My lady, excuse me," he said with a polite smile. "I fear we are fated continually to come flush on each other. I trust you have recovered from your taxing ordeal at Swinton Park."

Vanessa had no intention of speaking of her bruises, which were in locations she could not discuss in public. "I am fine. And you?"

He bent toward her and said in a conspiratorial whisper, "I landed on something softer than the earth."

She pressed her fan to her lips to silence her gasp at his forward words. She should be scandalized. She should ask him to leave and not to embarrass her again. She should have, but she began to smile. Lord Brickendon was never dull like the other men she had met; it was seldom she guessed what he might say or do. He was a scoundrel, but an intriguing one.

"It is a surprise," she said, "to see you back in Town so soon. Is the gathering over already?"

"I found Swinton's company distasteful." His grin became roguish. "Nearly as distasteful as that bully fop's constant gripping about landing in that hedgerow. He was still pulling sticks out of his hair when he returned to the house."

She laughed, although she knew she would not. Lord Brickendon's words resurrected the image of the outraged redhead firing furious words at her. Her amusement faded when the memory of his attempt to kiss her leapt to life. Softly, she said, "Mr. Swinton might have been better off if the switch had been applied years ago instead of during that ride."

"I can't help but be distressed at your cavalier disregard of my friends' hearts. I believe both Franklin and Swinton held a deep and sincere *tendre* for you."

"I fear you stretch the truth, my lord."

"Mayhap." He chuckled, his dark eyes twinkling with merry mischief. "I have to own that Swinton's only anxiety was if he would be able to win your fortune, but Sir Wilbur was unquestionably smitten by your feminine charms."

Vanessa was glad the brim of her bonnet could shadow her face from the viscount's intense gaze. Looking at a bone button at the top of his waistcoat, she said, "I regret causing the baronet any distress. However, even you must own, that to let him assume I had a fondness for him that did not, in truth, exist, would be more cruel than confronting him with the truth."

"Can it be that you have a gentle heart within you?"

"What a bizarre question!" she exclaimed, meeting his eyes. She wished she had not when she saw more amusement amid their ebony sparks. Taking a deep breath to steady her voice, which was too agitated, she said, "I can assure you, my lord, that I have a heart within my breast. That I choose not to give it to any of the men who have tried to win it does nothing to deny its existence."

He tilted his head to her. "I stand corrected. I should have guessed as much when I saw your resolve that each small duckling was given a bit of bread. Swinton would have been wise to chirp piteously to gain your attention."

Vanessa laughed with him. When she noticed the eager eyes watching them, she silenced herself. Enough tongues had wagged at her expense in the past fortnight. She did not need to give them more to chew about.

"Such a happy sound!" Aunt Carolyn offered her hand to Lord Brickendon and smiled as he bowed over it smoothly. "I am delighted that you have brought even a smile to Vanessa, my lord. She has been morose since our return from Swinton Park."

"She need worry herself no more," he answered, "for I can assure both of you that Mr. Swinton has made the most of his invisible injuries to obtain sympathy wherever he goes. I am sure that will ease your worries on his account, my lady."

He caught Vanessa's eyes before she could turn away. The good humor had vanished into their dark depths, and she could not guess what strong emotion glittered in them. She was relieved when Aunt Carolyn introduced the viscount to Lord Greybrooke. The formalities allowed her time to patch together her ragged poise. Lord Brickendon greeted Eveline as politely as he did the others, and Vanessa found herself relaxing. She had not realized until now that it was so important for her bosom-bow to be accepted by the viscount after Mr. Swinton's cruel comments.

"Do join us, my lord. Lord Greybrooke has taken a box, which will have room for another. We would enjoy your company." Carolyn turned to Vanessa. "Isn't that right, my dear?"

"Of course, we would be delighted to have you join us," Vanessa said automatically. Amazement spread through her as she discovered she spoke the truth. Unlike his friends, whom she had been eager to dismiss as swiftly as possible, Vanessa relished conversing with Lord Brickendon. Each time she encountered him was like a duel between respected, well-armed opponents. Using words to parry, a sharp barb here, a honed rejoinder there, gave her more enjoyment than anything had since her brother's departure and her father's death.

"How could I say no to such a generous invitation?" He offered his arm to Aunt Carolyn. "If I may be so bold . . ."

Vanessa found herself walking with Captain Hudson as they followed her aunt and the viscount up the stairs. Behind them, Lord Greybrooke and Eveline chattered like two Indian monkeys. Aware once more of the curious eyes upon them, Vanessa smiled. Aunt Carolyn should be careful, or *she* would become the source of rumor for the gossipmongers, for she had come to the theater with one gentleman and was allowing a second to escort her to their box.

"Your aunt is a wonderful woman," said Captain Hudson in a low voice.

"She would do anything to see those she loves happy."

"A grand tribute, which I had not expected from you."

Vanessa nearly paused on the steps, but the press of the crowd urged her forward. Looking at the blond man's taut face, she asked, "Would you explain that comment, sir?"

"Gladly, for I have no wish to see Carolyn miserable. She thinks only of your future." He cleared his throat, then said, "She will give no consideration to her future until you are settled."

"I know."

"Yet you play a coquette's game."

She shook her head, her voice as strained as his. "No, Captain, for *that* would break Aunt Carolyn's heart. If you would give more than a moment's thought to the situation, you would see that my aunt has no wish for me to wed unwisely."

Captain Hudson said nothing more as he held aside the curtain to allow her to enter the elegant box. The stiff line of his back signaled his vexation. Aunt Carolyn said she would return after speaking with Penelope Downing, who had taken a box only a short distance away. Vanessa took her seat behind Eveline and looked across the horseshoe shape of the theater. It was nearly full and more were crowding onto the floor and into the boxes.

Even before the curtain in the doorway had dropped back into place, Captain Hudson broke his silence to say, "If you will excuse me, ladies, gentlemen."

"Quite the transparent chap, isn't he?" Lord Brickendon leaned back in his chair opposite Vanessa's and chuckled. "He would be wise to give your aunt a bit of breathing room instead of chasing after her with such candid fervor. Your aunt does not seem the type of woman to dote on the chase."

Vanessa waved her fan. It was even more stuffy than the last time she and Aunt Carolyn had come to the crammed theater. "You fancy yourself an expert on women, my lord?"

"Hardly." He laughed again. "The man who thinks he knows everything about women is the greatest Tomdoodle of us all."

"So what have you learned?"

"Little, but I own that I have given it only a scant

portion of my time. I prefer sport where I know I can be the victor. The flirtations of the *ton* are set so a man loses his freedom and ends up with a wife and a family."

Vanessa doubted if Eveline and the earl, who were holding hands, had heard Lord Brickendon's cynical words. Even if they had taken note of them, they would have given them little credence as they laughed together, pausing only when the box attendant brought cooled wine.

"I agree." When she saw his surprise, she asked, "Why are you startled?"

"I have never heard such talk from anyone among the *élite.*" He bent toward her, his hand resting on the back of her chair. "Such sacrilege! The patronesses at Almack's shall oust you if they hear such words."

"I doubt if I could change *their* minds on this matter."

"Do you?"

Vanessa did not answer as she looked into his eyes which held such mysteries, yet portrayed his potent passions on every turn. In her lap, her fingers tingled, longing to touch the line of his jaw to discover if it was as unyielding as it appeared. The twists of black hair on his brow teased her to brush them back into place. She knew nothing of Lord Brickendon, but she began to believe that she wanted to learn, no matter how long such a study would take.

His hand grazed her shoulder, daringly stroking her bare skin. When his finger traced the line of her bonnet's ribbons from the curve of her chin to the sensitive silkiness behind her right ear, her lips parted with a soft sigh of indescribable delight.

In a husky whisper, he said, "You could make a man change his mind about many things." His hand slipped behind her nape to tilt her toward him.

Her eyes searched his face. The stern lines had not

softened, but the corners of his mouth tilted in a smile as his gaze caressed her face. With her heart pounding so fiercely she was sure he must hear it, her fingers rose to his wide shoulders.

Vanessa was jerked back to her senses by Eveline's laughter with her beau. Sitting straighter, she folded her hands in her lap. She avoided looking at Lord Bricken-don because she did not want him to see her reddened face. One moment, she had been espousing her determi-nation to keep her life from romantic entanglements. The next, she was letting him seduce her with sweet words and sweeter caresses.

She gasped when he put his finger under her chin and turned her face toward him. "My lord, please do not—"

"Say no more," he said with more equanimity than she possessed. "Shall we speak of other matters?"

"Yes," she breathed. She clutched onto the word as a safety line to pull her back from her own foolishness.

"Then choose a subject."

Her mind was a-jumble with the torrent of dulcet sen-sations left by his touch. Closing her eyes, she focused on the one thing that was a constant in her life. Corey needed her as much as she needed to escape from the tempting fantasy of Lord Brickendon's lips on hers.

Her voice was unsteady as she asked, "What have you heard about the war?"

"The war?" His brows were a dark punctuation of his question.

"If you would as lief speak of something else—"

"I am surprised *you* wish to speak of this. No, I should not be surprised about anything with you, my lady." His smile sprinted across his face so quickly she wondered if she had seen it. "I have heard nothing new. The government moves slower than an icebound river," he said as he folded his arms over his pristine white waistcoat and glowered across the theater. "If Boney himself popped up in Whitehall, I vow it would take the ministers a week before they decided if they should greet him and another to determine how."

"It is frustrating."

He rested his elbow on the edge of the box and faced her. His gaze drilled her. "Spoken like someone who is familiar with the government. You intimated at Swinton Park that you have had dealings with it."

"I would . . . if someone would listen to my appeal for information. I—" She labored to smile as her aunt stepped into the box. "Aunt Carolyn, we had begun to think you were going to miss the beginning of the show."

Vanessa let her aunt's conversation wash over her, drowning her in the comfort of normalcy. Feeling the viscount's curious gaze, she resisted looking at him. She had come so close to revealing too much of herself to this man who concealed so much.

When the performance began, she tried to lose herself in the funny moments and the tragedies. She could not. Always, she was aware of Lord Brickendon sitting nearby. She found herself listening for his laugh to discover what he thought was amusing and leaning toward him to hear his comments about the actors and the plays.

The first act came to an end, and she realized she could remember little of what she had heard and seen on stage. Yet every word and every smile from Lord Brickendon remained as clear as if they had happened only a moment before.

If her silence was noticed during the *entr'acte,* the others were too polite to mention it. She was glad when the program resumed, because she could hide her disquiet by pretending to be enthralled with the performances.

When the show reached its finale to polite applause,

Lord Brickendon held out his hand to Vanessa. She hesitated. To let him touch her when she was so unsettled might be want-witted. Then as she heard her aunt call for her not to dawdle, she knew it would be even more foolish to make a scene.

Lord Brickendon smiled as his fingers closed over hers. Slowly he drew her to her feet. In the close confines of the box, she stood too near to him . . . and too far away. She needed only to take a half step forward, and she would be in his arms. Looking up into his dark eyes, she saw an invitation she must not accept.

"Aunt Carolyn will grow worried if I linger here," she whispered.

"Then we must not make that fine lady anxious." Setting her hand on his arm, he pushed aside the heavy curtain. "I do not think you need to fret yourself. Lady Mansfield is smiling," he said in a low rumble. "She apparently enjoyed the show more than you did."

Vanessa wished he was not so observant. His friends had been easy to bamboozle because they had seen no further than their plans to win her fortune. Lord Brickendon would not be pushed out of her life so facilely. "I had an agreeable evening."

"Such sincerity!"

"I have had worse ones!" she averred stoutly.

"I shall accept that as a compliment." He slipped his hand from under her arm. Bowing to her and her aunt, he thanked Aunt Carolyn for their company and bid them a good evening.

As Vanessa descended the stairs, her eyes followed Lord Brickendon's tall form to the door. He was gone by the time they reached the portico. An odd emptiness twisted inside her. Lord Brickendon had said nothing about calling. Not that she had asked him to give her a look-in.

Perhaps she had convinced him that she had been

honest when she said she was not interested in leg-shackling herself to any man. Yet, as she rode away in the open carriage through the night, which was as ebony and deep as his eyes, she found herself thinking of the next time she might meet him and his mesmerizing gaze.

Chapter Eleven

Vanessa held a candle to the sealing wax and watched three drops fall onto the folded letter. Her father's signet ring was heavy as she pressed it into the blue wax.

Leaning back, she turned the letter to see the address she had written in bold letters. HIS ROYAL HIGHNESS, THE PRINCE REGENT She was astounded by her temerity, but she no longer knew any other way to find Corey. Yesterday a letter had arrived from the Prime Minister's secretary. He had been sorry to inform Lady Vanessa Wolfe that Lord Liverpool could not involve himself in the search for her brother's remains. She had no choice but to be more reckless. Perhaps the Prince Regent, who was rumored to have a streak of romance and daring about him, would offer the sympathetic ear she had so far been denied.

Before she could change her mind, Vanessa hurried to the ground floor. She had not wanted to ring for Quigley to come to her room, because that might draw Aunt Carolyn's attention. She had no worries about Eveline noticing anything. Her friend was lost in her mooning for the earl. An announcement must be imminent.

Quigley came across the foyer to meet her. He gravely accepted the letter. As he looked at the address, his face remained serene, save for a tic near his left eye.

"Please have it delivered as soon as possible," she said as calmly as if she wrote to the Regent daily.

"I shall endeavor to do so."

Vanessa watched the butler walk away, the tails of his somber livery fluttering like raven wings. Despair weighed on her as she went to the stairs. She had hoped she would never reach this desperate point. After this, there was nothing more she could do in England. A quake of fear ached across her shoulders as she gripped the mahogany bannister. If she could not get help in her homeland, she would have to go to France, despite the dangers of the war.

The twist of the doorbell jangled through the foyer. Vanessa continued up the stairs. Most likely, it was Lord Greybrooke giving Eveline a look-in as he did every afternoon.

Her feet faltered as she heard Lord Brickendon greeting the butler. Turning, she looked at his smile, which pulled her back into the enchanting web of dazzling seduction he had spun at the theater. She had heard nothing from him in the week since that night.

Aunt Carolyn had been distraught at his failure to call, but, for the first time, Vanessa had not been happy that she had succeeded in sending a gentleman from her side. She had been ambivalent, a very strange sensation. She had been disappointed to hear nothing from the handsome viscount, but she had reminded herself that she had no time for the dalliances he was reputed to enjoy. She must think only of Corey. Staring down at him, she could not. Her head was filled with thoughts of his lips so deliciously close to hers.

As Lord Brickendon handed his beaver to Quigley and brushed dust from the sleeve of his brown riding coat, indecision soldered her feet to the riser. She thought of his fingers on her skin, offering an invitation, but letting her make the choice. That choice had been denied her by other men who thought only of overmastering her heart. She had known exactly what they wanted. With the viscount she had no idea, and that was unsettling.

Both men gazed expectantly up the stairs, but she was unable to move. The words battering her lips she would not speak, for they were sure to embarrass her. She could well imagine Lord Brickendon's amusement if she demanded that he explain his intentions. No doubt, he would tell her she had made hers clear, and he had, too. Perhaps he had, but she remained all at sea.

Quigley shifted uneasily, then said, in a stentorian voice, "My lady, Lord Brickendon is calling. May I say that you are in?"

Vanessa heard a low laugh and saw the viscount trying to hide his mirth. The silliness of their situation shattered the paralysis holding her to the stair. How empty her garret must be to act like this! She descended and held out her hand to the viscount. He bowed over it, and she was shocked anew by the ravage of disappointment when he did not bring it to his lips.

"I am about to enjoy a ride in the Park," he said as Quigley moved away. "I thought, if you have nothing else planned, my lady, you might accept my invitation to ride together."

"I would like that. Very much." When she heard how breathless her voice sounded, she said quickly, "I am sure Eveline would be pleased to join us."

"Yes, do ask Miss Clarke." For once, his mocking smile had disappeared, and a genuine one had taken its place.

Vanessa abruptly realized the viscount still had possession of her fingers. His other hand covered them, and her vacillation vanished. She wanted to go on this ride to learn more about Lord Brickendon, whose smile had filled her thoughts every day and whose touch decorated her dreams each night.

Maybe this ride would give her the answer to settle her unsettled heart.

Aunt Carolyn gave permission for the ride, cautioning them not to become separated in the press of carriages and riders. Although they were riding earlier than the fashionable hour of five, the Park would be filled with those seeking to enjoy the fresh air and the fresh poker-talk.

"Go and change into something suitable, Vanessa," urged Aunt Carolyn. "Lord Brickendon and I shall have a nice chat."

Vanessa hesitated, knowing exactly the course their conversation would take. Lord Brickendon smiled as Aunt Carolyn shooed her out. His eye closed in a lazy wink when Vanessa glanced back to discover her aunt motioning for him to help himself to a cup of the chatter-water she had waiting for her callers.

She had no time to worry about what her aunt might say to Lord Brickendon, because Eveline urged her to hurry and get into her riding habit while she did the same. Amazed, Vanessa asked, "How did you know about the invitation?"

"I saw Lord Brickendon arrive." Eveline's smile was as bright as her hair. "Why else would he call in his riding clothes?"

"They are also proper attire for calls."

"True, but I cannot imagine Lord Brickendon paying a normal call. Can you?"

Laughing, Vanessa went into her room. She rang for Leale, but began to unhook her gown herself. She must hurry. Leaving the viscount to Aunt Carolyn's match-making any longer than necessary was sure to cause trouble for her. Nor, she had to own with a soft smile, did she want to waste even a moment of the time they could have together at the Park.

Her abigail popped out of the dressing room, Vanessa's red habit in her hands. The older woman's face was grim.

"Leale! Is something wrong?"

"You know quite well."

"If I knew quite well, there would be no need to ask." She settled the voluminous habit around her and waited for Leale to hook it into place. When her abigail remained by the bed, Vanessa faced her. "Leale, please tell me."

Leale pointed a thin finger at the writing table. Atop it sat an open bottle of ink and writing paper next to the sealing wax. Vanessa berated herself. She had been a perfect block not to hide the incriminating items before she took the letter to Quigley.

"Lady Mansfield told you to stop trying to find your brother," Leale stated with every ounce of her outrage. "You have not heeded her."

"I know."

"If she discovers this, she will be heart-shattered."

Keeping her hands on the back of her habit, so it did not slip off, she asked carefully, "If?"

With a weary shake of her head, Leale said, "My lady, I have been with you since you were a chip, and I know you for the hoyden you once were. Yet never have I known you to disregard another's feelings." Going to the table, she picked up a sheet of paper and crushed it. "This *must* stop, or I shall have no choice but to apprise Lady Mansfield of your disobedience."

"There will be no more letters."

"Can I believe that?"

"I shall swear that on anything you deem holy."

"And I believe you. I know you shall come to accept the truth."

Tears flowed into Vanessa's eyes. She wanted to be honest with Leale. If the missive to the Prince Regent gained her nothing, there would be no need for any more letters. She shivered, and Leale hastily closed up the back of the habit. The thick material would not halt this cold, because it came from her frightened heart.

Hurrying down the stairs, Vanessa noted that Lord Brickendon looked no worse for his conversation with Aunt Carolyn. Greeting Eveline warmly, Lord Brickendon thanked Quigley when the butler handed him his hat. Warm air and sunlight washed into the house when the butler opened the door.

Vanessa shoved aside her doldrums when she saw her favorite mount, a spirited white gelding, waiting. Settling her small whip in her hand, she watched as the viscount tossed Eveline up into the saddle of her horse.

Seeing his horse next to her gelding, she said, "I trust Maestro took no injury from the stone."

"None, and he is anxious to be away to the Park." Lord Brickendon helped her up onto the mounting block. With their eyes even, she saw how his crinkled with mirth.

"As anxious as his master?"

He chuckled. "I am always amused by your aunt's hospitality, my lady."

Deciding it would be wiser not to vent her curiosity about what he meant, Vanessa nodded when he asked if she was ready to mount. His wide hands caught her at the waist, their warmth oozing through her riding habit to tingle along her skin. He did not release her when she sat in the saddle.

"All set?" he asked.

"Yes." Her head spun with the force of the longing whirling through her. The gentle strength of his hands at her waist, the firmness of his chest against her leg, the soft stroke of his breath across her face as she looked down at him swept her away into fantasies of him holding her even closer.

"Shall we go then?"

Vanessa blinked, torn by his question from her dreams and thrown back into the commonplace world. He flashed her a smile and turned to mount his horse with the ease of a man long accustomed to riding. Abashed by her thoughts, she rode after the others, hoping no one had noticed her silly reaction to nothing.

Vanessa had no need to worry, for the viscount and Eveline set too rapid a pace for talking. The scent of early summer greenery mixed with dust from the road as they went deeper into the Park. Their pace did not slow, not even to greet friends. If those friends were astonished to see the viscount in her and Eveline's company, they had the decency to hide it.

When Vanessa heard even more rapid hoofbeats, she frowned. What leather-head was taking the bridle path at such a speed? Her eyes widened as she recognized the dark-haired man who drew his horse to a stop in front of them.

Lord Greybrooke smiled as he tipped his hat to them. The buttons on his stylish, black coat shone in the sunlight. "Ross, my friend, you are a fortunate man to have the company of the two loveliest ladies in this fair land."

"And you have none," Lord Brickendon answered. "If I was even an inch of a gentleman, I would ask you to join us in our ride."

"But you would as lief be a top-rate profligate." His grin negated his demure hit. "I am so pleased to chance meeting you like this, Eveline." He gulped and said, "I mean Miss Clarke."

"You need not pretend on my behalf," Vanessa answered with a laugh. "Anyone, who sees eyes glowing as Eveline's do when they meet yours, can guess you enjoy more than a causal friendship."

The earl squeezed Vanessa's hand swiftly. "You truly are in good pax with my dear Eveline. I am so indebted to you for allowing her to stay with you so we might have these weeks to become better acquainted."

"Will you ride with us along the Row, Edward?" Lord Brickendon asked.

Lord Greybrooke turned to Eveline. "If I may."

She said, "Of course you may . . . Edward." She smiled shyly.

Vanessa waited for Eveline or the earl to urge their horses ahead, but they continued to look at each other as if they had just discovered the solution to a rare alchemistic riddle. When Lord Brickendon tapped her shoulder and motioned with his head for her to follow him, Vanessa paused only long enough to do the same to Eveline. She looked back to be positive the spell between the two had broken long enough for them to recall themselves.

Laughing, as she rode with the viscount from sunlight to shadow beneath the trees, Vanessa teased, "You can hide your romantic side no longer, my lord. There was no surprise on Lord Greybrooke's face when he *chanced* upon us. You two had planned this outing before you called, didn't you? No wonder you were in such a rush to reach the Park."

He grimaced. "Spare giving me a mouthful of moonshine. The truth is that I broke Greybrooke's nose during a raucous game when we were in short pants. I felt such remorse I vowed to do anything he wished in return. For years, he has let that pledge lie quiescent. Last night, at Brooke's, he had the audacity to recall it." With an emoted sigh, he put his hand over his heart and said, "There was nothing a dashing knight could do but honor his promise."

"You could have refrained from breaking his boltsprit in the first place."

"True, but then what excuse would I have had to bring those two together?"

"The truth?"

"Which is?"

"That you wish happiness for your friend?"

Shaking his head, he said, "If giving up his free ways is what he wants, who am I to tell Edward he is a ninnyhammer?"

"So you believe marriage is the province of ninnyhammers?"

"Don't you?"

Vanessa faltered on her quick retort, not wanting to tell him that she had given the matter little thought. That would necessitate revealing the truth that her search for her brother precluded any thoughts of her own future. Yet lying to him was abhorrent. From the beginning, Lord Brickendon had treated her with an honesty no other man had offered.

"Marriage is right for Eveline and Lord Greybrooke," she hedged.

"Let's hope their sentiments are not infectious."

His answer was so dolorous, Vanessa laughed as they continued along Rotten Row. With no worry of carriages, for only the king and his family could drive down this *Route du Roi,* she let her horse have its head. The gentle pace suited her and the lazy breath of the breeze teasing her hair. Beside her, Lord Brickendon was silent, but there was no discomfort in the lack of conversation.

When a childish shriek broke into their contented quiet, Vanessa's first thought was exasperation. Then she chuckled.

Lord Brickendon asked, "Will you share what amuses you, my lady?"

She almost told him that she would as lief not, but heard herself saying, "I was bothered by a child's cry intruding on our ride."

"Then I must strive to rectify that." He slapped his hand against the black's flank.

Perplexed, she put her horse to a trot to follow. He drew in his mount by a stone wall along the Serpentine. When he peered over it, he dismounted. He lifted her from the saddle, his broad hands spanning her waist with ease. The lightning pulse raced through her again, but she had scant time to savor it. Setting her on the ground, he smiled as he slowly withdrew his hands.

"A minute, my lady." He handed her the reins for both horses.

"Yes," she whispered as she had in the Square, glad she had to say no more. Even one more word might reveal the wondrous tumult within her.

With the ease of one of the lads she could see standing by the river, he jumped over the stone wall and scampered down the bank toward the Serpentine. She walked the horses closer to the wall and saw a group of children who were clumped on the bank like reeds. A woman, who was as thin as a hen's head and was presumably their governess, was wringing her hands with dismay as a child tossed a rock and cried out in frustration when it vanished.

Vanessa guessed the children were trying to play ducks and drakes. Their lack of success was visible in their stiff motions. Resting her arms on the wall, she smiled as Lord Brickendon knelt to speak to the youngsters. The resonance of his voice rolled over her and through her, as enticing as the secrets in his dark eyes.

The viscount's hands were gentle as he assisted the littlest boy to take the proper stance to dance the stone across the water. The stone dropped with a tired plunk, but Lord Brickendon gave the child no chance to pout. Picking up another pebble, he patiently showed the little boy what he must do. The youngster crowed with delight when the stone skipped four times before disappearing into the ripples.

"Your turn," she heard Lord Brickendon say.

The child gave him a dubious look, but found another flat rock. He pulled back his arm, then paused, looking at the tall man. Lord Brickendon posed him correctly again.

Vanessa held her breath as the child sent the rock skimming across the water. It struck and bounced twice. She applauded wildly, not caring about the curious stares of those riding past.

The viscount tapped the child on the shoulder. When the little boy looked at him in confusion, Lord Brickendon pointed to where Vanessa stood. He bent to whisper to the youngster, who giggled, then bowed deeply to her.

"Bravo!" she called, acknowledging his bow with her own curtsy as Lord Brickendon turned to help the next child.

She had forgotten such innocent delight existed. In her headlong rush to find Corey and the mad swirl of the Season, she had not stopped to think of a child's battle to accomplish the mundane. Not mundane, she corrected herself instantly, but the singular satisfaction of achieving one's heart's desire, even if the heart forgot with the passage of time. Watching the viscount, who had given his hat to the bewildered governess, she recalled how Papa had spent hours teaching her to balance a gun and fire it, how he had sat with her by a pond as she struggled to put a worm on the hook, how he had cheered when she managed to sail the small sailboat through the waves beyond Wolfe Abbey. Never had he belittled her mistakes. Instead he had lauded her progress.

When each one of the children had succeeded, she heard Lord Brickendon say to the bare-bones woman, "I bid you good day, madam."

The woman stumbled over her attempt to thank him. He smiled as he took his beaver and set it on his sable hair. Tipping it to her, he climbed the bank and over the wall.

"You said you preferred sport you can master." Vanessa laughed. "Is this your favorite?"

He caught her hand between his and brought her a half step closer. No frivolity filled his eyes, for they were dark with stronger emotions. "Ducks and drakes," he said so softly she had to lean even nearer, "is easier to master than a woman's capricious heart, but sometimes the enjoyment gained from a sport comes from the attempt to conquer it."

"Is that what you wish?" She spoke no louder than he, for she wanted no passerby to overhear. "To conquer a woman's heart?"

"No, for something so precious must be freely given, or it is never truly won." He drew her hand to the ruffles on his shirt and pressed her fingers over the steady thump of his heart. She was glad he could not feel hers as it raced like an unbroken horse.

Suddenly he released her as, looking past her, he snarled, "Blast!"

Vanessa whirled, uncertain what she might see, angry that whatever it was had disturbed the perfection of Lord Brickendon's touch. When she saw Eveline and Lord Greybrooke race past, she sighed. She could not stand alone with the viscount nor could she allow her friend to be unchaperoned.

Thanking him for his assistance when he set her in the saddle, Vanessa slapped the reins against her horse's neck. The horse leapt forward, and she heard shouts as other riders scattered. In seconds, she had caught up with Eveline and Edward. Laughter brightened their faces as they tried—at the same time—to tell her about their mock wager.

Lord Brickendon said, "You should have more sense than to race along Rotten Row. I vow you nearly upset a dowager from her mount."

"Oh, dear." Eveline tried to look woeful, but failed, for her eyes sparkled. "What can you expect from a Clarke?"

"Do cut line!" Vanessa edged her horse between Eveline's and the earl's. Even knowing that her fury came from having that sweet moment interrupted, she could not still her lips. "Eveline, you are nothing like your mother. You have prided yourself on being a diamond of birth. All your life you have struggled against the preconceptions of those who would cast you in the mold of your mother. Do you intend now to give them the satisfaction of being right?"

Eveline's shoulders sagged. "You are right, Vanessa. Forgive me, Edward."

The earl grasped her hand. "Oh, my dearest, forgive me. Never would I intentionally besmirch your name which is as beautiful on the ears as you are on the eyes."

"It was my fault. I was thoughtless."

Vanessa moved her horse away from them as they continued to try to take full blame for the incident. Lord Brickendon asked, "Are calf-lovers always so sickening sweet to each other?"

"I pray not."

"And I pray you are right." He smiled and tipped back the brim of her tall hat. "If you ever chance to see me so syrupy, I beg you to give me a nob. That blow might put some sense in my skull."

Her fingers refused to be halted from curving along his rough cheek. Her craving to touch him was becoming an obsession. His hand covered hers, then drew it away. She swallowed her protest as he slowly slid off her glove. He brought her hand toward his lips. She held her breath, waiting for the powerful pleasure of his kiss. It became a gasp as he pressed his mouth to her palm, setting every inch of it afire with sensations that had no name.

As he lifted his head, she was caught again by his enchanting gaze. She waited for him to speak of the passions flashing there, but he handed her the glove and said, "We should ride on, my lady."

"But—" she choked, unwilling to let the magic slip away again.

"Edward and Miss Clarke are going to watch the parade by the barracks. We should join them."

Vanessa feared he was looking for an excuse to flee the delight. Mortification burned away her happiness. She had been so forward even as her words pretended she cared nothing for his touch. Had she mistaken the fervor in his kiss? No, she could not be so terribly wrong. Or could she? Trying to understand, but having no clue to his thoughts, she rode in self-conscious silence to where Eveline and Lord Greybrooke were watching the marching soldiers.

"Bring that Corsican monster to Tyburn!" called someone from the crowd gathered along the road. "We'll find a scragging-post to stretch his neck!"

Cheers met the brave words, but Vanessa noticed none of them. Horror clamped its suffocating hold around her as she stared at the uniforms. The blue was too familiar.

"Are you all right, my lady?" she heard Lord Brickendon ask.

"Don't you see?" she whispered, tears burning her

throat. "Captain Hudson was leading some of the troops." She pressed her bottom lip between her teeth before choking, "Can that mean anything but that he will be leaving to fight the filthy frogs soon? Oh, I wonder if Aunt Carolyn knows."

"He must have told her. I know Hudson. He's too much of a gentleman to leave without presenting his suit."

Too late, she could comprehend the captain's suppressed fury at the theater. "You don't understand! Aunt Carolyn will never accept his offer of marriage until I have found a husband." She swallowed roughly. "I have stood in the way of Aunt Carolyn's happiness too long. I shall never allow my aunt to suffer as I have since my brother left for France, thinking I meant the words I spoke to him in anger."

"What words?"

Tears flooded her eyes as she confessed her greatest shame. "I told Corey that if he went, knowing how he was breaking Papa's heart, I hoped I never would see him again. And I haven't!"

"So what will you do?"

She shook her head as she whispered, "I don't know."

Chapter Twelve

A shout resounded through the quiet halls. Pott grabbed his coat off the back of his chair in the kitchen and leapt to his feet.

"Lord have mercy!" gasped Mrs. Crumb, the house-keeper. "What can that be?"

Pott struggled to find his left sleeve. " 'Tis his lord-ship."

"Is he dying?"

The valet raced up the stairs. He panted as he reached the top. A man of his age and bulk should not be running like this. Lurching along the hall, he poked his bald head cautiously into his master's bedchamber. "My lord?"

He got no answer. He stared at the collar and cravat that had been tossed on the dark green rug to lie like a broken bird. A single shoe was half hidden beneath the gold curtains of the bed. He shivered. Perhaps Mrs. Crumb was correct. His lordship would not have left his private chamber in such a higgledy-piggledy state un-less he was fighting for his last breath against an in-truder.

"Pott!"

The valet flinched at the shout. "My lord, I am here. Where are you?"

Lord Brickendon stormed out of his dressing room, and the valet stared at him in disbelief. As disheveled as his chamber, the viscount had one shirttail hanging out of his breeches. His bare feet struck the carpet with such fury that Pott was sure Mrs. Crumb was ready to pray for their master's soul to be guided safely to heaven.

"When was this delivered?"

Pott squinted to try to make out what the viscount was holding in his clenched fist. It was a slip of paper, but beyond that he was not sure. Guessing, he said, "The invitation for Lady Mansfield's party—"

"Not that! This! From Franklin!"

The valet backpedaled as the irate viscount shoved a sheet of ivory paper in his face. He wrung his hands, uncertain how to deal with this raging boar. The viscount was usually calm, and Pott had been grateful for the serenity in the house since Lord Brickendon's mother's death last year. Now the viscount was raving as wildly as she had during her last fever.

With care, he took the page from the viscount's hand and peered at it. He could read, but slowly. Too slowly for his lordship, he discovered, when the viscount grabbed it back.

Lord Brickendon snarled, "Listen to this:

In light of recent events, I would like to ask you and Swinton to accept the withdrawal of my withdrawal from our wager. I intend to announce I am the winner before the end of the next fortnight. Buy a toast to me and my bride with the pound I wagered. I shall soon be your well-inlaid friend, the husband of Lady Vanessa Wolfe."

His black eyes were as furious as his voice as he looked at his valet. "It is signed Sir Wilbur Franklin. Blast it!"

"But I thought both the baronet and Mr. Swinton had

been trounced. Didn't you say last week that you considered this wager a pound it?"

"I *had* thought it was a sure thing." Ross glowered at his valet. The man had misplaced every reasonable thought. Could Pott not see the truth? His hands clenched. He should have guessed Vanessa would do something so idiotic when she had been so upset at the Park. But this? Blast that woman's stubbornness! "Lady Mansfield's party is this evening?"

Pott nodded, his collection of chins bobbing. "But, my lord, the hour is so late. If you had returned from Whitehall in midafternoon, I could have had a reply delivered to Lady Mansfield. You can't be considering attending the party when you haven't responded to the invitation."

"Blast convention! Get my best frock coat. I shall show that pluckless block that he cannot change the rules of this wager." He kicked aside his shoes and pointed toward the dressing room. "Hop to it, man! I shall not lose this wager now."

The ballroom in Lady Carolyn Mansfield's house had been roused from its usual duskiness to glitter like a dowager wearing all her family's gems. Fresh flowers admired themselves in the mirrors ringing the room between the paintings Lord Mansfield had collected during his travels before he settled himself with his young bride on Grosvenor Square. Soft music provided a melodious backdrop to conversation in the crowded room.

As Vanessa stood next to her aunt and welcomed each guest, she pretended she did not overhear the comments about Sir Wilbur Franklin's presence at the party. Eavesdropping was a deplorable habit, she wanted to remind herself, but she guessed the guests yearned for her to hear, so they could judge if she was agreeable to the baronet courting her again. That Lord Brickendon, who had been seen in her company recently, had made no appearance added to the gabble.

Vanessa wondered why the viscount had not replied to her aunt's invitation. He had said little during the ride back from the Park two days before. When he had not called the next day, she had guessed—had hoped—other obligations had demanded his attention. She had thought he would send his regrets if he could not attend tonight. There had been no answer.

Misery weighted her shoulders and seared her eyes, but she must not let anyone know. So she smiled a greeting to each guest and accepted their *bon mots* on her gown. Madame deBerg had outdone herself with the *appliquéd* sleeves, which reached no lower than the high bodice, and the matching silver ribbons along the frills on the skirt and woven in her hair. A single strand of pearls, a gift from her father on her sixteenth birthday, accented her white silk gown.

When Eveline rushed across the crowded room, she took Vanessa's hands and drew her to one side. "I must tell you. I cannot bear to wait another minute."

"What is it?" she asked, although she already knew. Dismay thickened around her. She should not covet her friend's joy, but she wished she could flee the mire of dreariness.

Eveline whispered, "Edward just asked me to be his wife. I know we must wait for Papa's permission to wed, but I am sure he will give it. Now Papa will not have to return from the country for the Little Season, and I shall be Edward's wife. Oh, Vanessa, can anything be more wonderful?"

"I can imagine nothing more wonderful than seeing my dearest friend happy with a man she loves." When Eveline's smile faltered, Vanessa asked with growing concern, "You do love him, don't you?"

"I think so." Her green eyes widened with childish bafflement. "But how am I to know? I have never been in love before. How am I supposed to feel?"

"I have heard that you know you are in love if your heart is filled with joyous anticipation each time you think you might meet."

Eveline pressed her hands to the bodice of her creamy gown. "I do look forward to seeing Edward. He never fails to bring me a small token to show his unending affection." She held up her left arm. A sapphire bracelet sparkled over her kid gloves. "A secret betrothal gift."

Laughing, as her friend's happiness swept over her, cleansing her of her anguish, Vanessa embraced Eveline. "It shall stay secret only the shortest time, for your face betrays your jubilation." She stepped aside as Lord Greybrooke neared. "I believe your future husband can bear no more time away from you."

Eveline hugged Vanessa again and fairly flew back to where the earl welcomed her with a broad smile. Vanessa watched for a moment, then looked away, embarrassed by the honesty of their emotion.

"Quite the surprising couple, aren't they?" Sir Wilbur's rumbling laugh grated on her ears.

Vanessa needed all her will to keep her smile in place. The baronet's sedate black frock made no attempt to cover the expanse of his belly. His white breeches and silk stockings suited him as well as a crown on a pig. Telling herself she must overlook the fact he was a puff-guts if there was to be any chance for a successful marriage between them, she quelled her shudder.

"I am not surprised at all, Sir Wilbur," she said stiffly. She would forgive other faults, but not animadversions to her bosom-bow. "Lord Greybrooke is a genuine gentleman, who has had the good sense to win the heart of the Season's most beautiful woman. As Eveline is as sweet as she is pretty, they seem a perfect match."

"Do you think they will wed?"

"Shall we wait until they tell us their plans? There is scanty use in wasting our breath on discussing something about which we know little."

Sir Wilbur was not abashed by her admonition, for he laughed. "Lady Mansfield urged me to ask you to stand up with me for the first dance. It is impolite to keep one's guests waiting too long, you know."

Vanessa's smile faltered as she put her hand on his pudgy arm. Her fingers recalled the strength of Lord Brickendon's muscles beneath them. She kept her fingers from recoiling, because that would insult the baronet anew. Not that he would take insult. He was too anxious for this match. His eagerness to reassure her that he was gracious enough to forgive her for having him thrown into the street was as false as her smile. If she had been a willow, lacking both fortune and title, he would have never called upon her in the first place.

As they stood in the middle of the otherwise empty dance floor, with every eye upon them and many tongues wagging, Vanessa looked across the room to where her aunt had her arm linked with Captain Hudson's. Aunt Carolyn wore the same expression of happiness as Eveline. Vanessa took a deep breath and put her hand in the baronet's.

Vanessa nearly changed her mind by the fifth time Sir Wilbur's foot came down on her silk slippers as he turned her about the room with no attempt to keep to the waltz's tempo. Her thin slippers could endure only a little abuse, and she feared she would end the evening with at least one broken toe.

When the baronet suddenly stopped in the midst of one enthusiastic whirl, Vanessa rocked back into something hard. She turned and gasped as she saw Lord

Brickendon's warm smile and warmer gaze. Knowing she should offer him a gracious greeting, she could do no more than stare up into his eyes. Her heart thumped like a child's ball on the cobbles. She heard Sir Wilbur grumble something, but she paid him no more mind than she did the cut of the viscount's black velvet coat which, with its stand-fall collar and tails reaching to just above his knees, accented the breathtaking breadth of his shoulders.

"I am sorry I am late, my lady," Lord Brickendon said with a smile that sent the deliciously familiar spiral of delight through her. He looked from her to the blustery baronet. "May I hope that I am not too late?"

Sir Wilbur interjected, "Now see here—"

"May I?" Lord Brickendon asked, ignoring the baronet as he held his hand out to Vanessa.

She was astounded how well her slender fingers fit on his broad palm. His other hand settled at her waist as he spun her into the intoxicating pattern of the waltz. He led her about the floor with as much ease as if he had spent many hours of practice with her as her dancing-master. She was certain that Lord Brickendon truly became the master of any skill he attempted.

"So quiet?" he teased. "Can I believe I am forgiven for my tardiness?"

"I had feared you would not come," she whispered, too happy to be coy.

"I had considered letting you stew in your own juices if you were jobbernowl enough to set your cap on that tripes and trillibubs simply to give your aunt a chance to marry."

"But you didn't."

"No, for the lesson would be too painful even for an obstinate woman like you to suffer through." His low laugh coaxed a smile from her. "All the world and his wife are rumbling about your abrupt change of partners.

You are, as ever, kind to give them something to prattle about."

"My lord—"

"Would it unnerve you too much to call me Ross?"

She said with the honesty she always could use with him, "I would like that."

"So would I . . . Vanessa."

Her name on his lips was a caress even more fervent than his fingers on hers. Letting him draw her closer, she found his gaze holding hers as the music washed over them, its gentle rhythms a countermelody to her heartbeat. She was unsure when one dance ended, and the next began, but she swirled through each one with him. When he murmured that he needed to speak to her alone, she walked with him out of the ballroom, not caring a rap about what anyone thought of her odd actions, and down the stairs to her aunt's blue sitting room.

The distant sound of the music followed them as Ross sat next to her on the settee. With her hands between his, he said, "You never answered my question. Am I too late to keep you from accepting Franklin's offer of marriage?"

Sorrow clamped around her heart, stifling all joy, as his words reminded her that this must be nothing more than a rapturous interlude. She must marry, so she no longer stood in the way of Aunt Carolyn's betrothal. "No, but nothing has changed."

"That is true."

She looked at him, mystified, as she heard his amusement. She pulled her hands away from his. If he thought her plight so humorous, she would as lief he had remained distant.

"Don't fire that baleful glower at me," he continued in the same light voice. "Nothing *has* changed. It took a bit of searching, but I finally convinced someone to tell me about Hudson's men. They are to stay in garrison here in Town."

"Here? He shall not be going to France, too?" She could not hold back her tears. Covering her face with her hands, she wept, for her aunt's happiness and for her own that she need not throw away.

"I did not mean to bring you to tears." Ross pulled a handkerchief from under his coat. "I have been accused of many misdeeds, many which I would not inflict upon your tender ears, but never have I been accused of causing a woman to cry simply because I told her that her aunt was set to wed a carpet-knight."

Vanessa took the square of lawn and dabbed at her eyes. "Forgive me. I hate being a wet-goose."

His finger beneath her chin tipped her face up. The warm caress of his gaze stroked her face, and her lips parted as an eager breath urged her to put her hand over his. "Sweet Vanessa, when I first met you I saw in you a strength I've seen in few others, but be cautious it does not betray you. Tears are meant to be shed. Joy is meant to be spread with laughter. Grief is meant to be shared. Why do you hide yours?"

Blinking back more tears, she set herself on her feet. His words pierced her to the heart, for they were undeniably the truth. The very same truth she had been ignoring as she continued her single-minded pursuit of Corey's whereabouts. Ross had never failed to be honest with her. Mayhap that was why she had found it impossible to be anything less than the same in return. He made her smile and laugh and want to be happy again. Not only happy, but to want a rapture that came from the caress of his fingers and the longing for his mouth upon hers. She kept her back to him as her yearning to be honest warred with her fear he would call her an air-dreamer as everyone, even Aunt Carolyn, had.

Looking down at the damp handkerchief, she whispered, "I have tried to share my grief, to find someone who could ease it, but no one wishes to listen. I believe my brother Corey is alive somewhere in France."

"I thought he was dead."

Vanessa faced him as he stood. "There is no proof he is not alive." She clenched her fingers on the handkerchief. "By all that's blue, I wish someone would do more than tell me there is nothing anyone can do."

His hand stroked hers, teasing her fist to soften. "Have you given thought to the fact there may be nothing anyone can do?"

"No."

"That is no surprise." He brushed the back of his hand against her wet cheek. "You dare to believe the impossible."

"Ross . . ." She shook her head. "No, I cannot say it."

"Yes, you can. Tell me what is gnawing at you."

The ice around her heart splintered as she knew she must trust him as she had no one else. "Ross, you said you have connections in the government. I have asked someone to check into the reports from Corey's commanders. They will not answer my queries. I have written to everyone."

"Including my uncle?" A smile pulled at his lips. "Was that why you had the misfortune to call on him that day?"

"Yes," she whispered, unable to halt the color crawling up her face. "I had hoped he could help. I had hoped Lord Liverpool's ministers would help. I even wrote to Lord Liverpool himself. When he did nothing, I sent a letter to the Prince Regent. If he does not—"

His finger against her lips silenced her growing agitation. "I shall ask." Before she could thank him, he frowned. "That is all I pledge. I cannot promise that my questions will receive any more attention than your ardent ones."

"But you will try. That is more than anyone has done before." She wrapped her hand around the finger he had held to her lips. "Thank you, Ross. Thank you so very much."

Rising on tiptoe, she leaned forward to kiss his cheek. She gasped as his arms enfolded her and pulled her tight to his firm body. The kiss she had planned to place on his cheek was met instead by his lips. The flame she had seen sparking in his intriguing eyes seared her mouth. Slowly her arms rose to encircle his shoulders, ceding herself to the potent pleasure of his touch.

When he drew his mouth from hers, she heard his command to open her eyes. She wanted to ignore it, to linger in this dream. With his arms around her, with his mouth against hers, with his promise to help her, she could imagine nothing more wondrous.

She looked up at him and smiled as she ran a daring finger along the cleft in his chin and up the firm line of his jaw. Turning his head, he teased her fingers with a light kiss. He murmured her name as he captured her lips again. She returned his kiss with all the hunger in her soul.

A choked curse behind her wrenched Vanessa from the ecstasy. She looked over her shoulder to see Sir Wilbur standing in the half-open door.

"Did you wish something, Franklin?"

She was shocked by the frigidity of Ross's voice. The baronet must have been, too, for, when he tried to speak, his voice cracked on the first word.

"Make sense, man," ordered Ross, "instead of squeaking like a blasted stuck pig. Otherwise, begone."

Sir Wilbur stamped out, slamming the door behind him so hard a vase on a table next to it bounced. Vanessa ran to steady it, then reached for the door. When a broad hand covered hers on the latch, she turned to Ross.

"I must . . ."

"You must what?" he asked, the tenderness returning to his voice. His finger played along her bare shoulder, teasing and tantalizing.

"Aunt Carolyn will be in a flutter," she whispered, her voice growing fainter on every word as he turned her back into his arms. "She is so concerned about my reputation."

"It is tainted." He pressed his lips to the curve of her neck. Through a flurry of fiery kisses, he whispered, "There is nothing left but for you to say you will marry me."

"Marry you?" Each word was a separate battle as she longed to sink into the sea of sweet passion, which was deepened by each touch of his mouth against her. "That would salvage my standing, but what would it do to your reputation as a rogue of the first order if you leg-shackled yourself to me?"

Framing her face with his hands, he waited until her eyes focused on his handsome face. "I am not jesting you, Vanessa. Marry me."

"Not jesting?" She drew away, trying to make her mind work. Every warning she had ever heard about Ross's reputation raced through her head. So many women he had dallied with, so many mysteries surrounded him, so often he had taunted her. She must think about this sensibly. Even now, she should not trust him, although he might be the very man to help her find Corey . . . and although his touch left her weak with the longing for his arms enfolding her to his hard chest. "But I thought—"

"That I wished nothing but to tease you, so that your eyes sparkled like twin sunlit pools? Or that I would be satisfied to hold you in my arms only when we twirled to the staid tempo of a waltz?" His hands on her shoulders brought her back against him. " 'Tis no lark, Vanessa, when I tell you that I wish to have you as my wife. Tell me you wish me for your husband."

She opened her mouth to answer, but the sound vanished beneath his lips. Unwilling to fight the dulcet assault on her senses, she knew there could be but one answer. She loved Ross. She was sure of it, for her days were empty without him. Mayhap everything said about him was true, and she was an air-dreamer to believe he loved her as she had come to love him. Mayhap that was so, but she knew her heart would offer her no answer save one.

"Yes," she whispered, her lips only a breath from his, "if you think that marrying you will make you as happy as it will make me, yes, I will be your wife."

He laughed. "If I think? I was like a man infected by the madness of a Midsummer Moon tonight when I thought I might be too late to keep you from marrying Franklin." Leaning her head on his shoulder, she could hear the smile in his voice as he said, "I have never been as certain of anything as I am that I would have done anything to win your heart."

Chapter Thirteen

". . . and a party!" Eveline danced around the breakfast-parlor. "We must have a grand party to announce Vanessa's betrothal!"

Aunt Carolyn had not stopped smiling since Vanessa had shared the news of Ross's proposal nearly an hour before. She raised her cup of cocoa, then lowered it, for it had grown cold while they had talked. "Penelope Downing is having a small gathering tonight. No more than fifty people." She stretched across the round, oak table to take her niece's hand. "What do you say to announcing your betrothal to Lord Brickendon this evening?"

Eveline interjected, "Do you think she could keep it a secret any longer?" Laughing, she sat and propped her elbows on the table. The *Morning Chronicle* crinkled beneath them.

"And you?" Vanessa asked, her happiness brightening every word. "How long can you keep your secret?"

When Aunt Carolyn insisted on being told the rest of the news, her smile grew broader. Standing, she folded her hands in front of her. "We have much to do. Eveline, you must write to your father posthaste. I realize Lord Greybrooke intends to call on him to present his suit, but your father should hear such wondrous tidings from your hand. I shall send a message to Penelope that I must speak with her this afternoon." She tapped a finger against her chin as Eveline rushed out to do as she had been bid. "If I tell Penelope that we wish to announce your betrothal, she is sure to spill the secret on any ear that will heed her. And Eveline—"

"She is a prattle-box," Vanessa owned.

"She must stay in today, or she'll babble the news to the whole *Beau Monde*. I must discuss this with Victor. Oh, he should be here any minute." Without looking at Vanessa, she went out of the room, still debating aloud how she would handle the ticklish problem.

Vanessa, left alone, leaned back in her chair. Ross would be amused if he saw how flustered Aunt Carolyn was. Last night, he had urged her to delay announcing their betrothal until he could be sure his friends would be present, for he wanted to share their happiness with them. She jumped to her feet as she realized she must send him a note, so he could let Penelope know which of his friends to invite. How would he explain that to Penelope? She laughed. Ross would charm her neighbor into believing any loud one he devised.

Going into the blue sitting room, Vanessa took a sheet from the writing table. It was a delicious feeling to know this letter did not have to be written in secret. If Ross was able to break through the stone wall set up by the government, she would never need to write another clandestine letter. Once Corey was safe, her last missive to the government would be a thank you.

"My lady?"

"What is it, Quigley?" she asked without looking up as she reached for a bottle of ink.

"Lord Brickendon, my lady."

Her fingers halted inches from the bottle, and she drew them back slowly. A mixture of excitement and

astonishment flowed through her that Ross had beat up
her quarters, but she presented a serene face to the butler. Rising, she said, "Show him in."

The butler nodded.

Hoping she did not look a complete rump, Vanessa
wished for a glass bigger than the one over the mantel.
She adjusted her short sleeves, which were the same li-
lac as her muslin skirt. The white bodice matched the
flounce at the hem. Realizing her hair was loose about
her shoulders, she pulled a ribbon from the trio edging
the Vandyke ruff and tied her hair back at her nape. She
had no time to do more before she heard Ross's asser-
tive footsteps.

When he entered, she admired the flattering cut of his
coat and the way his shining boots followed his lean
legs. He held out his hands, and she put hers in them.

"I was just about to write a note to you," she said, her
delight at seeing him adding music to her voice. "Aunt
Carolyn suggests we announce our betrothal at the
Downings' *soirée* this evening. If you will tell me
whom you wish to invite, I shall arrange for them to be
there."

He did not return her smile. Instead he enfolded her
hands in his. "I must speak with you. Now! Alone!"

"Ross—"

"It is about your brother."

Vanessa was glad he held her hands as her suddenly
weak knees threatened to dump her face first onto the
floor. She whispered, "The garden."

"Is it private?"

"I don't know." She tightened her hold on his hands.
"Ross, what is wrong?"

"I shall tell you in the garden."

The stern set of his jaw warned her that prying his
message from him would be impossible. She had waited

for so long to hear of Corey. She must wait a few moments longer. But what had Ross discovered so quickly?

Going down the back stairs, she led him across the brick terrace to a small arbor set in the very center of the garden. Rose vines arced over it, leaving the interior scented with freshly overturned earth and cool with shadows.

Vanessa sat on the wooden bench. Ross did not sit next to her until she reached up to take his hand with both of hers. The lace at his cuffs tickled her icy fingers as she whispered, "You told me that grief is meant to be shared. Is that why you hesitate? Is the news about Corey so bad?"

"Your aunt is in?"

"Yes, but she shall be leaving soon with Captain Hudson."

He smiled swiftly. "Are you certain ours will be the only announcement tonight? Those two are as close as a court plaster, and this party would offer a most convenient opportunity for them to proclaim their own plans."

"Aunt Carolyn has said nothing of that."

"Words are not always necessary." He stroked her cheek with a single finger. "Haven't you discovered that, Vanessa?"

Although she wanted to surrender to the bliss of his touch, she asked, "What have you learned of Corey?"

"Your brother is alive."

She gripped his sleeve and searched his face, fearing she might discover he was teasing her. She could not believe how swiftly he had obtained the information she had sought so long. "Alive? Are you certain?"

He smiled gently. "Aren't you?"

She rose and put her hands on the splintered edges of the arbor. Looking across the empty garden, she whispered, "I had thought I was. I wanted to believe it with all my heart, but I have listened to other doubts too long."

"Then listen to me, Vanessa." He put his hands on her shoulders and drew her back to rest against him. "He is alive. He is a prisoner of war, but he is alive."

She put her hand on his chest. "A prisoner?"

"If my sources are correct—and they always have been—your brother is a prisoner in a *château* on the Loire."

"Then we can retrieve him."

He walked away. His hands tightened into fists as impotent fury scored his voice. "Blast it to perdition! Those damn castles are as impenetrable as a spinster's heart."

"There is no way he could escape?"

"If there is, he has not found it yet."

"Oh, Corey," she choked. She pressed her face to his shoulder and wept.

Ross stroked her back, wishing he could find some words—any words—to ease her tears. Resting his cheek against the silken softness of her hair, he listened to the ragged sound of her sobs. They threatened to shatter her, but she was strong enough to combat even this.

"Vanessa," he called softly. When she continued to cry, he led her back to the arbor. He sat next to her and repeated her name. Her tear-streaked face rose, so he could see the agony in her expressive eyes.

"I told him I never wanted him to return," she choked. "Now he is a prisoner of that Corsican beast!" Clutching his ruffled shirt, she gasped, "There must be something we can do. Bribery?"

"It would take more money than even the Wolfes possess."

"Could an exchange be arranged?"

"I asked, and I was told Napoleon refuses to release your brother in any prisoner exchange." His jaw grew taut with his furious frustration. "There is an accusation of spying against him."

"But they will kill him!"

"They have not killed him yet," he answered gently. The wild expression faded from her eyes. Brushing the tips of his fingers against her damp cheek, he watched as she closed her eyes and leaned toward him, trust in every motion.

Ross stood and locked his hands behind his back. She rose, too, and looked up at him, astonished. Not that he blamed her, because she had come to have faith in him. Damn, he had been a stupe to bring her this information today. If he had waited until after this evening, he might not feel like such a blackguard.

"I must do something," she whispered. "I cannot let him die thinking I hate him. What can I do, Ross?"

"Do nothing now."

"Nothing?"

"Give me a chance to learn more. I have secured an appointment with the Prime Minister on the morrow. I vow that I shall endeavor to do everything I can to bring Lord Wulfric home to England alive." He brushed her hair back from her damp face. "You believe me, don't you?"

"Yes," she whispered, leaning her head against his chest again.

Ross was glad she could not see his face as he heard the unwavering trust in her voice. He knew how little he deserved it.

Pink silk swirled around Vanessa's ankles as she turned so she could see herself from every angle in the cheval glass. The pink slip ended in a row of flounces below her new gown of white, French gauze. Her gown's short sleeves and deeply rounded neckline were decorated with the same silk roses as those flowing along its skirt. The edges of her demi-skirt flared as she reached up to her hair which Leale had styled *à la grecque*. Curls edged her face, but her hair was pulled back sharply and held in place by roses of the same soft shade as her slip.

Leale clucked like a mother hen with a single chick as she brought Vanessa's elbow-length gloves. "You look perfect, my lady."

"I must tonight." She bent to be certain the laces on her soft slippers were tied according to Cocker about her ankles. Her open-work stockings peeked from beneath the hem of her slip. Smiling, she opened the bottom drawer of her writing table and took out the locked box.

Her fingers paused on Corey's last letter, but she did not open it as she had so often. She slipped it into her bodice before lifting a gold choker with a single diamond from the box. It was the one piece of her mother's jewelry she had never been able to bring herself to put on, because her mother had been wearing it the night she fell ill with the fever that had taken her life. Tonight Vanessa wanted to have a bit of each member of her family with her.

"Leale, please bring me the small, velvet box from the back of the armoire," she said as she ran her fingers along the gold strand. If only her mother could be with her tonight to see that the lessons Lady Wulfric had tried to inspire in her recalcitrant daughter had been learned.

Leale was unusually discomposed as she handed Vanessa the box that was no larger than a half crown. Vanessa opened it and took out the signet ring. She slipped it over her middle finger. With the bulk of her gloves beneath it, the ring fit. She ran her finger over the crest of the Marquess of Wulfric. She had wanted her father to wear this ring to his grave, but her aunt had insisted it must be kept for his heir. Aunt Carolyn has assumed that Vanessa would send it to Papa's cousin who, with Corey's supposed death, could claim the title. Now she knew for sure that Corey was alive. With luck and Ross's help, she soon would be able to give this ring to Corey.

Vanessa endured her aunt's fussing and then stood for Eveline's inspection. They concurred with Leale, although she saw her aunt give the signet ring an odd look. Aunt Carolyn said nothing as Quigley announced Lord Greybrooke.

The earl seemed distracted, for his greeting was perfunctory. He swept Eveline out the door to walk her the few steps to the house next door.

"Could Mr. Clarke have so quickly rejected the earl's plea for Eveline's hand?" Vanessa asked.

Her aunt wore a puzzled expression as she turned from the window where she was watching for Captain Hudson. "What are you prattling about, Vanessa?"

"Lord Greybrooke. He was quite terse."

"Dear child," she said with a laugh, "it is not unusual for gentlemen to be overwhelmed by the hubbub of a betrothal."

"But my betrothal is a secret still."

"Do you think Eveline could refrain from sharing the news with her fiancé?" Patting Vanessa's arm, she turned back to the window. "Have pity for poor Lord Greybrooke. Probably he is anticipating—with much foreboding—when *he* is the butt of jokes by his tiemates on the end of his bachelor days."

Vanessa was not convinced, but said no more as Captain Hudson entered the house a step ahead of Ross. Following her aunt and her beau out of the house, Vanessa considered mentioning her concerns to Ross. She missed her chance, for they were greeted by an exuberant Penelope Downing.

Kissing Vanessa's cheek, she exclaimed, "How happy I am for you, my dear! And for me! I'm so pleased you are going to announce—"

"Penelope!" warned Aunt Carolyn in a low voice. "Hold your tongue. It shall not be long before you can loosen it to flap as you wish."

"But I am so happy." She continued to twitter like an overweight songbird as Vanessa walked with Ross up the curved stairs and into the ballroom.

The room was a near twin to the one in Aunt Carolyn's house, but was decorated in flamboyant scarlet silk on the walls and an endless swath of gold across the ceiling. Chairs followed the walls, but no one sat. The guests turned to watch Vanessa enter the room on Ross's arm. She was sure many of them had guessed an announcement was forthcoming. Penelope could hide nothing.

"Do not be so down-pinned," Ross said beneath the lilting tune being played by a small orchestra.

"I shall not!" She gave him her happiest smile. "Think how excited Corey shall be for me when he returns to find me married. He used to tease me that no man would want to marry an ugly hoyden like me."

Ross scanned the gilded room. "Your Season has proven your brother quite wrong."

She wondered whom he sought with his intense stare. "Ross, is something bothering you?"

"I wish this night was over." He smiled dimly.

Recalling Aunt Carolyn's words, Vanessa did not pursue the matter. Ross would survive the hazing of his friends easily. She smiled as she imagined them—many years from now—laughing together over their nervousness tonight.

The hours passed in a blur of music and dancing with Ross and listening to her aunt's anxious questions. Was Vanessa nervous? Did Vanessa want some wine to put roses in her cheeks? Did Vanessa think she should sit and rest? Her color was too high, wasn't it?

Soothing her aunt, who was fretting her gizzard, Vanessa saw Eveline gesture to her, but had no chance to talk to her as Aunt Carolyn urged her to come to stand near the orchestra where Ross was waiting. Aunt Carolyn puffed Vanessa's sleeves and fluttered about, pulling a bow here, adjusting a flounce there.

Ross watched with a smile. Taking Vanessa's hand, he said, "You are trembling. Are you frightened?"

"I shall be happy when this night is over, too." She was astonished when his smile wavered. It returned, but it was the cool one he had worn when they first met. As if he had shouted it, she knew something was bothering him. "Ross, what is wrong?"

Eveline pushed through the arc of the crowd and hissed, "Vanessa, I must speak with you!"

"Now?" She glanced at Ross who had not answered her. He was gazing at the opposite end of the room, his face naked of expression. Something must be wrong, but what could it be?

"Please, Vanessa," Eveline whispered. "I must speak with you. Now!"

"What—?" She was interrupted when a glass of champagne was thrust into her hand. Offering Eveline a regretful smile, she had no time for more because her aunt was raising her glass.

Joy filled Aunt Carolyn's voice. "Drink with me to the health of Lord Brickendon and the future Lady Brickendon, my niece Lady Vanessa Wolfe."

Cheers drowned out the sound of crystal clinking as the toast was drunk to the soon-to-be newlyweds. Vanessa struggled to smile when Ross offered her a sip from his glass, but she gave up when she saw Eveline turn away, tears awash on her face.

Looking back at Ross, she discovered his gaze was on Eveline, too, as her friend pushed her way through the well-wishers. His smile remained steady, but Vanessa was even more certain something was wrong.

Terribly wrong.

Vanessa sighed as she climbed the last step to the second floor. From the ballroom, she heard the strains of her favorite waltz and the enthusiastic cacophony of conversation.

But Eveline Clarke and Lord Greybrooke were no longer among the Downings' guests. After searching nearly every room of the house for her friend, Vanessa guessed they must have departed. Eveline should have known better than to leave without a chaperone, but that did not worry Vanessa as much as her bosom-bow's tears. She had to know why Eveline had needed to speak to her so desperately. She prayed it had nothing to do with Ross's peculiar behavior since the betrothal announcement. After a single dance, he had vanished as completely as Eveline.

Voices sounded from the other side of the hall. Hope burst forth. Could Eveline and her earl have been so close all along?

Vanessa reached for the half-opened door. Her fingers froze as she identified the speakers. Sir Wilbur Franklin! Bruce Swinton! Could *these* be the friends Ross had insisted must attend tonight?

"We are a pair of catollers," said Mr. Swinton. "We should have known better than to try to best you at your own sport, Brickendon. You have proven to be the victor in this wager by winning Lady Vanessa Wolfe's hand."

"Yes," said the baronet, "and what do you do next?

Do you wed her? Or is simply winning the wager the end of it for you?"

Vanessa pressed her hands to her mouth to silence her cry of heart-deep despair as she saw Mr. Swinton toss several coins on the table. Sir Wilbur grumbled, then followed suit. Ross's satisfied smile as he scooped them up told her the heinous truth. She meant nothing to any of these men other than the chance to win a pot.

"When will the wedding bells toll the death of your bachelor life?" Sir Wilbur persisted. A sly grin was taut on his lips. "Or shall you take yourself a wife and continue your ways? The lady is clearly unhappy here in Town. Wed her, get her with an heir to your title, and send her off to the country alone."

"You have my life all mapped out for me," Ross answered. "It is most convenient to have friends who care so much about my well-being. Or could it be that you wish to win back these coins?"

"As Franklin boasted too soon, *you* will have no need of these few pennies now that Vanessa Wolfe and the Wolfe fortune are yours," came Swinton's answer. "We are stuffing a fat pig in the tail by paying off this wager."

Hearing Ross's triumphant laugh, Vanessa fled. She could listen to no more. How could a man she had believed loved her treat her heart in such a cavalier manner?

She avoided the ballroom. Tears scorched her face, and she would let no one learn of her shame. No one, but the three men who had considered her to be of such small value that they were willing to make a May game of her.

She closed her eyes as she dropped to a settee in an empty room at the back of the house. Eveline must have learned of the wager and had tried to warn her. It was too late, for she had swallowed Ross's clanker. Hiding her face in her hands, she surrendered to tears at her betrayal by the one man she had dared to trust.

Chapter Fourteen

Vanessa said nothing to Ross as she loosened the ribbons to her bonnet in the foyer of her aunt's house. The betrothal ball had, at long last, reached its ignoble end. She wished she could disavow the truth, but Ross's laugh as he collected his winnings, which seemed more important to him than her heart, rang through her memory. It was a reminder that his love was only goat's wool.

Once she had been able to stop the flood from her eyes, she had washed her face and returned to the ballroom. Avoiding Sir Wilbur and Mr. Swinton had been simple, for they must have left immediately after their conversation with Ross. She doubted if anyone had noted her long silences and, if they had, she was sure they would have labeled it wedding nerves. She had danced with many of the guests, but had managed to avoid suffering through a waltz with Ross. If she had been in his arms, her pretense and her poise would have been shattered.

Aware of Quigley, an ever-vigilant watchdog, waiting in the shadows, she said, "Good night, Ross." She did not meet his gaze. The sweet fires in his eyes might lure her into forgiving him for toying with her as if she was no more important than the turn of a card.

He stroked her arm in a gentle invitation to the rapture she had believed was genuine. "Must you go so soon? I thought we might have a glass of wine for a private celebration. I had not guessed I would be prevented from saying more than a score of words to you all evening by those drearily cheerful well-wishers. Are you so tired you cannot spend a few minutes with your fiancé?" His soft laugh sent warm ripples through her.

She suppressed them. That she should be thrilled by the sound of his voice when he had betwattled her added to her shame and anguish. She had been a cabbage-head to believe him once. She must not again.

"I am quite fatigued." It was the truth. She was tired of his deceptions.

"That is no surprise. A full evening following the distressing news I brought you this afternoon is enough to sap anyone."

She almost asked him what he was speaking about, then realized she had forgotten Corey's misery while she suffered her own. "I have had worse days."

"I know, but I wish you never had to abide another." He brushed a strand of hair away from her cheek, and she flinched at his beguiling touch. His volatile expression became a frown. "You are as skittish as a spring lamb. What is wrong?"

"I told you. I am fatigued."

He seemed to accept her swapper. And why not? *She* had never been false with him, save hiding the truth of her hopes for Corey. Even that, she had revealed to him.

"May I come by to take you for a ride in the Park tomorrow after my meeting with Lord Liverpool?" He tipped her chin up with a single finger, so she could not avoid his eyes. His smile had not changed, but she asked herself why she would expect it to. He never had been honest with her. "I thought we might ride along the Serpentine again, but where we shall not be interrupted by troops of soldiers and children."

Stepping away, she said, "I am so exhausted, Ross. I think I shall stay late abed."

"I shall not call until three." She heard his amusement as he went on, "By exactly two, Mrs. Downing will be clattering her carriage through the Square, so sleep shall be impossible." He grew serious again. "I hope to have something to tell you after my meeting with Lord Liverpool, but do not be disappointed if it takes a few days for even the Prime Minister to obtain the intelligence we need."

"If you call here—"

"I would as lief that no one but you and me knew the course of my conversation with the Prime Minister."

"Aunt Carolyn—"

"Has too many friends who delight in gobbling like brainless geese. I feared Penelope Downing would explode before our betrothal was announced." Taking her fingers, he pressed them to his cheek. "Say you will ride with me in the Park tomorrow afternoon."

"Yes," she whispered, willing to accede to almost anything to have him be gone. In another moment, all on end, she might throw herself into his sturdy arms and beg him to soothe her with his bewitching kisses. He was sure to repeat her own words back to her, reminding her that eavesdropping was a deplorable habit. Yet if she had not chanced to hear the damning conversation, she would be ignorant of Ross's true reason for winning her heart.

She should demand that he be honest with her, but she was afraid he would be. That would complete the defilement of her dreams. *Not tonight,* she told herself. *Not yet.*

"Are you sure you are suffering from just fatigue?" he asked when she drew away.

His concern nearly broke through the thick wall of her pain, but she simply said, "I need time to come to terms with all I have learned today."

His fingers stroked her shoulder. Bending to place a kiss on the downy skin beneath her ear, he chuckled when she gasped involuntarily. She tried to submerge the delight his touch invoked, but it was impossible. He was a profligate, who knew so well how to twist a woman's heart into believing him when he lied with a hatchet, but she loved him.

She whispered another good night and scurried up the stairs. Although she was tempted to look back, she resisted. She must find some way of ending this betrothal, which would be easier to put aside than the pain eating at her heart.

Sending Leale away, Vanessa pulled out the tear-stained letter from the bottom drawer as she had so many nights. "Corey, he lied about loving me. Was he as false about helping to find you?" She lowered the letter to her lap. "I trusted him as I dared trust no one else, but he proved that I was a noodle. But I shall not be a noodle again, nor shall I be diverted from searching for you until you are home for good and all. Never again."

The gray light of morning had barely peeked over the houses on the eastern side of the Square when Eveline burst into Vanessa's room. Still dressed in her nightgown and her muslin wrapper, the redhead asked, "Did I wake you?"

Vanessa almost laughed. Her one attempt to escape her anguish in sleep had left her in the midst of a nightmare nearly as horrifying as the truth. She had used the night to map out what she must do next. Although the answer had been simple, she had sought to discover a more uncomplicated way to bring her shattered dreams to fruition. She had found none, so she had the choice of doing what she must . . . or letting her brother die at the hands of Boney's soldiers.

Standing with a rustle of the green crêpe gown she had put on more than an hour before, she motioned for her friend to sit by the window. "You did not wake me."

Eveline perched on the very edge of the chair and was silent while Vanessa dropped to the window seat. She wrung her hands until her knuckles bleached. "I have been grappling with my conscience all night, and I can bear it no longer. I must speak with you as I should have last night. Oh, dear, how can I say this?"

"You find the idea of me marrying Ross repulsive." Vanessa did not make it a question. There was no need, because she knew Eveline better than she knew herself. Certainly better than she knew her heart, which had led her so foolishly into this predicament.

"Vanessa, I was so thrilled for you until last night. I wanted you to be as happy as I am with Edward. But then I heard about . . ." She shivered.

"I know what you have heard. Do not berate yourself that you had no idea of it before last night. It was—to say very the least—a surprise." She stared across the Square and saw little as fog obscured everything beyond the walkway. Nothing was clear any longer. Corey was alive, but a prisoner of this appalling war. Ross was dallying with her heart as it was rumored he had with so many others.

"I do wish you would reconsider this betrothal."

"You know as well as I do that breaking a betrothal is not something to be done lightly."

Eveline's eyes lit with green fire. "Then you *are* thinking of putting an end to it?"

"What bride has not had second thoughts?" Vanessa asked, looking away before Eveline could discern the depth of her pain.

"Please have second thoughts and third thoughts and more, Vanessa." Eveline's dressing gown whispered as she stood. "Edward was so distressed when we spoke of this."

"I am curious how he learned about Ross's plan when I remained as wise as Waltham's calf until last night."

Eveline put her hands on Vanessa's arms and brought her to face her. When Vanessa saw her sorrow mirrored on her friend's face, she struggled to restrain her tears. That Ross had played her false was crime enough. He should not have been allowed to hurt Eveline as well. She moaned as she thought of Aunt Carolyn's grief when she learned the truth.

"Edward and the viscount are friends of long standing." Eveline strangled on a sob. "I should as lief say they *were* friends of long standing. Last night, Edward said, if his fears are true, he hopes never to come face to face with the viscount again. I pray he gets his wish, for, on their next meeting, Edward might demand that the viscount name his friends for grass before breakfast in the Park."

"A duel? No!" Although Ross had speared her heart with his cruel antics, she did not want to imagine him dead or—more likely—ostracized because he had killed the earl.

"You must listen to this." Eveline urged her to sit.

"Eveline, talking of this helps nothing."

"I insist you listen to the whole."

Vanessa sighed and nodded. "If you must."

"I must." Eveline clasped her hands in front of her mouth as she thought deeply. Then, just when Vanessa was about to demand she get this over with, she said, "Edward and the viscount both belong to Brook's. When the viscount spent little time there during this Season, Edward became concerned. The viscount was seldom there last year, because of his mother's ill health. After she died, just after the beginning of last year's Season—"

"I did not know that." Vanessa blinked back tears while Eveline paced. How much else of himself had Ross hidden from her?

"—Edward expected, with the end of mourning, Lord Brickendon would resume his old habits of stopping into Brooks's regularly. Lord Brickendon still has patronized the club infrequently. Even when he came in, he avoided the gaming room. It is whispered that the viscount is about to leave the key under the door."

"Bankrupt?" Vanessa shook her head. "Impossible."

"Edward is beginning to ask questions among their mutual friends and business acquaintances, but he fears the viscount wishes to wed you solely for the Wolfe fortune."

"Impossible," she said again. "Ross knows that the fortune is not—" She faltered, not wanting to share, even with her bosom-bow, that Ross had reassured her that Corey was still alive. Then comprehension struck her. By telling her that he would assist in the search for her brother, he was keeping her from doing anything. Citing the slow rumblings of the government, he could delay giving her a definitive answer until after they wed and he could lay claim to her father's money. Would he do something that horrible? With a shudder, she knew, even if it was truth, that treachery seemed less despicable than his other subterfuge of betting on her heart with his friends. "Is this all you wanted to tell me last night?"

"All?" Eveline whirled, her face almost as ruddy as her hair. "You mean there is more?"

For the first time in her life, Vanessa lied to Eveline. She reassured her friend that she appreciated being told about what Lord Greybrooke had discovered. Nodding when Eveline said that the earl was searching for proof of the rumors and hoped to have something to tell them soon, Vanessa was glad when her friend left.

Sitting on the window seat again, Vanessa leaned her head against the cool glass. She had never guessed that happiness could be so fleeting.

Vanessa owed her aunt the duty of the truth. Now that she knew the truth, Vanessa needed have no worry about marrying the baronet, who was as culpable as Ross in this bizarre bet, to ensure her aunt's happiness, but she wanted Aunt Carolyn to learn of the truth from her instead of when she was upon the gad.

When Vanessa came with trepidation into the breakfast-parlor, her aunt poked at the newspaper. "See? Right here in the *Morning Chronicle?* The announcement of your betrothal. I have made an appointment with Madame deBerg. She will be coming here just before tea." She smiled, for the *couturière* seldom called on patrons at their homes. "We must make plans for your wedding trousseau."

"Aunt Carolyn," she said, gripping the back of one of the oak chairs, "I must speak to you of an important matter."

Folding the paper, the older woman shook her head. "I shall hear nothing about the wedding being held at Wolfe Abbey. I know it has been a tradition since the house was established in Good King Hal's time, but you shall have a wedding here in Town. By the elevens, half of our intended guests have never been so far from London." With a wag of her finger, she stood. "Do not look at me like a forlorn kitten. You must listen to my experience in these matters."

"But, Aunt Carolyn—"

"Victor is calling within the hour, and I must look presentable."

"So early? But, Aunt Carolyn, I must speak with you about—"

"Cut line, Vanessa!" she said with more fervor than Vanessa had expected. "Now that I have you settled, I can think of my own life. Did you think that I would sit on the shelf forever?" Coming around the table, she kissed Vanessa's cheek. "I wish only to be as happy as you must be right now."

"Aunt Carolyn, this is important."

"Of course, Vanessa. I—" The clatter of carriage wheels slowing in front of the house added pretty color to Aunt Carolyn's face. "That must be Victor. Do go and talk with him while I get my pelisse." She paused by the door and smiled. "My dear, I promise you we shall have time to talk about all these important details many times before your wedding." The ruffles on the bottom of her light blue gown bounced as she hurried from the room.

Vanessa went to a window to watch Captain Hudson emerging from his carriage. Writhing fingers of fog were losing their grip on the cobbles, and she could see the shadow of the houses on the other sides of the Square. She closed her eyes to the familiar sight and turned from the window as she heard Quigley greeting the captain.

"Good morning, my lady," Captain Hudson said with a genuine smile as Vanessa entered the foyer.

"Aunt Carolyn will be here directly."

"Then I shall take the opportunity to say again that I wish you every happiness in your marriage to the viscount." He put one booted foot on the lowest riser and leaned on the bannister. His blond hair caught fire in the light from the candles overhead.

Without a preamble, she said, "Captain Hudson, I would like to see the reports of my brother's disappearance."

His nonchalance vanished as he straightened. Shock raised his voice. "My lady, surely you must realize that such reports can be seen only by the eyes of our military leaders."

"I want to know the truth about the events of that day."

"That is impossible."

Taking a slow breath, she asked, "Could *you* see them?"

"No, he cannot." Vanessa looked up the stairs to see her aunt coming toward them. Aunt Carolyn patted the captain's arm gently, but her lips were tight with irritation as she turned to her niece. "Vanessa, I thought I had made it clear that you were to have nothing more to do with this senseless, worthless search for your brother's remains."

"For my brother! He is not dead!"

"Vanessa!" Her aunt gripped her arm. "Child, you must put this madness from your head. It shall ruin your life. I shall hear no more of it. Nor will you pester Victor with your cockle-brained demands, or—"

Knowing she sounded like a petulant child, but not caring, Vanessa demanded, "Or what? What can you hold over my head now that I have done as you wished and arranged to leg-shackle myself to Ross?" She nearly strangled on the angry words.

Aunt Carolyn did not answer her. Instead, she said to the overmastered captain, "Excuse her, Victor. I believe she is overwrought from the excitement of the past few days. Once she has rested, she will be much her winsome self again."

Captain Hudson glanced back at Vanessa as he let Aunt Carolyn herd him out of the house. Seeing Quigley coming into the foyer, Vanessa did not wait to see his chastising frown at her sharp words to her aunt. She rushed up the stairs.

New tears added to the ones already clogging her eyes. Clenching her hands, she acknowledged the truth. She could wait no longer for anyone else to help her. She would do what must be done . . . now . . . alone.

Vanessa heard the chiming of the tall-case clock as she opened her chamber's door. In one hand, she carried the letter she had written, in the other, a small satchel. She could not take more, for that would garner attention she wanted to avoid. Keeping the satchel hidden beneath her full cloak of blue Vigonia cloth, she descended to the foyer.

It was two. Ross would be calling before the hour was over to take her for a ride. By then, she must be far from London. Deceit troubled her, but Ross had been deceitful from the first. If she wished to salvage even a small part of her happiness, she must do this.

The few words of the note to Ross played through her head.

Meet me at Madame deBerg's shop. It is on Bond Street near Mr. Willoughby's apothecary. My appointment will be completed by half-past three.

She had not signed it, not wanting to put her name to such a blatant plumper.

"The carriage is waiting, my lady," Quigley said as she crossed the foyer. "Lady Mansfield will wish to know when you expect to return."

Vanessa hated the tears that billowed into her eyes when she discerned that the butler was concerned about her going out alone. More than anyone, she loathed being false with him, for he had never failed to be honest with her.

"Tell Aunt Carolyn I may be late for the appointment

she has set with Madame deBerg." She longed to tell
him more, but she could not. If he suspected the truth,
he would prevent her from leaving. Holding out the
note, as if it was unimportant, she asked, "Will you give
this to Lord Brickendon?"

"If you are expecting his lordship—"

"I must hurry, or I shall be late." She rushed out the
door, so she did not have to tell him another out-and-
outer.

The tiger assisted her into the carriage and nodded
when she instructed the coachman to take her to Madame deBerg's shop. Sitting back against the thick cush-
ions, she stared at the familiar front of her aunt's house.
The immensity of what she was about to attempt struck
her, stealing her breath, but not for a moment did she
consider turning back. It was time to go forward with
her life. She would not return to Grosvenor Square
without her brother.

When they reached Madame deBerg's shop, Vanessa
did not alight from the carriage. She asked the tiger to
have the coachman come to speak to her. She noted the
dandies strolling along the street and wanted to avoid
any chance of a confrontation with the Bond Street
Loungers, who held the street as their own territory during the afternoon. The brilliantly dressed gabies made a
great cake of themselves, but their pranks were bother-
some.

"Yes, my lady?" asked Scoville with a tip of his tall
hat. "Did you wish to speak with me?"

"I assume these horses are fresh."

"Yes, my lady." The coachman's brow threaded, cak-
ing the dust and soot that had come up off the street.

"They are strong?"

"The best of the stable, my lady. On my word, the
black can—"

Vanessa had no interest in hearing a litany of the horse's genealogy and talents. "I wish to go to Dover."

"Dover?" he gasped.

"Immediately."

"Dover?" he asked again, glancing uneasily at the lad on his right. "Today?"

"At once, Scoville. You do know the way?"

"Y-y-yes, my lady." He aimed a hand at the boy's ear and growled an order for the tiger to get back into his place at the rear of the carriage.

Vanessa ignored the small voice in her head. She must not give anyone a chance to persuade her to give up her mad determination to sneak into France and arrange to free Corey. Otherwise she might accede to their good sense. She was queer in her attic to attempt this, but she would not turn back when she was sure no one else cared about Corey as she did.

And when she had no one who cared for her as much as he did.

No one at all.

Chapter Fifteen

Once Vanessa's carriage had left London behind, the fog dissolved into mist, then to rain that fought its way past the curtained windows of the carriage to soak Vanessa's cloak. The cheerless countryside was brightened by their arrival at the cathedral city of Rochester. She considered calling for a stop at the Crown. The fine hostelry was known even in London, and, for that reason, she did nothing to stay Scoville's hand from the whip. They would have to stop for the night, but not in such a well-known place. If they could reach Chatham before they paused, they could reach the docks of Dover before the next night's high tide had the smugglers underway.

Vanessa kept her satchel close and hoped no knight of the pad would set his men upon her carriage. The bag contained what money she had and her mother's diamond necklace. She was not sure how much an interloper would demand in exchange for taking her across the Channel, but she had to be certain she had enough money to buy Corey's freedom and get them back to England.

She tried to make plans, but her eyes wore lead manacles on each lash. Each time she blinked, she found it more of an effort to reopen her eyes. A night without sleep was exacting its price on her. She drew aside one of the leather curtains, hoping she could stay awake by watching the sights they passed. An icy wind and driving rain forced her to lower it again.

She slumped against the seat, which rattled with the roughness of the feather-bed lane. Her excitement had disintegrated into grim resolve. Nothing now must be allowed to turn her back from rescuing her brother and begging his forgiveness for the words that haunted her sleep. Then they would go home to Wolfe Abbey, leaving behind only her illusions of finding a man she could love and trust as a casualty of what would be her sole Season in Town.

Finally she could fight her exhaustion no longer. Telling herself she must be rested by the time she reached Dover and truly began her adventure, she gave herself to sleep.

The carriage slowed. Half asleep, Vanessa noted the change in the tempo of the horses' iron shoes upon the road. Not a dirt road, but cobbles, for the noise was sharp. With a smile, she nestled more deeply into the comfort of the seat and thought about the comfortable bed she would hire when Scoville halted the carriage in the yard of a fine inn here in Chatham.

Another sound intruded on her. A low thud resounded near her ear. She considered opening her eyes, but she was too enmeshed in sleep to let the curious sound draw her back into the world.

Rain, she told herself. It must be the patter of raindrops into puddles in the street. Instead of waking, she would as lief stay in the satisfying sweetness of her dreamworld. She did not want to escape the dream where her brother stood nearby as she was warm in Ross's embrace. That could be just a dream. She would find Corey, but she must never let her heart be betrayed again.

When the pattern of the storm's thunder never changed, her curiosity refused to be ignored. She opened her eyes to discover that, although the sky was gray, night's darkness had not yet arrived. But, if it was not dark, they could not have reached Chatham yet. What—?

Her unuttered question vanished from her head as warm lips covered hers. As her dream came to life, she slid her hands up a worsted coat to encircle broad shoulders. The lips became more demanding, and she surrendered to them, wanting to give every bit of herself to the ecstasy.

Suddenly Vanessa pulled away. She stared in disbelief at Ross, who was grinning at her like a fool. "You should not be here!" she cried, not caring how silly her words sounded.

"True." His hand cupped her chin and brought her lips to his again. When she drew back, he laughed. "It appears I have compromised you, Vanessa, by my un-chaperoned company in your carriage. I am afraid I shall have no choice but to buckle myself to you."

"No!" Her mind was clearing from the tendrils of sleep. "I do not want to marry you. Not now. Not ever."

His smile dropped into a forbidding frown. Folding his arms over the front of his double-breasted, black wool redingote, he set one Hessian on the opposite knee. Not fooled by his easygoing pose, she regarded him with an expression as uncompromising.

"This is, indeed, a surprising announcement," he said in a tone so calm she could have almost believed he was indifferent. A single glance at his eyes, which blazed with rage, warned her to caution. "Surprising in lieu of the fact we announced our plans to our friends last night."

"So we did, but I fear I have distressed my bosom-bows with our announcement. In light of that, I have reconsidered your offer of marriage."

"Without so much as a reasonable explanation?" When she hesitated, he added sharply, "You owe me that much, Vanessa."

Knowing he was right, but fearing if she said much more her tears would fall to add to her humiliation, Vanessa turned to look out the window and gasped when she realized the beau-traps she had heard beneath the horses' hoofs belonged to Bond Street. "What are we doing in London? I was going to—"

"Meet me at Madame deBerg's shop, so it is somehow just that you would open your eyes just as we are passing it."

"But I cannot be in London. I was going—"

Ross grasped her shoulders and brought her to look at him. His eyes narrowed with the fury that tightened his lips until he nearly spat each word at her. "Imagine my surprise and consternation when I arrived at Madame deBerg's shop to discover the *modiste* was to come to your aunt's house before tea. It took me only a short time to convince Quigley to blow the gab of where I might find Lady Mansfield. She shared my astonishment at your subterfuge, and I left her in a pool of tears while I chased you." His face became as hard as sculptured stone and his voice as unfeeling. "You need to be cut for the simples. What in blazes did you think you were doing?"

Easing out of his grip, Vanessa clasped her fingers to keep him from seeing how they trembled as she met his gaze without flinching. "Me? I would venture you are the one suffering from hey-go-mad humors if you have ridden after me only to ask such a question."

"You're correct. I am twice over a thick to come chasing after you to prevent your fool's quest."

"Quest? I fear you are mistaken, my lord. I was enjoying a ride in the country."

"Your man says you are on your way to Dover, as I suspected when no one knew where you might be. You are a poor liar. You bite off each word as if it was distasteful, which it should be." He caught her hand and held it when she tried to pull away. "Good fortune offered me her favor when I discovered you so soundly asleep that you did not know I had joined you on your return journey to London."

"I have no wish to return to Town."

"You would as lief go to France. Blast it, Vanessa! You must be a paper-skull to trot blithely into that maelstrom. What could you do in France beyond ending up in circumstances as dire as those of Lord Wulfric's?"

Her voice broke. "You learned something else about Corey from Lord Liverpool?"

Instead of answering, Ross asked, "Did you think I would let you flee like this? Your aunt is waiting—no doubt, having a *crise de nerfs* for you while her abigail gets the burnt feathers—at her house."

"Aunt Carolyn never has a *crise de nerfs*. We Wolfe women would not—"

"Ever show an ounce of sense," he interrupted yet again. "I am taking you back home where you belong."

"Where I belong is with my brother."

"Have you lost every bit of wits you ever possessed?" Sorrow clamped around each word he spoke in a near whisper. "Why didn't you come to. me? I am your fiancé." He laughed with raw pain. "At least, I thought I was when I set out to halt you."

Vanessa sat in glum silence. Her grand plan had ended in the bitter ashes of the ruin of her dreams, but she could not give up. As the carriage came to a stop before her aunt's house, she swallowed her tears as she recalled her vow never to come back here until she returned with her brother.

Ross opened the door. Getting out, he held up his hand. Vanessa saw—from the edge of her eye—the furious expression on her coachman's face as he jumped down from the box. Scoville did not want a Wolfe to submerge her will to another's commands.

"Are you going to sit forever in the carriage, Vanessa?"

"If you would step aside and close the door, I could continue on my journey."

To Scoville, Ross asked with an adder's tongue, "What say you, coachee? Do you wish to see your lady a guest of Napoleon's soldiers?"

The coachman dug his toe between the cobbles as he mumbled, " 'Tweren't right for her to go in the first place, but—"

Ross snapped, "Listen to him if you will not listen to me."

She recognized defeat, but it would not be her companion for long. Somehow—she had no idea how—she would obtain her brother his freedom. Yet her urgency to find out what Ross might have learned about Corey overmastered every other consideration.

With regal disdain, Vanessa allowed Ross to assist her to the walkway. She watched as Scoville untied Ross's horse's reins from the back of the carriage, but she did not pause as she walked to the door. Ross would not leave until he was sure she was fully acquainted with her folly.

Quigley opened the door. Aunt Carolyn burst through to throw her arms around Vanessa. Her sobs sliced into Vanessa as her aunt begged her to forgive her the harsh comments earlier.

"I forgive you," she said to assuage her aunt's grief.

"Your words did not hurt me. I knew how anxious you were for this wedding."

"Finally you are speaking sense," Ross interjected. He took Vanessa's arm in his strong hand. When she stared at him in disbelief at his cavalier behavior, he said to her aunt, "Lady Mansfield, I beg your indulgence and ask you to allow me a moment to speak to your headstrong niece in private. Perhaps I might convince her to explain why she took this maggot in her head to go to France."

Amazement and horror widened Aunt Carolyn's eyes. "France? She was going to France?"

"Need the two of you ignore me as if I were a naughty child?" Vanessa demanded.

"When you have acted the limb, you should expect to be treated as one," returned Ross. When she flinched at the insult, he looked back to Aunt Carolyn, "My lady?"

Wringing her hands, Aunt Carolyn said, "You may use my sitting room, my lord."

Quigley took Vanessa's damp cloak. "There is wine in there, my lady. If you would like something warm, I can have Cook heat some rum for you."

"That is not necessary," she answered in a choked voice as she saw how he avoided her eyes.

"My lord?" Quigley asked Ross. "Would you like—?"

"I said it wasn't necessary!" she said with rare heat.

The butler arched his brows, but said nothing. He gave a half bow in her direction and, taking her cloak and Ross's coat, backed out of the foyer. Aunt Carolyn rushed after him.

Vanessa considered balking at Ross's assumption that she would go meekly with him up the stairs. A single glance at the hard line of his jaw warned her that, if she hesitated, he would toss her over his shoulder like a farmer carrying a calf.

He closed the door of the sitting room. A lone lamp

lit the shadowed room. When she heard the latch click, she shivered, knowing he would not let her leave until he had wrested from her every answer he wanted. Indignation straightened her back as she sat primly on the rosewood settee. *He* had no cause to be infuriated when he had blown upon her at every turn. That he expected honesty from her when he had lathered her with swack-ups was the ultimate conceit.

Ross crossed the room to the sideboard where a decanter and glasses waited. Mud, that was splattered on his breeches and had ruined the sheen of his boots, told of his wild ride to catch her carriage. His coattails snapped on every step, accenting his unspoken fury.

"I think I am due an explanation," he said with the feigned equanimity he had used in the carriage.

"I fail to understand why any is necessary." Splaying her hands across the lap of her wrinkled gown, she continued to regard him with her most severe expression. If her composure faltered, even for a moment, she feared it would forever. "You clearly knew my destination. Can there be any question of my purpose in going to Dover and on to France?"

"Only that you are determined to suffuse yourself in arrant nonsense." He put his hands on the back of a chair as he tried to pin her in place with a glare. "I should anoint you thoroughly, but I have never raised my hand to a woman. Maybe I am a goosecap for not letting you fry in your own grease."

"My lord, I—"

His eyes became dusky slits. " 'My lord'? Can I believe that you have brought not only our betrothal to an end, but have spiflicated our friendship as well?"

"*My lord,*" she repeated more forcefully, "I left you a message to let you know that I would not be going for a ride with you in the Park. As I have told you that our betrothal is over, that was all that needed concern you. My destination was not your bread and butter."

"You left me lies apurpose."

"You are an odd one to be accusing another of being false." All her grief focused in her voice as she cried, "I thought I could trust you!"

"You can."

"No, for you have used your fascinating arts to convince me to let you play booty with my heart. I shall never believe another word you speak."

Ross straightened, and she resisted recoiling from the wrath tightening his face. "So you have said before. I have lied to you? I would like you to illuminate me on that statement, if nothing else."

"I know of your wager with those sons of a sow you call your friends." Vanessa raised her chin in a weak pose of defiance. "What you did not wager on, my lord, is that I would discover the truth of your abhorrent game."

He went back to the sideboard. She closed her eyes as she was filled with renewed pain. Even to the moment she had confronted him with the truth, she had prayed Ross would disavow her accusations, telling her that her eavesdropping ears had been mistaken. Now she knew the truth. The wager had been real.

Pouring a glass of wine, he brought it to her. With an icy smile, he said, "I have not lied to you before, Vanessa, and I shall not now. Yes, I wagered with Franklin and Swinton that I would win your heart and your hand before the Season came to an end."

Her fingers tightened around the stem of the glass until its jeweled facets cut into her palm. Standing, she put the glass on a table and took a steadying breath. "I appreciate your honesty, my lord, no matter how belated it might be. I trust you will find mine as welcome. I ask you to please leave my aunt's house and not return."

"If that is your wish."

"It is."

He tipped her face toward him. When she quivered at the luscious warmth of his touch, he said softly, "Speak the truth, Vanessa, for I tire of the huffs and puffs of your half-truths. Do you truthfully wish me to leave and never return? Do you wish to return to your hopeless, empty life? I have seen the fires burning in your eyes and tasted the heat on your honeyed lips. Can you forget—can you truthfully forget what we have savored?"

Vanessa turned away. Her face was sure to expose the truth that her heart had not changed. It cherished the love that she wished to give only to Ross, but she could not ignore the question that thudded through her on every beat. She loved Ross, but not once had he spoken of love.

"What we have had is over, for it was based on balms." Still not looking at him, she said, "It is in the air, my lord, that you are mucked out."

"What does the state of my pockets matter to you?"

Taken aback by his calm question, she whirled to face him. "Could you have forgotten that, if Corey fails to return alive, I shall be one of England's richest women? A woman with a title that shall bring honor and prestige to your children?"

"Damn, Vanessa," he snapped, coming around the chair, so there was only open floor between them, "no matter what nonsense you have had your head filled with, I never intended to marry the mixen for the sake of the muck. Forget your father's blasted title and to perdition with that blunt!"

She recoiled from his fury. Even the Wolfe temper was dimmed by the rage burning in his eyes. Quietly, she said, struggling to keep her voice even, "You are the one who forgets yourself with such cant, my lord."

He gave a mocking bow in her direction. "Then I beg your pardon. And may I say that you have become blind to the truth? You discount what I say to you, so why should I tell you that you have listened unwisely to those who have reason to hurt you?"

"Eveline would never hurt me." She pressed her hands to her mouth when she saw how her answer stunned him. Her hand started to reach for him, but she pulled it back. Longing to ease his pain was want-witted when he was the source of hers.

"Miss Clarke has been carrying these bangers to you?" He locked his hands behind his coat and walked to the window. "I suppose that she heard these stories from her lover. Odd, that Edward would think—" He sighed, and she could not mistake the genuine regret in his voice. "You have had your revenge, Vanessa, if you yearned for me to suffer as you have, because I have in truth been wounded by one I believed to be a bosom-bow." Fury blazed again in his eyes as he faced her. "However, I have not betrayed you. I have just been aboveboard with you about that witless wager. Would I have been so forthright if I had wished to continue to bronze you?"

Slowly she sat and rubbed her numb fingers together. No matter how he might be twisting his words, she must be honest with him. "I do not know. I have no idea which of your words are on the square any longer."

He swore so viciously her face burned. Having no pity on her delicacy of mind, he crossed the room to take her hands and bring her back to her feet. "You have been seeking what you want for so long that you cannot see what you need is here in front of you."

"And you are what I need, my lord?" She lifted her chin again, so the tears in her eyes did not course along her cheeks. "Do I need a rogue who risks my heart on the turn of a card?"

"You need me."

Vanessa was astonished when he added nothing more. Then she realized there was nothing more to be said. This was the truth. Picking up her glass, she sipped slowly, but the wine's warmth could not lessen the chill within her. She could not make her dreams come true by wistful thinking.

"Lord Brickendon," she said, finding it ever more difficult to keep her voice from quivering, "I bid you good day."

As she walked toward the door, he said to her back, "Perhaps before you have me ejected as you did Franklin, you might wish to hear what I learned from the Prime Minister."

She turned. "I wish to hear it all."

"All? There is no all." He took a deep drink of his wine and leaned his elbow on the back of her aunt's favorite chair. "There is only the same. The government fears making any bargains with Napoleon at this juncture. They believe the war will come to an end before the year does, although I think they are being optimistic. If they were to strike a deal with Boney, the English people would be furious."

"Even to rescue a fellow Englishman?"

He sniffed with disdain. "My dear Vanessa, there is nothing the English love better than a martyr. No one denies Nelson was a hero at Trafalgar, but how much more acclaim he received because he died while protecting English interests! Becoming a dead hero will enshrine your brother in history along with Nelson and Richard the Third's nephews in the Tower. Alive, he is only a bother to this government. I have pestered and exasperated every man I know in the government, but they seem as obdurate as you."

"Thank you for your help." She reached for the latch.

"So what will you do now?"

Vanessa owed him no reply, for he had not apologized for the wager nor had he defended himself by speaking of love. Yet she said before she could stop herself, "I have not decided, but I shall not sit on my hands and weep while my brother faces death."

"What you mean is that you will sneak away again to try to rescue him." He finished his wine, then put the glass on the sideboard. When he faced her, his expression was as blank as Quigley's. "You leave me no choice. I shall go to France and dig your brother out of whatever hole that dirty Corsican has imprisoned him in."

"*You* are going to France?"

He shrugged. "Why not? I was looking for something to entertain me for the rest of the Season. Fool that I was, I thought I would find the wager and your company diverting. That has come to an end, so why shouldn't I cross the Channel in your place?"

"But Corey is *my* brother."

"A fact no one contests." He laughed coldly as he closed the distance between them until she had to tilt her head back against the door to look up into his eyes. She was aware of every inch of his strong body, although he did not touch her. "My dear Vanessa, you have been looking for a knight of yore from the moment your aunt fired you off. A dashing air-dreamer who will risk his last breath to obtain you your heart's desire. So often I have jested with you on that very matter, little perceiving that you would settle for nothing less. Now I stand before you ready to embark on this cocklebrained crusade."

"No."

His eyebrows rose in an unspoken contradiction.

"It is my place to get Corey," she said quietly. "It is right that I risk my life for my brother."

"You cannot believe that I will allow you to send

yourself on a quest that will take you into Napoleon's domain?"

"I shall not argue with you about the sense of this journey, but the fact remains that *I* should go."

He settled his hands on her shoulders. "And the fact remains that I shall not let you go."

His hands did not imprison her. He would release her if that was her wish. It was not. When he drew her to him, so her head rested over the gentle thump of his heart, two tears edged along her cheeks. She still was unsure of anything about him. She wanted to trust him as she had wanted nothing else in her life. Even her yearning to apologize to her brother was dimmed by her craving to trust Ross.

Softly she said, "If you are going, I must go with you."

"You?" He stepped back and edged her face with his broad hands. "Are you truly off the hooks? I shall be blowed before I allow you to cross the Channel into the hell of war."

She put her hands over his. Sorrow stabbed her as she drew them away. "Ross, you have no choice. If you do not take me with you, I shall go alone."

"You are a blasted stubborn woman." He strode across the room. Pouring himself another glass of wine, he raised it to his lips. He put it down without taking a drink. Slowly he turned to look at her. "Very well. It is clear I cannot bring you to your bearings on this. Perhaps you are right. We may have a better chance of reaching him and setting him free if we work together. You will have to trust me, Vanessa."

"I will try."

The glint returned to his eyes. "I suppose I can ask for nothing more. Meet me at the Appletree Inn on the Dover Road by six tomorrow morning. The Mail coach leaves from there for Dover." He lifted his glass in her direction. "May good fortune continue to grant both of us her favors."

Chapter Sixteen

A stable boy ran forward as Vanessa entered the stable yard behind the Appletree Inn. Grinning, he scratched one side of his ragged shirt.

"Take yer 'orse fer ye, milady?" His words whistled through gaps in his teeth.

She gave him the reins, but held her breath. The lad must have been sleeping in droppings, for he stank as much as the stable behind him. Handing him a coin, which she had taken from her purse before she entered the inn's yard, because she wanted no one to suspect how much money she might be carrying, she motioned for him to take her bag from the back of the horse.

Searching the inn's yard, Vanessa was startled it was so empty. An upended wagon sat in the thick shadows below the tiers of galleries on the building's four stories. Stacked next to it were barrels and bundles wrapped in canvas. Something dripped on her head, and Vanessa looked up to see one of the inn's denizens hanging wet linen over the uppermost railing. She took a step back, but was careful to avoid the trough beside the pump.

She had expected to see dozens of people and packages waiting to board the Mail. Squinting, she tried to determine where the coach could be hidden in the murky stable.

"I am looking for a gentleman," she said when the stable boy handed her the small bag.

"Anyone in particular?" He eyed her with renewed interest. "The Appletree ain't no academy, milady, but there be gents who ain't really no gents. They always be lookin' fer a bona roba."

Vanessa drew the length of her blue pelisse closer to her as she said, "Young man, I am no Cyprian! I am looking for a gentleman of my acquaintance."

"Then why can't ye see fer yerself if 'e be 'bout the yard?"

Owning to the uselessness of this conversation and the fact the lad was right, Vanessa pointed to a half-open door set beneath the inn's trademark sign of a blossoming apple tree. "May I wait in there?"

"The master don't take to naturals usin' the inn without givin' 'im a cut."

"I told you I am not—Oh, cut line!"

The lad laughed as Vanessa hurried to the door. She peeked in, but the room beyond the door was lost even more to shadows than the stable. Ross had said he would meet her at the inn, not inside it, but she took a tentative step inside, although it went against her pluck.

The scent of sour ale mixed with the odors from the stable. Rushes crunched beneath her feet, but she doubted if they had been changed since the beginning of the year. Each step raised more offensive smells until she feared she would gag.

When her eyes adjusted to the stygian bleakness of the room, she noted a keg set on a table at one end. Stained tankards hung from the low rafters, and a quartet of men, who sat near the table, were watching her with a variety of expressions from leering admiration to apathy. The man, with an indifferent expression, wore an apron, and she hoped he was the keeper of the inn.

She edged toward him, glad to keep a trestle table between herself and the man with the lustful grin.

" 'Elp ye?" grumbled the man in the apron. He glanced at her and away.

"Can you tell me where I should wait for the Mail for Dover?"

" 'Ere."

"Right here?"

He splashed water perfunctorily in a glass and placed it on a dirty shelf behind him. "In the yard be best. But ain't no use in waitin' now. It left."

"The coach has departed?" Vanessa put out a hand to steady herself, but pulled it back from the filthy table. "When?"

"Most of an hour past." He paused to fill another mug for one of the shadowy creatures. "If'n ye want to stay, ye need to order."

Vanessa was sure her stomach would rebel if she ate anything on one of these filthy tables. The reek of the dirty room blocked out the odor of the unwashed bodies, but added to the discomfort in her middle.

"How long before the next coach?"

"Midday."

"But that is too late. I need to get to Dover right away."

He shrugged with indifference, the sleeves of his shirt clinging to his thick muscles. "The coach leaves at midday. Ye stayin' or no?"

"Can I rent a carriage?"

" 'Ave to talk to them in the stables on that. I don't tend to carriages."

More laughter followed Vanessa as she went back out in the morning sunshine. Not just the laughter from the suck-pints inside, but the memory of Ross's deep laugh. The innkeeper's few words told her that Ross had bleared her eyes with her own trickery and must be in a fair way to Dover by now. By playing—with much more success—the prank she had tried to pull on him yesterday, he had managed to delay her from taking the Mail with him.

By the elevens, she would not let him spend the day chatting to his fellow riders about her gullibility! She had been a widgeon to trust him again, but she would show him that she would not be left behind.

"Boy!" Vanessa called.

"Yes, milady?" The stable boy popped out from behind the pump. "Can I 'elp ye?"

"I must rent a carriage."

"None to be let."

Vanessa frowned. "None?"

"It be let, milady."

"Then bring my horse."

" 'E be gettin' 'is feed now, milady."

With a sigh, she pulled another coin from her purse and dropped it into his hand. She had no idea where he hid it among his rags. With a tip of his cap, he urged her to wait while he got her horse.

By now, Aunt Carolyn might have discovered her absence. She could not return to Grosvenor Square for a carriage. There was no choice but to ride to Dover. She winced at the thought of traveling seventy miles on horseback, then smiled. If she galloped hell-for-leather, she would easily catch the Mail, unless some young blood had paid to drive it at a neck-or-nothing speed. Once she overtook the coach, she would insist that she be allowed to ride, even if she must sit in the rear box.

She gasped as her own thoughts scandalized her. No lady of quality rode in the rear box, but her reputation was of little import now. She was too close to finding Corey to turn back.

The lad brought her horse. Giving him her bag, she asked him to tie it in place again behind her saddle.

"Lady Vanessa!"

She whirled at the familiar voice and stared into the triumphant face of her tiger. The lad leapt from his horse and ran toward her.

"What are you doing here, Albert?"

"My lady, you must come back with me to Lady Mansfield's house. Bang-off!" He grabbed her horse's halter. "You mustn't delay."

"I am riding to Dover." She climbed onto the mounting block and settled herself into the saddle. Frowning when she saw Albert still held her horse, she said, "If you wish to ride with me, you may. If not, step aside."

He lowered his voice. "My lady, I urge you to come with me posthaste."

"I—"

"There are pad-thieves lurking here." He glanced toward the stable. "They're eyeing your horse and your purse. My lady, I beg you to come away from this place with me."

"How did you know to find me here?"

"The note from Lord Brickendon, my lady." Guilt lengthened his face. "He sent a note asking your aunt to send someone for you at the Appletree Inn by six this morning. Said he would be away from London for a few weeks, but would call when he returned. Thank goodness, Lady Mansfield found his note. Your aunt was ready to search all over Town for you when—"

Furiously, Vanessa said, "By all that's blue, that man vexes me! He vows to be truthful, then the next word out of his mouth is a lie."

"This was to be delivered to you, my lady. Lord Brickendon wanted you to have it straightaway."

Vanessa opened the slip of paper the tiger handed her and read:

My dearest Vanessa,

You have no reason to take heed of these words when you must believe that I have played you false yet again. If you recall, I told you only that the Mail leaves from the Appletree Inn, not that we would travel on it. I go to France alone. Do not follow, for I shall be gone from England before you reach Dover. Put your trust in me. I look forward to the hour when I watch you welcome your brother home. Until that hour, I remain

Your (I pray) trusted servant,

"Ross," she whispered and folded the page closed. Her gloved fingers lingered on it as she looked south toward the Dover Road. What had her determination to win Corey's freedom wrought? She should have guessed Ross would not be so easily persuaded by her high-handed demand that she accompany him across the Channel. Now he was facing the danger alone.

Bitter bile tainted her throat as she realized he was trying, by rescuing Corey, to recompense her for the pain he had caused with the wager. Yet, if Eveline was correct, Ross had nothing with which to bribe the French officials to release Corey.

Albert fidgeted, rubbing one foot against the back of his other leg. "My lady, we must return to the Square immediately. Lady Mansfield told me to tell you not to delay a moment."

Vanessa hesitated. There was no reason not to go to Dover as she had planned except that Ross had asked her to trust him. Did she? She turned her horse toward Grosvenor Square, knowing she must trust Ross completely . . . for the first and maybe, as he went into the midst of the war, for the last time.

* * *

Quigley threw open the door as Vanessa slid from the saddle. He rushed out without his coat. That the normally fastidious butler was so untidy surprised her more than anything else on this astonishing day.

"Is Aunt Carolyn ill?" she asked while they climbed the steps. She could think of nothing else that would send his mouth to jerking as if from a palsy.

"No." He kept his eyes averted. "Let me take your coat, my lady." He grabbed her bag from Albert and set it on the floor.

"Quigley!"

The butler's hands were trembling as he looked at her. She gasped when she saw happiness brightening his usually dour features. "He is here, my lady," he said in a near whisper.

"He?" Ross must have realized that he was a Tomnoddy to go to France alone. She would tell him in minute detail how furious she was with him for abandoning her in that disgusting inn's yard. She would chastise him for daring to bronze her with her own trick. She would urge him to tell her—without the harsh words they had spoken yesterday—the truth about the claims against him. She would—

"Nessa!"

Her eyes widened at the name she once had hated, then had despaired of ever hearing again. Only one person living called her that. Not Aunt Carolyn. Not Ross. Only—

"Corey!" she cried as she ran forward to fling her arms around her beloved brother. Sobbing against his neck, she clung to him, sure that if she released him, he would disappear as he had after so many dreams on so many nights.

"Gently, Nessa." He laughed. "Don't knock me to the floor and complete what Boney's lads failed to do."

She stepped back to see the scars of war etched into

him. His healthy color had bleached to a sickly, wan shade, and a patch concealed his right eye. She moaned when she saw that he leaned on a cane.

"Oh, Corey . . ."

"Have no pity for me," Corey cautioned her with the same determination she had heard when he argued with her and Papa that every able man had an obligation to fight for England. "Going was my choice, both to France and into battle that day."

"You could have died!"

"But I did not." He put his arm around her shoulders, and she gazed up at his beloved face. His smile was unchanged, and she knew that eventually she would learn to ignore the patch. Just to have him back . . .

"It must have been horrible."

"It was." He never had minced words to ease her feelings. "So often, the thought of my contrary sister waiting for me at home was the only thing that kept me alive. I knew you would never forget me. My thoughts went out to you every day. Did you think I would cock up my toes and free you from my funning?"

Vanessa did not wipe away the tears running along her face as they slowly climbed the stairs. She was astonished how well Corey could manage with his cane, but that thought was muted by what she had yearned to say since minutes after he had stormed out of Wolfe Abbey. "Corey, I am so sorry for what I said that last night before you left."

"You said?" He tweaked her nose as they reached the first floor where Aunt Carolyn was standing beside Captain Hudson. Their grins were so wide Vanessa wondered if they would leap from their faces. "What did you say, Nessa, that clearly has been plaguing you all these long months?"

"You don't remember?"

He shook his head, sending his too long black hair fall-

ing into his face. Pushing it aside, he said, "I remember
only how much I've wanted to apologize to you for saying that you were siding with Papa because you were
worried about having to manage the Abbey if he died before I returned."

"You said that?"

Limping into the sitting room, he dropped with a
grateful sigh into a chair. "We both said hateful things
that night. At least we can apologize to each other. I
cannot ever retract the words I made to Papa."

She took off her bonnet and knelt next to him. "Papa
prayed for you to come home alive. Some of his last
words were for you."

"Only *some* of his words?" His smile returned.

"You know his very last words were demands for the
reforms for the poor that he had harangued the Lords
for since before we were born."

He ruffled her hair. "Dear Papa. I am glad he never
changed. Nor have you, Nessa. Scaring old Aunt
Carolyn that way by piking off like a conveyancer trying to elude the Watch."

Aunt Carolyn came into the room and sat across from
him. " 'Old', am I, lad? I think you shall find me far
younger than you remember." She rose to kiss him
lightly on the forehead before sitting next to Captain
Hudson, who still smiled broadly. "Vanessa, if you had
not been so cork-brained as to take off as you did, you
would have been here when Corey came home. Why
you did something so jobbernowl just now when—"

"Corey is home," Vanessa finished, halting her aunt
from continuing the scold.

With a smile, he put his hand over his sister's. "Not
yet truly home. Do you long, as I do, for the draughty
hallways of Wolf Abbey?"

"We shall take a walk along the strand below the Abbey before the month is out."

Again his smile dimmed. "And I shall go to the churchyard and tell Papa that he was right. I was a paper-skull to run off to fight when I had no idea of what awaited me. I thought I would be a grand hero like those whose pictures hang in the gallery, but I was just a blithering block."

Aunt Carolyn squeezed his hand. "The important thing is that you are home, Corey. Today you must rest, but on the morrow, we must—"

"The first thing we must do," he said with an echo of the authority that had filled his father's voice, "is call upon Lord Brickendon. From what I understand, this homecoming would have been impossible without him badgering the Prime Minister."

"Ross?" Vanessa whispered. "Oh, my dear God, no!" Her joy had blinded her to the catastrophe yet waiting to happen. Sitting back on her heels, she pressed her hand to her lips and stared at the Square beyond the windows. Ross should be here to share their joy.

Corey must not have heard her because he continued, "Aunt Carolyn tells me that I shall come to know my savior well, for he is to become my brother-in-law. Don't you think that such a familial relationship would excuse us from calling upon him at such an unusual hour?"

"Ross is not at home." Vanessa saw her brother's brow knit at her faint answer. She rose, groping for the sofa, and carefully lowered her stiff body to it.

"What is wrong?" Corey asked. "Nessa, you have no more color in your face than in your best gown!"

"Ross is on his way to France to free you. He could be killed because I believed that he . . ." Her voice splintered into sobs.

"What's wrong?" Eveline rushed in with a flurry of white silk. "Corey!" She hugged him enthusiastically, motioned for her fiancé to come into the room, then turned to the others. When she realized that Vanessa was still crying, she said soothingly, "Happy tears will wash away the pain of those months of not knowing what was happening to your brother."

Vanessa raised her head and whispered, "Ross is on his way to France."

"To France?" Eveline's brow furrowed in bafflement. "To escape dun territory and his creditors?"

"Eveline!" gasped Vanessa and Lord Greybrooke at the same time.

The earl added in shock, "Didn't I ask you to say nothing of that?"

The redhead faced him defiantly. "I told only Vanessa. She needed to know that her fiancé is about to become a fallen angel."

"Bankrupt?" Aunt Carolyn shook her head. "I have heard no such talk about Lord Brickendon."

"Nor should you now," the earl answered with an remorseful smile. "I have no more than suspicions caused by my friend's peculiar behavior of late. When I mentioned them to Eveline and said I intended to discover what was amiss with Ross, she must have misunderstood."

"Then he isn't purse-pinched?" Eveline whirled to Vanessa. "I did not mean—"

"I do not care a rush if Ross is well-inlaid or a shagbag," Vanessa said, trying to restrain the endless flow of tears. Behaving out of hand had led to Ross risking his life needlessly. She could not let her tears now add to the disaster. She turned to her brother. "We must stop him."

"You are right. We cannot allow him to go to France. I shall not allow any man, especially the one who saved my life, endure what I had to." Corey stood awkwardly, but waved aside his sister's help. "If I leave immediately, I have a chance to halt him."

"I will ride with you," said the earl. "With all hands to the pump, the two of us can search the docks faster than you alone."

Captain Hudson rose. "I shall go with you as well, too." His lips tilted in a surprisingly abashed grin. "After all, it would not do for me to sit here like a cowhearted chucklehead while my future nephew-in-law heads into such jeopardy."

Vanessa gave her aunt a quick smile, but the time to rejoice about Aunt Carolyn's good news must be after Ross was safe. "I must go with you." She shivered as she recalled saying those same words to Ross.

"Nessa—"

"I shall not brangle with you about this, Corey." She gripped his hands. "Don't make me suffer again as I did while I waited and waited never knowing if you would come home. I must go with you."

Pride filled his eyes. "That you must." He put his hand on her shoulder. "We shall find him somehow, Nessa."

Chapter Seventeen

Rain streamed along the pier and congregated between every cobble. Shadows huddled next to bundles, which had been unloaded from one of the ships clinging to the long pier, but only a skinny dog moved through the storm. The stench of the city was muted as the smoke was washed away into the churning waters of the Channel.

Vanessa peered through the carriage window. She had wanted for sense when she allowed Corey to persuade her to remain in the carriage. Wringing her gloved fingers together, she wondered how long it would take them to find someone who might have seen Ross.

She looked back toward the city. The clanging of church bells marked the late hour and were a bleak reminder that they must meet Lord Greybrooke and Captain Hudson at the inn near the base of Castle Hill before the next hour was chimed. Through the rain, she could see little of the huge castle, save for a few lights kept for the guard, who patrolled Dover, which was closer to France than any other British city.

An uneven footfall came toward the carriage. Vanessa threw open the door.

"Sorry," Corey said when rain dripped from his greatcoat onto her cloak.

She gripped his arm, not caring about the wet. "Have you found Ross?"

"News of him." He hoisted himself into the carriage and reached forward to strike his hand against the roof. He called an order to take them to the inn. Sagging against the seat, he grimaced when more water poured from his cocked hat to his shoulders.

"What did you learn?"

He put his hand over hers, and she wondered how his fingers, which were soaked, could be warmer than hers. "Dear sister, if that lurcher I spoke with is to be believed, and I paid him enough to buy every truth he knows, Ross sailed an hour ago."

"Oh, no!" She turned away and put her hand to her mouth to muffle the sobs that had been battering at her lips during the long, rough ride from Town.

"This storm made the captain shove along." He sighed. "I was told by every sea-crab I met that no one can catch the smuggler Ross sailed with. He has eluded the authorities for years, both here and in France."

"We must sail after him."

"Impossible. Not a single captain would consider putting to sea in this blow."

Vanessa saw her despair mirrored in his eyes. "But, Corey, if we delay until the morrow, we may never be able to halt him."

"We must delay." He drew her head down to his shoulder. "There is nothing else we can do now, save praying that he will survive the French."

Corey insisted that Vanessa change into dry clothes before she joined the others in the dining room of the small inn. Too heart-weary for a dagger-drawing, she climbed the narrow, twisting stairs. When she bumped her head on the low ceiling, a sob burst from her. Her breath snagged on her aching heart as Ross's face burst into her mind. Had anyone ever been as much of a goosecap as Vanessa Wolfe? If she had trusted him— just this one more time—he would not be sailing to his death.

As she inched along the dark hallway, searching for the second door on the left and the room Corey had hired for her, she was consumed in remorse. She had seen how difficult it was for Ross to dismantle the brick wall around him to invite her to share his life, but she had acted as if his efforts meant nothing.

The door opened beneath Vanessa's cautious fingers. She stared at the fly-specked gray walls. An iron bed with a thick coverlet was set next to a stand holding an empty pitcher and bowl. A knock on the half-open door was her only warning before a broad woman bustled into the room. Rosy-cheeked, with her graying hair drawn back beneath a starched mobcap, the large woman carried a bucket of water.

She splashed it into the bowl and filled the pitcher as she said, "Mayhap it be none of my business, milady, but I was 'earin' what yer menfolk be sayin' down in the tavern. Ye lookin' fer a friend?"

Vanessa took off her bonnet and poked at the drenched flowers. They were all to pieces . . . just like her dreams. Tossing the hat onto the bed, she sat on the lumpy mattress. "We are looking for my fiancé, but we missed his sailing tonight. There is no hope of following him until the morrow, and that may be too late."

"La!" the woman said in a burst of sympathy. "Yer man be gone 'cross the Channel to those frogs?"

"Yes."

"Bad sort they be. So's I hear." Pulling a towel from beneath her apron, she put it on the stand and asked, "Does yer man speak that parleyvoo?"

"What—?" In spite of fear, Vanessa smiled weakly.

"Oh, you mean French. I have no doubt Ross has mastered French as he has everything else."

"Includin' yer heart." The old woman chuckled and backed toward the door. "Yer sup will be waitin' fer ye when yer ready fer it, milady."

Vanessa forced another smile, which lasted only until the door closed and she was left to confront her fearful thoughts. This was completely her doing. She wanted for sense as much as Sir Wilbur and was as manipulating as Mr. Swinton.

Going to the glass over the table, she saw fright clouding her eyes. Her fingers rose to brush her hair back from her face. They paused as she lowered her gaze from her own recriminations, but there was no escaping the truth. If she had been brave enough to believe her heart, which had urged her to believe Ross, she would be sitting, snug and happy, in her aunt's parlor as they toasted Corey's return with smuggled French brandy.

Hoping that Captain Hudson or Lord Greybrooke would have good news to share—although she could not fathom what it might be—Vanessa washed tearstains from her face and went down. She followed the sound of familiar voices to the other side of the narrow, stone corridor. Rafters crisscrossed the dining room from the huge hearth to the door. A pair of windows, with diamond mullions, were awash with rain. At one of the trio of long tables, her brother sat with the earl and Captain Hudson.

The men set themselves on their feet as she entered. Her opaque hopes collapsed when she saw their somber faces. They were silent while she walked across the narrow room to their table. Captain Hudson stepped aside to motion for her to take the sole chair.

"I found no one who was willing to set his boat upon the waves before the storm comes to an end," he said before she could ask what he had learned. He inclined his head toward the earl who was refilling his glass from a brandy bottle in the middle of the table. "His lordship had no better luck."

"Good fortune has kept her favors for Ross," Vanessa said softly. When her brother asked her what she had said, she was spared from answering by a door opening.

Aromas of a roasting joint preceded the innkeeper. The nearly bald man carried a huge platter in his thin arms. He offered Vanessa a smile as he set the platter with its steaming collection of meat and vegetables in front of her. "Milady, a glass of wine?"

"Yes." She nodded her thanks when a young girl set it beside the platter. Tempted to ask for the full bottle to sand away the rough edges of her pain, she listened while her brother spoke with their host.

"Bad blow," the innkeeper said. "Surprised any of the lads was willin' to set sail tonight. Yer friend must have a large purse of gold or the cap'n a burning greed to get his sea-coal from France. Some milord must be anxious for his brandy." He blanched. "Beggin' yer pardons, milords. Meant nothin' by it, I did."

Corey stabbed a slice of the juicy meat and set it on the trencher before Vanessa. "No insult taken, my good man. We will be wanting another bottle later."

"Aye, Milord Wulfric." The innkeeper backed away from the table, shooing the young girl ahead of him into the kitchen.

"I wonder how long it will take before I grow accustomed to hearing that said to me," Corey mused darkly, then shook himself. "This meal looks just right for us after our soaking."

Vanessa watched as the men served themselves. They ate with relish, even as they began to debate what they would do in the morning.

"You cannot seriously be contemplating crossing the channel yourself, Lord Greybrooke," Captain Hudson said to deflate the earl's grandiose plan he was spinning between sips of brandy. "I shall go. I am a military man. I shall find him in a pig's whistle."

"But you have seen no action more dangerous than a runaway cart in Covent Garden. In France, you could hang by the eyelids," argued Lord Greybrooke. "Ross is my friend, and I am beholden to him to save his bacon myself. What think you, Wulfric?"

"I think I should go."

"No!" Vanessa gripped the edge of the table, but lowered her voice as she added, "I shall not allow you to go back to that horrible country until Boney is defeated once and for all."

His eyes sparked, and she thought he would howl with fury as her father had when his wishes were thwarted. The other men grew silent when Corey looked at them, but Vanessa braved his glare. She was not afraid of the fierce Wolfe temper.

"There is no use quarreling when we have no idea how long the storm will last." Lowering his voice, Corey said, "You must eat, Nessa. You do not want to insult our good host, do you?"

She looked across the room to see the door was ajar. The broad tips of the Boniface's fingers gripped it. She doubted if many guests of quality came to this tiny inn of courts.

Lifting her knife, she put it back onto the table. "I fear I shall embarrass all of us if I try to swallow a single bite."

Corey rubbed her trembling hand and murmured, "I wish I could tell you that it would be all right, but—"

"Please say no more. If you give voice to what I fear in my heart, I do not believe I could bear a moment more of this horror." She blinked back hot tears. "Why did I insist that he go on this madman's quest?"

Lord Greybrooke said, "Be strong, my lady. Ross Hogarth is a resourceful man and full of pluck." He smiled gently. "After all, he won your heart when every other man in London despaired of achieving such a feat." His smile became a scowl when cool air blew into the room, followed by the slamming of a door beyond the dining chamber. "What sap is abroad on a night like this?"

"Other than us?" Corey asked wryly as he chewed a bite of the meat.

As the men began to discuss anew what they would do on the morrow, a tall shadow unfurled in the doorway. Vanessa's heart cramped with desperate hope as she stared at it.

"Ross!" she gasped.

Rain sprayed from his redingote as he charged across the room. Fury hardened his face. He grabbed her arms and jerked her to her feet. "I did not believe it could be true! I did not want to believe you could be so stupid!"

"You are alive," she whispered, touching the salt-stained sleeves of his coat.

His anger did not diminish as he snapped, "Not only did you chase after me, but I have no doubt you planned to catch the next available boat to the continent."

"I thought I would never see you again." Her fingers swept up his muscular arms. She had to touch him to assure herself he was real.

"When are you going to accept that you gave *me* the rôle of the knight errant? You are supposed to be the lady guarding over her castle while I slay French dragons." He shook her gently. "Vanessa, I vow I shall see you locked up in the most inaccessible tower of Wolfe Abbey before I take another chance of you following me into that blasted war."

"Wolfe Abbey does not have any towers."

"A true shame." His lips twitched, but his eyes still blazed with the emotions she found so beguiling. With his voice no longer echoing among the rafters, he said, "You are the most blasted woman I have ever known."

"And you are the most incorrigible man I have ever known."

He laughed as he swept her to him and caressed her lips with the longing that ached within her. Holding him, unable to believe a second miracle had occurred, she whispered his name softly when he raised his mouth from hers. She touched his face, which was roughened with whiskers, and smiled.

"What are *you* doing here?"

At Captain Hudson's startled question, Ross looked past her, his frown returning. "Are you a part of this, too? I should have known you would prove you have more guts than brains. And Edward! This is quite a surprise after your tales that I am about to become a public man without a farthing in my pocket."

"A misunderstanding," Lord Greybrooke said, flustered.

"Ross," Vanessa said softly, "we all worried for your safety."

"You needed have no worry." He shrugged off his coat and tossed it on the back of her chair. "The storm was even too much for even the best interloper. We turned back before we were set awash." He brushed his hand against her cheek as he added, "That was when I learned you were searching for me, Vanessa. I should have known I would break yet another vow when I finally caught up with you."

"What vow?"

Devilment twinkled in his eyes. "I swore before half the crew that I would give you a lacing like the one

your father should have given you long ago. Not a man
among those brave lads doubted that you might not deserve a taste of leather."

She rested against his broad chest, delighting in the
steady rhythm of his heartbeat beneath her ear. It quick-
ened as she whispered, "But you decided on another
punishment? What scold am I due because I love you so
much that I would dare the wrath of Boney himself to
see you safe?"

His hands encircled her face as he drew her head
back. Just as he was tilting her mouth toward his again,
he froze at the sound of a throat being cleared.

Vanessa laughed as she saw Corey's face was bright
with amusement. "Ross, this is my brother."

"Your brother?" he choked. "I thought—"

"You should have had more patience," said Corey
with a laugh. "With your pestering questions added to
Nessa's, I fear any government's bulwark of bureauc-
racy was doomed to fall before you."

Ross held out his hand. "This is a meeting I have anticipated greatly, Lord Wulfric. I must own I had not
expected it to be under such comparatively pleasant
conditions."

"I owe you more than I can ever hope to repay."

"Grant your blessing upon the marriage of your sister
to me, and all debts shall be null." He laughed when Vanessa blushed. "Am I assuming too much, Vanessa, by
believing that your avowal of love means you are once
again willing to become my wife?"

Vanessa glanced uneasily at the other men. Lord
Greybrooke mumbled something and motioned for the
captain and her brother to join him in the contemplation
of the fire on the hearth. When they were out of earshot,
she said, "I would as lief ask if you are willing once
more to have me as your wife? With Corey's return, I

have no claim to Wolfe Abbey or to my father's legacy."

Bringing her to him, he whispered, "What will it take to persuade you that I love you, not that blasted fortune."

"You love me?" She was sure her heart would burst with happiness on the very next beat.

"Would I have asked you to be my wife otherwise?" He laughed and put his finger to her lips. "Nay, do not answer. Listen instead. I swear I have loved you since the first. I must have been on the wrong side of the hedge when brains were given away to convince Franklin and Swinton to take part in that blasted wager."

"No," she said slowly as she lowered herself to the bench. When he took a piece of meat off the platter before he sat next to her, she smiled and pushed the plate closer to him. "I was determined to let no man turn my head with his gentle words until I could rid myself of the burden of the legacy that was truly Corey's."

"As I was determined to let no woman intrude on my life." He touched her cheek lightly. "I fear you changed my mind for me, sweetheart."

"My mind was changed by your resolve to win both my heart and your wager." She laughed. "How much did you win?"

"In addition to your heart?" He snagged another slice and chewed on it before saying, "A pound from each of them."

"Only a pound?"

He laughed. "Would you have preferred me to put a century on the table?"

"No, because the money is not important to me. I will love you if you are as poor as a Job's turkey."

His amusement faded as he ran his finger along her lips, sending swirls of joy through her. "Your sentiments are charming, Vanessa, but rumors of my coming bank-ruptcy are only prattle. My bank is in bang-up prime."

"But Lord Greybrooke said you were so seldom at your club that he became distressed."

He picked up a generous piece of meat and took a large bite. "Perhaps we both have learned a lesson in trusting others." He downed half the wine in her glass. "Excuse me, Vanessa, but I've had nothing to eat since breakfast." With a grin, he said, "I have a wolf in my stomach as well as in my heart."

Longing to surrender to that teasing grin, she resisted. "But about your club? Lord Greybrooke said—"

"How would I have had time to enjoy an evening at the table of green cloth when I have been busy for the past month badgering everyone in the government to find me the answer I prayed would bring a glitter of happiness into your eyes?"

"The past month?"

His nonplussed expression belonged to a naughty child. "I peeked into the letter you sent my uncle, for I doubted you would have been doing something as com-monplace as inviting that old boor to a party. Although he wished to have nothing to do with your quest, I was block enough to try." His finger twisted a tendril of her hair as he said softly, "It is true that, at first, I thought only of using the information to best Franklin and Swinton at our game. I had no idea when I first sug-gested that blasted bet to entertain us, I would end up spending less time at my club, because I became re-solved that I would discover the truth for you."

"You did offer to be my dashing knight."

He finished the wine and reached for the platter again.

"You are making a pig of yourself," she said. "Save some for the others."

"If you do not wish me to assuage that hunger, there

is but one way to satisfy me." He pulled her to him. As his mouth lowered to hers, he whispered, "And I wager this is one feast this pig-widgeon shall never tire of."

ZEBRA REGENCIES
ARE
THE TALK OF THE TON!

A REFORMED RAKE   (4499, $3.99)
by Jeanne Savery

After governess Harriet Cole helped her young charge flee to
France — and the designs of a despicable suitor, more trouble soon
arrived in the person of a London rake. Sir Frederick Carrington
insisted on providing safe escort back to England. Harriet
deemed Carrington more dangerous than any band of brigands,
but secretly relished matching wits with him. But after being
taken in his arms for a tender kiss, she found herself wondering —
could a lady find love with an irresistible rogue?

A SCANDALOUS PROPOSAL   (4504, $4.99)
by Teresa DesJardien

After only two weeks into the London season, Lady Pamela
Premington has already received her first offer of marriage. If
only it hadn't come from the *ton's* most notorious rake, Lord
Marchmont. Pamela had already set her sights on the distin-
guished Lieutenant Penford, who had the heroism and honor that
made him the ideal match. Now she had to keep from falling
under the spell of the seductive Lord so she could pursue the man
more worthy of her love. Or was he?

A LADY'S CHAMPION   (4535, $3.99)
by Janice Bennett

Miss Daphne, art mistress of the Selwood Academy for Young
Ladies, greeted the notion of ghosts haunting the academy with
skepticism. However, to avoid rumors frightening off students,
she found herself turning to Mr. Adrian Carstairs, sent by her
uncle to be her "protector" against the "ghosts." Although,
Daphne would accept no interference in her life, she *would* accept
aid in exposing any spectral spirits. What she never expected was
for Adrian to expose the secret wishes of her hidden heart . . .

CHARITY'S GAMBIT   (4537, $3.99)
by Marcy Stewart

Charity Abercrombie reluctantly embarks on a London season in
hopes of making a suitable match. However she cannot forget the
mysterious Dominic Castille — and the kiss they shared — when he
fell from a tree as she strolled through the woods. Charity does
not know that the dark and dashing captain harbors a dangerous
secret that will ensnare them both in its web — leaving Charity to
risk certain ruin and losing the man she so passionately loves . . .

*Available wherever paperbacks are sold, or order direct from the
Publisher. Send cover price plus 50¢ per copy for mailing and
handling to Penguin USA, P.O. Box 999, c/o Dept. 17109,
Bergenfield, NJ 07621. Residents of New York and Tennessee
must include sales tax. DO NOT SEND CASH.*

ELEGANT LOVE STILL FLOURISHES —
Wrap yourself in a Zebra Regency Romance.

A MATCHMAKER'S MATCH   (3783, $3.50/$4.50)
by Nina Porter

To save herself from a loveless marriage, Lady Psyche Veringham pre-
tends to be a bluestocking. Resigned to spinsterhood at twenty-three,
Psyche sets her keen mind to snaring a husband for her young charge,
Amanda. She sets her cap for long-time bachelor, Justin St. James. This
man of the world has had his fill of frothy-headed debutantes and turns
the tables on Psyche. Can a bluestocking and a man about town find true
love?

FIRES IN THE SNOW   (3809, $3.99/$4.99)
by Janis Laden

Because of an unhappy occurrence, Diana Ruskin knew that a secure
marriage was not in her future. She was content to assist her physician
father and follow in his footsteps . . . until now. After meeting Adam,
Duke of Marchmaine, Diana's precise world is shattered. She would simply have to avoid the temptation of his gentle touch and stunning phy-
sique — and by doing so break her own heart!

FIRST SEASON   (3810, $3.50/$4.50)
by Anne Baldwin

When country heiress Laetitia Biddle arrives in London for the Season,
she harbors dreams of triumph and applause. Instead, she becomes the
laughingstock of drawing rooms and ballrooms, alike. This headstrong
miss blames the rakish Lord Wakeford for her miserable debut, and she
vows to rise above her many faux pas. Vowing to become an Original,
Letty proves that she's more than a match for this eligible, seasoned Lord.

AN UNCOMMON INTRIGUE   (3701, $3.99/$4.99)
by Georgina Devon

Miss Mary Elizabeth Sinclair was rather startled when the British Home
Office employed her as a spy. Posing as "Tasha," an exotic fortune-teller,
she expected to encounter unforeseen dangers. However, nothing could
have prepared her for Lord Eric Stewart, her dashing and infuriating partner. Giving her heart to this haughty rogue would be the most reckless
hazard of all.

A MADDENING MINX   (3702, $3.50/$4.50)
by Mary Kingsley

After a curricle accident, Miss Sarah Chadwick is literally thrust into the
arms of Philip Thornton. While other women shy away from Thornton's
eyepatch and aloof exterior, Sarah finds herself drawn to discover why
this man is physically and emotionally scarred.

*Available wherever paperbacks are sold, or order direct from the
Publisher. Send cover price plus 50¢ per copy for mailing and
handling to Penguin USA, P.O. Box 999, c/o Dept. 17109,
Bergenfield, NJ 07621. Residents of New York and Tennessee
must include sales tax. DO NOT SEND CASH.*

TODAY'S HOTTEST READS
ARE TOMORROW'S SUPERSTARS

VICTORY'S WOMAN   (4484, $4.50)
by Gretchen Genet
Andrew—the carefree soldier who sought glory on the battlefield, and returned a shattered man . . . Niall—the legandary frontiersman and a former Shawnee captive, tormented by his past . . . Roger—the troubled youth, who would rise up to claim a shocking legacy . . . and Clarice—the passionate beauty bound by one man, and hopelessly in love with another. Set against the backdrop of the American revolution, three men fight for their heritage—and one woman is destined to change all their lives forever!

FORBIDDEN   (4488, $4.99)
by Jo Beverley
While fleeing from her brothers, who are attempting to sell her into a loveless marriage, Serena Riverton accepts a carriage ride from a stranger—who is the handsomest man she has ever seen. Lord Middlethorpe, himself, is actually contemplating marriage to a dull daughter of the aristocracy, when he encounters the breathtaking Serena. She arouses him as no woman ever has. And after a night of thrilling intimacy—a forbidden liaison—Serena must choose between a lady's place and a woman's passion!

WINDS OF DESTINY   (4489, $4.99)
by Victoria Thompson
Becky Tate is a half-breed outcast—branded by her Comanche heritage. Then she meets a rugged stranger who awakens her heart to the magic and mystery of passion. Hiding a desperate past, Texas Ranger Clint Masterson has ridden into cattle country to bring peace to a divided land. But a greater battle rages inside him when he dares to desire the beautiful Becky!

WILDEST HEART   (4456, $4.99)
by Virginia Brown
Maggie Malone had come to cattle country to forge her future as a healer. Now she was faced by Devon Conrad, an outlaw wounded body and soul by his shadowy past . . . whose eyes blazed with fury even as his burning caress sent her spiraling with desire. They came together in a Texas town about to explode in sin and scandal. Danger was their destiny—and there was nothing they wouldn't dare for love!

Available wherever paperbacks are sold, or order direct from the Publisher. Send cover price plus 50¢ per copy for mailing and handling to Penguin USA, P.O. Box 999, c/o Dept. 17109, Bergenfield, NJ 07621. Residents of New York and Tennessee must include sales tax. DO NOT SEND CASH.

JANELLE TAYLOR

ZEBRA'S BEST-SELLING AUTHOR

DON'T MISS ANY OF HER
EXCEPTIONAL, EXHILARATING, EXCITING

ECSTASY SERIES

SAVAGE ECSTASY   (3496-2, $4.95/$5.95)

DEFIANT ECSTASY   (3497-0, $4.95/$5.95)

FORBIDDEN ECSTASY   (3498-9, $4.95/$5.95)

BRAZEN ECSTASY   (3499-7, $4.99/$5.99)

TENDER ECSTASY   (3500-4, $4.99/$5.99)

STOLEN ECSTASY   (3501-2, $4.99/$5.99)

DISCOVER DEANA JAMES!

CAPTIVE ANGEL   (2524, $4.50/$5.50)
Abandoned, penniless, and suddenly responsible for the biggest
tobacco plantation in Colleton County, distraught Caroline Gil-
lard had no time to dissolve into tears. By day the willowy redhead labored to exhaustion beside her slaves . . . but each night
left her restless with longing for her wayward husband. She'd
make the sea captain regret his betrayal until he begged her to
take him back!

MASQUE OF SAPPHIRE   (2885, $4.50/$5.50)
Judith Talbot-Harrow left England with a heavy heart. She was
going to America to join a father she despised and a sister she
distrusted. She was certainly in no mood to put up with the in-
sulting actions of the arrogant Yankee privateer who boarded her
ship, ransacked her things, then "apologized" with an indecent,
brazen kiss! She vowed that someday he'd pay dearly for the lib-
erties he had taken and the desires he had awakened.

SPEAK ONLY LOVE   (3439, $4.95/$5.95)
Long ago, the shock of her mother's death had robbed Vivian
Marleigh of the power of speech. Now she was being forced to
marry a bitter man with brandy on his breath. But she could not
say what was in her heart. It was up to the viscount to spark the
fires that would melt her icy reserve.

WILD TEXAS HEART   (3205, $4.95/$5.95)
Fan Breckenridge was terrified when the stranger found her near-
naked and shivering beneath the Texas stars. Unable to remember
who she was or what had happened, all she had in the world was
the deed to a patch of land that might yield oil . . . and the fierce
loving of this wildcatter who called himself Irons.

*Available wherever paperbacks are sold, or order direct from the
Publisher. Send cover price plus 50¢ per copy for mailing and
handling to Penguin USA, P.O. Box 999, c/o Dept. 17109,
Bergenfield, NJ 07621. Residents of New York and Tennessee
must include sales tax. DO NOT SEND CASH.*